A BLOODCURDLING VISION OF HELL

The room had a concave glass dome that gave perfect clarity to the vast array of stars and constellations above. Black night poured like velvet; the moon hung low and bright. The weight of the stars pressed down and formed a vortex, swirling incredible colors.

The Earth was in its infancy, burning volcanoes spewing across vast oceans. Then blue sky and grass as birds soared in the air and the oceans filled with ships. A blinding light blotted out all life, before man once more rose to civilization again. This was the Cataclysm and the Dark Time that followed, when men cowered in fear and forgot all they had ever learned.

The images faded—the journey across countless millennia had taken only minutes. But the vision had only shown the past—not the future. The stars would not tell what would befall them across the sea in the terrible city of Kuba . . .

"*The Haven* is a superb creation and I have been recommending it to all. The Haven stories are a wonderful experience."
—Andre Norton

DUNGEONS OF KUBA

ADVENTURES OF THE EMPIRE PRINCESS #2
BY GRAHAM DIAMOND

PLAYBOY PRESS
PAPERBACKS

TO MIRIAM
FOR SPECIAL TIMES
AND SPECIAL MEMORIES

DUNGEONS OF KUBA

Copyright © 1979 by Graham Diamond

Cover and interior illustrations by Jose Gonzalez: Copyright © 1979 by Playboy

All rights reserved. No part of this book may be reproduced, stored in a retrieval system or transmitted in any form by an electronic, mechanical, photocopying, recording means or otherwise without prior written permission of the author.

Published simultaneously in the United States and Canada by Playboy Press, Chicago, Illinois. Printed in the United States of America. Library of Congress Catalog Card Number: 78-71423. First edition.

Books are available at quantity discounts for promotional and industrial use. For further information, write our sales-promotion agency: Ventura Associates, 40 East 49th Street, New York, New York 10017.

First printing, May 1979.

CASCA'S TALE

Casca, the forest wolf, growled contentedly and stretched luxuriously before the fire. It was a cold winter's evening, and the warmth of the crackling fire reminded him of bright summer days under the shade of the sycamore tree. Outside, the snow deepened. The storm had lasted for days. In his youth, of course, Casca would never have dreamed of hiding from it inside the house. But now, as the long years had begun to mount, he was glad to be away from his beloved forest and spend his time among men and their children.

How he loved the children! Like cubs they were; he had sired seven of his own and now had four times that many grandchildren. And now, for the first time, there were great-grandchildren on the way. Casca was proud and more than eager to return home to the forest in spring to see them for the first time.

The forest had changed, though, and that made him sad. In the old days, when he was a hunter and lord of his pack, he could roam the wood wild and free and never find signs of men. Now men had built roads that crisscrossed his land; horses and rumbling wagons passed over them almost every day. The old days were gone and he was sorry for it; yet he was also glad. The roads were links between the forests and the valleys and the mountains, between men's cities and ports, farms and rivers. The whole world had changed, and in his small way he had helped it all come about—no small feat for a mere forest wolf—but the real credit, he knew, went to the girl whom men called Anastasia, the Empire Princess.

Casca, like all wolves, knew her not as Anastasia or even as Stacy but as Khalea—Khalea, the wolf queen, who had brought peace and civilization throughout the world. He was proud of his association with her, proud of the friendship that had begun when they were both cubs in the forest so long ago. But so much had changed since then—so much, so many tales to tell.

Casca was a storyteller, like most wolves, excelling in the craft. But there were so many tales of the Princess, it was difficult for him to remember them all! Sometimes he wished he were a man (he'd never admit it openly, of course), for at least men were able to put onto paper the experiences they wished to recount. A wolf had to rely only on memory. And when you were speaking of someone like Stacy, that could be a difficult task. But, good storyteller that he was, he always managed to tell them properly, as they had actually happened, and with vivid detail. If sometimes he was forced to exaggerate to make a point, well, no one seemed to mind. Certainly not the children. Wide-eyed and eager, they were always willing to accept every word he said as fact.

So, as the snow fell and the fire glowed warmly, Casca lazily opened his eyes and turned to the handful of young children sitting beside him.

"Tell us the tale about the taking of the Shrouded Castle!" cried one young boy.

"No," pouted his sister. "Tell us the story of how the Princess came to the Land of Jewels."

Casca shook his head and growled in the common tongue. Those were short tales, he knew, and this was the beginning of a long evening. He would choose none of those.

"Let him decide which saga to tell us," said a third in the group.

Here Casca's eyes brightened. "How many of you know about the time the Princess almost lost the Empire?" he asked.

The children glanced at one another with surprise. It was clear from their puzzled expressions that none of them did. He felt his heart beign to beat faster. It was a harrowing tale and frightening—more than enough to while away this cold, dark night. And of course it was all true. Once Khalea had been put into such great peril that not only had the Empire almost been lost; the entire world had nearly been forced back into the ages of the Dark Time.

The children were eager with anticipation. They knew that a story such as this would prove to be far more than a mere adventure. It was a story for grown-ups, the kind told in whispers when children were about. And now their friend Casca was about to share it with them.

The young boy tossed his locks from his eyes and asked, "Where does the story begin?"

In true wolf fashion, Casca replied dryly, "At its beginning. And it all happened not so very long ago...."

The children sat back breathlessly, eagerly waiting.

Casca smiled. He enjoyed having such a willing audience. "It was a summer's day, if I recall," he began. "Life in Rhonnda-by-the-Sea was peaceful and quiet. The story begins not here, however, but in a strange land far, far across the sea. It was there that the dark plot was first hatched...."

And so they listened, hanging on his every word. Herein lies the fable that he told, one of the most difficult adventures ever faced, as only Stacy could have lived it: the saga of the Empire Princess.

PART ONE

WHY STACY WAS FORCED TO LEAVE HER BELOVED RHONNDA-BY-THE-SEA

The Rani of Kuba sat back upon her throne, her face half covered by the deepening shadows of night. She was waiting, patiently. The hour was at hand; her agent would arrive any moment. Only her eyes hinted at the anger that swelled like a tidal wave inside her. Once that wrath was unleashed, few powers save those in heaven could control it.

Sigried, the Rani, was a beautiful woman. Long yellow hair fell over her shoulders, flowing over a skin that was a blend of dark cream stirred to gold. Her face was elfin, her cheekbones high. It took only a single glance to know she was a woman of high birth. But her power was in her ice-blue eyes, framed by long black lashes. Round and large, slightly slanted at the corners, her eyes were like the sea in winter, like the sky on a frigid day. Men were enchanted by her; her glance alone had often imprisoned hearts and minds, and knowingly her lovers had let themselves be used, even wasted, so that her will might be done.

Such a woman was the Rani. Many tales told of her charms, of her intelligence, of her cruelty. She wielded her authority as boldly as any man and had forged her realm into a mighty power. Except for one, Kuba was the most powerful empire in the world, and if Sigried could have her way, it would be second to none.

For years she had harbored hate for the Empire Princess. The day rarely passed when Sigried did not reflect bitterly on the fate that had made her empire second. But, more than that, Sigried's perfect body still bore a scar from the sting of Anastasia's dagger. Once they had fought each other in the Black Pit of Satra, and Anastasia had used accursed wolf tricks to beat her. Sigried would never forget. One day—and that day would be soon—payment would be made in full.

Now she heard the clamor of footsteps approach. She smiled thinly. The dragoon mercenary had come at last.

A dark, broad-shouldered man entered the dim room. Tall, with a strong build, he strode hurriedly across the tiled floor toward the throne. Under thick brows, his cold eyes brooded. He glanced at the mosaic map designed into the tile and noted the arc of dark blue that represented the Kuban empire.

The dragoon pushed aside his cloak and shortsword and bowed low before the Rani. Then, lifting his head, he glanced up, waiting for permission to rise.

For a long moment Sigried let him stay kneeling before her. His eyes looked tired, she noticed. The voyage must have been long and hard. She toyed with the gold bracelets on her wrist and shifted slightly in the chair; then she bade him stand. "What have you to tell me, Dimitri?" she asked. Her voice was as soft and musical as a nightingale's.

The dragoon stretched his cramped muscles and grinned. "I have been given duty in the Empire Legion," he said, "a duty that keeps me close to the palace itself. They have come to trust me—or should I say, at least not to suspect me of being in your employ."

Sigried smiled. The seeds of her plans had borne fruit. The waiting had been worth while. "Then you have managed to get close to *her*?" The last word was spoken contemptuously.

"Only once, Mistress. In Azura, when the Empire, using Satrian and Russak troops, put down the Azurian insurrection. The Empire Princess herself came to lead her army."

"You saw her, then?"

"Yes, Mistress. I positioned myself as close to her as I could. Had I reached out, I think I could have actually touched her."

Sigried winced. "You were *that* close and you let her live? You have failed me, Dimitri! You should have killed her as we planned, right there and then."

The dragoon's face dropped at the sight of her anger. He shook his head warily. "I couldn't, Mistress; I swear it! If I could . . ."

The Rani sat back to hear the rest, but the bitterness she felt over this missed opportunity would not leave.

"It was impossible for me to have touched her," said Dimitri ruefully, with the sad voice of a man not used to failure. "Believe me. She surrounds herself with a fierce bodyguard. Each and every one is sworn to give his life to protect her. And there were wolves—two fiery beasts with malice in their eyes and fangs poised to strike. The red fur of those devils made me bristle with fear, and you know I am no coward."

Sigried nodded; she would grant that much. As a mercenary for hire, Dimitri had come with the highest credentials. She had used him before and he had led her troops well.

"So the Azurian barbarians fell to her handful of Satrians and Russak savages? Where was the Empire Cavalry? Her Rhonnda troops?"

"She needed them not. Anastasia unleashed her wolves. How can *any* man fight such a force? No wonder her army is the most powerful on earth."

Siggy laughed caustically. "So her wolves defeated the Azurians. And now her army will be tied down in occupying Azura."

The Dragoon looked away. "No, the Azurians were allowed to remain free."

The Rani paled. "She let her enemies go free?"

"She did—on the provision that they accept her rule and fly the maroon and blue Empire flag."

"The bitch! She wins the hearts of her foes and claims half the world because of it!"

Dimitri nodded ruefully. He let his eyes scan the map on the floor, noting that the red of the Empire loomed twice as large as the Kuban blue. The Western Isles, the Land of the Russaks, the coasts of the Long Continent —all these were red. Now Azura would have to be added as well.

"But is it not so, Rani? Their empire grows daily. It was only a short time ago that Azura was even discovered. Your own ships had been burned—"

"I don't need a geography lesson!"

"Face the reality, Mistress. Even Satra, the city closest to Kuba, is ruled by her allies."

"I know full well the extent of her empire," she hissed. "I know the Empire Fleet sails the Seven Seas in quest of new lands and further riches for her banner. That was why I brought you here. But even you have failed me. I'm surrounded by clowns and idiots!"

The burning in her eyes frightened the mercenary; but he knew that the sting of her words was unjust.

"I have not failed," he replied coolly.

Her ice-blue eyes flashed. "You were sent to Rhonnda-by-the-Sea to kill Anastasia, yet you yourself tell me she still lives. I call that failure, Dimitri. Do you have another word for it?"

He watched disconcertedly as her right hand slid down toward the knife strapped onto her belt. Her prowess with it was known throughout the world. He wanted to run from her, from the gaze of those piercing eyes; yet strangely he was locked by them and felt drawn toward her, even if it meant his own death was at hand. Mixed with dread rose desire. He glanced at her body, watched the gentle heave of her breasts, the taunting, seductive curve of her mouth. More than anything else in the world, he wanted her. It was this very desire that had brought him to her in the first place.

Well aware of his thoughts, knowledgeable of her ability to manipulate, she sneered and said, "Why should I allow you to live?"

He swallowed hard. "Because I know a way to get at the Princess that will make her beg at your feet."

She leaned forward to listen, chin on her hand. If the dragoon indeed had a plan worthy of his reputation, then she would reward him with her pleasures this very night; but it had better be a good plan. If he began to snivel and make excuses, she would slit his throat. Her father had not left the throne of Kuba to a fool. She had invested too much time already in this dragoon. He should be well aware that he was already living on borrowed time.

"Spin your scheme for me, mercenary," she said in a voice so low he could hardly hear.

He smiled. The Rani was interested, he realized; he had just bought back his life. "For me to murder the Princess directly," he said bluntly, "is not possible. My life would be forfeit before I even tried. Yet there are other ways. . . ."

"Speak plainly, Dimitri; I have little time for riddles and games. Anastasia has been a thorn in my side for too long. Now I must be rid of her. The Empire must crumble and the Fleet be destroyed, her allies forced to bicker among themselves. But this can be done only with Anastasia out of the way. Now, tell me your scheme."

With a sly smile across his face, the dragoon began to speak. In a hushed voice he told her all she had hoped to hear and more. His plan was ingenious.

Tingling with excitement, Siggy laughed deep in her throat. It was perilous, to be sure. It would involve great risks to her carefully placed spies within the Rhonnda palace. If the plan failed, she could expect the Empire Fleet to burn every Kuban port in revenge; but if it worked, it would leave the Princess shattered and her empire in ruin. And Sigried would be there to pick up the pieces.

She arose from her throne, took his hand and led him slowly toward her private chambers. "Come, Dimitri," she whispered. "The night is long, and we'll share it together. Then in the morning, after you have rested, you'll make all haste back to Rhonnda and complete your task. And hurry, my darling. Keep in mind that I'll be here with open arms to wait for your return."

To the golden port of Rhonnda-by-the-Sea came the ships, scores at a time, all flying the many different banners of the Empire. Fast lateen-rigged cargo vessels bringing spice and cloth from the desert kingdoms of Sytherna came from the south; lumbering cogs laden with strange and exotic wares and produce sailed slowly in convoy from the mysterious Western Isles; sleek longboats groaning under the weight of minerals and precious stone drawn from Satra in the north. Crude artifacts and weapons were brought from the land of the Russaks; there was silver from the mines of Rhonnda's own southern shores, marble from the quarries of the Newfoundland River, timber and cloth and wild horses from the Free Land Mountains. All this and more came in a steady flow to the richest city in the world.

As the purple towers and golden spires came into view, all ships raised the maroon and blue Empire colors proudly, even above the flags of their own lands, for Rhonnda-by-the-Sea was the center of the Empire, the very heart of the world. It throbbed with a pulse and beat of its own, unlike any other. It was the jewel, the crown. The palace, built at the site of the old High Castle, loomed atop the highest hill and looked majestically down not only upon the city but also upon the sea.

At the mouth of the harbor the warships lay at

anchor—always ready on a moment's notice to sail forth and track down any foreign vessel or mercenary ship bent on plunder. Because of this vigilance, pirates were few across the Three Seas of Rhonnda. And even as these warships kept the shipping lanes open and free, the Empire Fleet combed the Seven Seas of the world in search of new lands, its presence protecting as well the far-flung shores already under the maroon and blue colors of the Empire Princess.

There was no war with Kuba, only an uneasy truce; but trade between the two powers was nonexistent, and vessels of that land were closely watched as they crossed Empire waters to their own northern and eastern ports. No Empire warship would interfere; but a wary eye was always needed. Kuban privateers often plied the seas in the guise of merchant vessels, preying like unseen spiders on the unsuspecting.

War was a luxury that could not be afforded; the Princess knew that all too well. For countless years such wars had torn apart the very fabric of the world. Anastasia was desperately trying to put it back together.

The golden spires and purple towers glistened in the late-afternoon sun. A multitude of gulls flew across the bay, high against the sky. The city was quiet, as always on a late spring day. Merchants closed their stalls early; shoppers spent their time lazing under the shade of the trees in the many parks and gardens.

From where Stacy stood, at the tower of the west wing of her palace, she could see the heat shimmering and rising over the resplendent domes below. Beneath the wall was a large courtyard filled with sparkling fountains. Long winding hedges, tall and trimmed, ran alongside the stone walks and weaved their way toward the high black iron gates of the palace. Outside the gate a small bridge arched over a shallow brook, which in turn led down to the main road and to the ever-busy squares and markets of the city.

From the height of the wall, Stacy could see nearly all of her beloved Rhonnda-by-the-Sea and beyond it the blue range of dark mountains. How very much she missed the forest and her friends there—the wondrous home of her earliest memories, where she had wandered free and wild under the stars. These rugged Rhonnda hills were a good second, though, she had to admit, what with their dense, looming trees and multitude of wild flowers. It was the only shelter she could turn to and at least for a short while forget the heavy burdens placed upon her shoulders, burdens that too often were more than she could bear. For Stacy had never sought to gain her famed title; far from it. The office of Empire Princess had been thrust upon her. She had been little more than a wide-eyed girl when by demand of the Empire Council all of Rhonnda's new and growing empire was laid at her feet. Even then she had wavered, feeling that her destiny as foretold by the stargazer Alryc and the dead mystical poet Bartok could best be served in other ways.

It was the people themselves who had changed her mind, the crowds of sincere citizens who had swept her away from the ancient Valley in the south and brought her once again to Rhonnda. Stacy was now their leader, her will virtually supreme; yet she was every bit as much their servant, seeing their interests and those of her land always above her own.

And she had served them well. She had brought the Empire to new heights of riches and glory. It was awesome power, frightening and terrible power, all at her fingertips. A single command might bring the entire world to war, a countercommand might save it. Stacy had not been on the throne for very long, and so much was left to be done, she knew. Her dream to reunite the world would not be easily realized. It was this knowledge and this knowledge alone that kept her resolute in her will to continue as Rhonnda's princess. This selfless desire to right the wrongs of history had cost her much, she knew. Her life was not her own, nor would it ever be until the day she could leave the palace forever and find her own happiness.

Stacy leaned with her back against the wall and gazed bemusedly toward the tiny park within the palace grounds. Hand in hand, children were playing, forming a large circle and merrily singing an old children's rhyme. She sighed and closed her eyes. How much she wanted children of her own.

The Empire Princess could never be as other women —luckier women, she thought. They could choose to have a husband and a family, but Stacy's duty to the Empire came first, and those were choices she would not be allowed to make on her own. Duty could never be divided.

An older girl appeared on the scene and took charge of the group of children. Stacy watched her with a touch of envy. It was Maralisa, the only child of Stacy's dear sister, Lorna. Again Stacy felt her heart sink. Both Lorna and her husband had died tragically some years before, leaving Stacy the only one to care for Mara. Too close in age to be a mother to her, the Empire Princess had come to love the girl as a younger sister. Mara was now almost 18. Stacy was 27 and she envied Mara: Mara was free, as free as the great soaring birds above the bay, and for that freedom Stacy knew she would gladly trade everything she had.

Except for Elias, the commander of the Empire Fleet, Stacy loved the girl more than anything else in the world. She was intent on seeing that Mara's youthful happiness never be lost.

Mara was now leading the children to rest beneath the shady trees beside the rock garden. Off to the side of a leafy sycamore, two large wolves lay in the grass.

Seemingly they were asleep; but Stacy knew better. The slightest whiff of danger would send them bounding to their feet, fangs bared. Wolves were the best guardians any child could have. They were loyal and trustworthy, as well as perfect companions. And who but Stacy should know better? She who had virtually been raised by the fearsome packs of the faraway forests?

She turned her gaze from the garden toward the distant, ever-blue sea, her only rival for her beloved Elias. The blue water kept Stacy entranced, that mysterious sea across which she and Elias had made their first journey together. How long ago it all seemed now—she, the young aristocrat set on adventure; he, the dashing captain of the *Brora*, the first Empire ship to venture across the ocean. They had blindly sought the fabulous mountain city of Satra and faced together a year of terrible danger. Now, a handful of years later, Satra itself was a part of her empire, and its foremost ally in Stacy's wish to bring the world out of its Dark Time. Prince Sumavand himself, liege of Satra, had been the man to bestow the title of Princess upon her for saving his city from doom. Now almost half the known world flew the Rhonnda banner.

She gazed out toward the distant horizon. The Empire Fleet was at last due home again; it might arrive at any time. And with her fleet would come Elias back from his latest adventure, back with a thousand gifts and tales of strange lands—most of all, back into her arms. She thought of his touch, his lips upon her mouth, the feel of his sea-hardened body pressed against her own. And she whispered his name.

The sea had always burned in Elias's soul, a beckoning siren whose call he could never refuse. Sometimes Stacy hated him for it. It was the sea, she would think bitterly, who would wed Elias; the sea with whom she could never compete. Elias was the finest captain in the Empire, if not the world. Stacy had given him her powerful fleet to command, to sail the Seven Seas and reap new riches for Rhonnda. Elias had done his job well—too well, perhaps. It was duty and love of the Empire that kept them apart, kept them from the marriage they had hoped for.

So intense was her gaze that she was not aware of the tall figure approaching along the landing.

"It won't be long before you can see the sails," said the voice.

Stacy turned and smiled at the sight of the lumbering figure before her, a giant of a man with a thick crop of silver hair and piercing eyes. With his hand on his staff and his crimson robe flowing in the breeze, he looked down at her and smiled.

Stacy clasped her hands and sighed. "When will they arrive, Alryc?" she asked softly. "Why don't they hurry?"

Alryc's eyes burned through her own. "Elias will make all haste to return to you, my lady," the mystic stargazer told her. "He always does. You know that his heart cries out as much as your own."

Stacy forced a grateful smile. Somehow Alryc always knew the right words for the moment. It had always been that way. She raised herself high on her toes and kissed his cheek. "What would I ever do without you?" She squeezed his hand.

"Don't be bitter," he said. "One day things will be different for you."

Stacy shook her head. "I used to believe that," she said wistfully, "but not anymore. Too much time has passed. Soon it will be too late." She bit her lip.

He looked at her sharply. "What would you do, Stacy? Turn away from the throne? Let a lesser woman or man lead?" He answered his own question with a shake of his head. "No, my lady. Destiny cannot be altered. If life seems hard for you now, always remember that happiness will be found when the journey is done."

Stacy laughed caustically. "I want Elias now, Alryc. I want to be a wife now, to have children, to cook for my family, to be waiting for my husband in the evening."

"Rhonnda needs Elias," Alryc said.

Stacy's eyes flashed. "Well, so do I! Let another sea captain take charge of the Fleet. It's time he stayed home with me."

The aging astronomer furrowed his bushy silver brows. "You're more upset than I realized, my princess, and I think it's more than just because Elias is away. What is it, Stacy?"

She avoided his eyes. "I'm tired of seeing our fleet sail half the world to force its will upon peoples who would be better off left to themselves." Now she looked at him. "I don't want to see any more men die—on either side."

"Then the battle at Azura still grieves your heart."

"The blood of all those soldiers," she whispered. "It's on my hands. They died fighting either for or against me. Their deaths were all because of me."

Alryc's eyes darkened. "We did what must be done. You know that as well as I. They were a warlike nation and, as such, a threat not just to Rhonnda but to all the world."

Stacy nodded. The war had been forced, she knew. Both she and Alryc had tried desperately to avert it; but there was no running from the truth. If Azura had remained a hostile land, then neither Rhonnda nor any of her allies would ever have been safe in southern waters.

"So we've gained another land," she said in a hushed voice. "Won ourselves another piece of territory. But that won't bring back the dead."

Alryc's face grew stern, like that of a schoolmaster

angered at his pupil. "In a world torn apart by anarchy, it takes a forceful hand to stem the raging tides of destruction. Have you forgotten the Darkness, Stacy? The terrible Dark Time that shrouded us all?"

She shook her head. The black shadow across the world could never leave her thoughts. Throughout every continent there remained only the pitiful remnants of once mighty civilizations. It was a decayed, bleak and dying world.

Alryc stretched out his arms as if to encompass the harbor, where the sun was beginning to set. "Count the flags, Stacy. Look at the ships. A few years ago none of this would have been possible. There was no trade. Crossing the sea was thought impossible. There was no contact between civilizations, no peace in any land. Rhonnda's banner has brought law, and with law has come peace. It is Rhonnda's task to rebuild the world. This was your own vision, Stacy. Have you forgotten? It was this vision that brought you to lead. And now you can see it all coming true before your eyes. Please, child, don't throw it all away. Finish your work as only you can."

"You make it sound so easy." She sighed. "There were those who schemed against us when we began; there are those who still do. Have you forgotten the savage ruthlessness we faced when Satra was torn between aligning with us or standing beside Kuba and the Rani's banner? It took our fleet and armies a year to restore matters. And when Kuba broke relations, do you recall the bitterness? The armed fight to keep the Disputed Islands out of Sigried's control?"

Alryc nodded glumly. "Kuba has gone her own way, that is true, but perhaps not forever. Long ago when I first read your stars, I knew that the roads for you would be difficult. I knew you would be deprived of that which other women take for granted. But you are no ordinary woman, Stacy, and you knew even then that these tasks must be fulfilled and took the burdens on your shoulders."

Stacy closed her eyes. "Those burdens have grown so heavy, Alryc. Forgive me. I can no longer be as selfless as before."

Alyrc buried her in his arms and caressed her softly. "Be strong, my princess," he whispered soothingly.

Stacy leaned against him, gaining renewed strength from his.

The soft shuffle of shoes against stone suddenly broke into their thoughts. They both turned, startled, to see Maralisa racing up the steps. Skirt swirling as she ran, her eyes bright and her pretty face flushed, she reached the landing and came breathlessly toward them.

"Didn't you hear me shouting to you?" she asked, looking first to Alryc and then to Stacy.

Stacy shook her head. "We didn't hear you. What is it, Mara? Is anything wrong?"

Mara laughed and clapped her hands girlishly. "Wrong? *A'zi,* no! Look! Both of you!"

Stacy turned breathlessly to the wall. Her heart pounding like a kettledrum, she strained to see past the long purple shadows crossing the city and the mountains. There was the speck of a ship in the distance moving toward them from the horizon, a tall ship . . .

"The Fleet!" she cried. "It's the flagship, the *Southwind!*"

Slowly the fighting ship came into view—triple-masted with sails of gold emblazoned with the crest of Rhonnda. And behind the *Southwind* came the others: sleek, fast warships, all with the blue and maroon banners of Rhonnda aflutter from stem to stern.

All at once for Stacy the world seemed beautiful again. She stared transfixed and with every breath whispered his name: Elias. Elias! *Elias!* She smiled through her tears. "Fara above!" she exclaimed. "It seems so long."

Mara laughed. "Only nine weeks, Stacy."

"It felt like a year. The Southern Coast is so far away."

"May I watch the Fleet sail into port from the High Tower?" Mara asked with a young girl's eager anticipation.

Alryc glanced at her sternly. "It will be hours before they reach the quay," he said. "Long past your bedtime, young princess."

Mara's eyes betrayed her hurt.

Stacy saw the disappointment and sighed. "Very well, Mara, but be sure you're accompanied by someone."

Mara laughed, and with her skirt flaring, she turned and hurried back down the winding steps.

Alryc watched her approvingly. "Young, handsome lords will swarm to her like bees to honey," he mused aloud once she had gone.

Stacy's smile assured full agreement. She also knew something of a young woman's charms and understood all too well how much good or evil could be wrought using feminine wiles. "I pray Mara never knows my burdens," she said sadly, thinking of the day when Mara would take her place within the palace and become a princess in her own right.

"Mara is every bit as strong as you are, my lady," assured Alryc, comfortingly.

Stacy nodded slowly. "Perhaps. But she's so filled with the joys of life—a young girl's joys. I don't want her ever to have to lose that."

The stargazer furrowed his brows. "You cannot see the child's strength," he said. "Your eyes see her almost through a mother's eyes. But I can see it more clearly. You've raised her well, Stacy, been more than a parent. From the very beginning you've been her inspiration. You taught her well the ways of the forests and the wolves, taught her to stand alone in the face of adversity. Mara's will is her own now, and when her time to lead does come, she will do it skillfully, have no doubts."

Stacy shook her head. She pushed hair from her eyes. "You have all the right words, don't you, Alryc? But Mara's still just a child."

"And how old were you, my princess, when the throne was thrust upon you? You were little more than a child yourself; yet you overcame the many difficulties that faced you."

"What choice did I have?" she asked. "There was no one else to turn to. How many of us had seen and known what had become of the world across the Seven Seas? Only a handful of us realized what had to be done, if only for our own sakes."

"Now half of that very world flies your banner," Alryc reminded her. "When Mara's time comes, it will be no less."

Stacy leaned over the wall, resting her head in her hands. Alryc was perhaps the best friend she had ever had, she knew. She trusted his visions and insight more than she trusted her own. And somehow his prophecies had always proven true. She hoped his prophecy for Mara would be all that he said.

The flagship loomed larger through the strong currents of the bay. Stacy closed her eyes and pictured Elias, pictured him as he would be this very moment on the bridge of the ship, hands clenched firmly behind his back, dark, curly hair blowing gently in the breeze, eyes gazing out toward the palace on the hill and the woman he loved. His face would show his strain and fatigue from the long, arduous voyage, but his resolve would bring him home without a single minute's rest. Commands would be barked; his crew would scamper across the broad decks and raise the blue and maroon banners. And then, after so many weeks, the ships would come to berth.

Stacy clenched her fists and dreamed of the feel of

his arms. *Let him come soon,* she prayed. *Don't make me wait too long. The sea may claim his very soul, but tonight his being belongs to me....*

"They should berth before midnight," said Alryc, unknowingly disturbing her thoughts. "Why not come back inside and prepare yourself to greet him? I'll schedule the War Council briefing for tomorrow morning."

She looked at Alryc with an impish grin, then laughed grandly. Again he had read her every thought. "Make it *late* tomorrow morning, First Minister," she said, addressing him by his formal title.

He saw the young lover's mischief in her dark, brooding eyes and smiled. "*Very* late, my princess," he replied with a bow. "I know you and he will have much to discuss, and I don't want you to be disturbed."

The hour was late, well past midnight. Stacy lay still, leisurely stretched out across the wide bed partly covered by a soft Satrian quilt thrown across dark-blue silk sheets. All candles and lamps were out; the room was bathed in gentle shadows. A thin needle of light glowed from beneath the door. Outside the window a hazy half-moon peeked down at her; slanted moonbeams poured through the curtains and washed the hanging plants in silver. The breeze was calm; the curtains rustled ever so gingerly. Restless for his arrival, she counted stars and sang to them sweetly, the way wolves do. Entranced by the countless number of glittering stars, she gazed at the patterns they formed and wondered what hidden message they were telling. She was not a star reader or a mystic; but belief in their wisdom was common among her people. The stars guided her ships to distant shores, then brought them safely back home. Mystics, like Alryc, believed that when a man died, his soul swept to the heavens and took its place in the sky, yet another glimmering bauble to help show the way to the lost mariners below.

Her many years of sea experience had taught her much. She could plot a course as well as any sailor, could follow the constellations with an expert's eye and name them all. Yet the mystery of the night skies had always eluded her. It was the one goal she had never achieved. Perhaps one day, she mused, there would be time even for this; but that day was far off. Until then, better to leave such work to men like Alryc.

The air was stuffy; she opened her robe and lifted the slim copper band from her hair, letting it flow freely against the sheets. For over an hour she had exulted in a hot bath scented with pine, applied traces of perfume and brushed her long hair until it bounced with life— all this to pass the time until he came. The night waned slowly. Where was he? Why was he so late? Could there have been trouble abroad the ship? Perhaps he was injured, hurt upon the shores of some hostile land . . .

She knew she was letting her imagination run away. Elias was safe. If he was late, there was good reason. But she cursed the Fates for keeping him from her.

Just then she heard footsteps from the adjoining room and the sound of a door being opened and shut. Her heart raced. The bronze doorknob began to turn. She held her breath. The room flooded with soft globe-light. She saw his silhouette enter and pause. Stirring slightly, she pretended to be asleep.

Elias watched her with a smile, then quietly closed the door behind him. For a long moment he stood over the bed looking down at her, his eyes showing the fatigue of the long voyage home. He was a tall, broad man, ruggedly handsome, with a short-clipped black beard now liberally flecked with gray at the sides. The deep lines around his mouth told of the years of strong sea winds he had faced. His eyes were deep-set, brooding, under thick brows.

He bent over, hesitant about waking her. Perhaps he should leave her now, he thought, and come to her in the morning.

From behind the quilt she smiled and opened her eyes. "Don't you dare leave!"

He grinned boyishly and kissed her softly.

She pulled his head down against her. Tingling excitement raced through her as she threw back the quilt.

"I've come home, my princess," he said in a very low voice. "The Fleet was delayed. We ran into strong gales in the—"

"I don't want to hear about the Fleet," she whispered, "or anything else."

His mouth pressed firmly against hers; she felt his warm breath. With nimble fingers she unbuttoned his tunic and unbuckled his belt. They fell to the floor. His own hands reached out, tugged at her robe and scanned her tanned, supple body as the robe fell in folds to the floor. Her golden skin glowed in soft moonlight, and in her stance he saw the soft savagery of the young wolf huntress who had captured his heart so very long ago. His fingers pressed against the firm flesh of her thighs, palms growing wet with need and burning desire.

Stacy drew close and with her hand at the back of his neck, drew him to her. Soft kisses smothered her face and neck. She peered at him through slitted feline eyes and gasped with pleasure.

"Elias, Elias, it's been too long. . . ."

Hushing her, he pushed her slightly back, just enough so he could see her fully before him. She moved her hands to her side, breasts heaving with every labored breath. His eyes pored over her: her stomach, hips, long, shapely legs. Taking her hand, he brought her near again, unable to dim the surging need that rose in every muscle in his body.

Stacy smiled, sharing the need. She threw back her head, black hair falling over her rounded shoulders, and teasingly began to sway before him ever so slowly. "Do I still please you?" she whispered in a low, throaty voice.

The look in his eyes told her his response. He lay back upon the wide bed, breathing slow, deep breaths as her breasts swayed back and forth along his chest. His hands caressed her, fingers lightly running from her sides over her thighs, then back up along her breasts. Stacy squealed at the sensation, recalling vividly their first lovemaking so long ago and how, with the passing of time, their need for each other had only heightened.

His hands moved lower again, across her abdomen in small circles. She moved beside him and side by side they lay, touching, feeling. Suddenly she tensed as his hand knowingly caressed a sensitive spot. She squirmed and he took his hand away. Then the movements began anew. Her hips rose slightly, fell back and rose again. Her hands moved over him; she heard his soft moan of pleasure. His body stiffened at the feel of her tongue wetly toying at the sides of his mouth. His mouth opened to kiss her, strongly, passionately, with increasing urgency.

The time of teasing and games was almost done, they both knew. Gently he pushed her shoulders down; she closed her arms around him and brought him to her. The sensations came in towering waves, each rising to a higher peak than the last. He slipped inside her, and with deep, purposely slow movements they made love, discovering each other's mysteries anew.

Stacy squeezed as his thrusts grew deeper. A series of spasms shook her being; she lost herself and all control as the last fresh wave of feeling ran through every inch of her body. Then down, down, down she tumbled, savoring every last diminished sensation until it was gone and only the afterglow remained.

They rested in each other's arms, bathing luxuriantly in the moon's silver light, bodies aglow in perspiration.

The thin curtains danced as a cool sea breeze pushed inside the darkened chamber. Elias reached out and ran his fingers through her hair, toying with the endless curls twirling over his chest. He kissed her tenderly: her eyes, her hair, her cheeks, her mouth. She smiled and asked if he was ready again. He shook his head and with a grin said, "Soon." For now he was content just to be touching her again and gazing into her dark, mysterious, wolflike eyes.

Stacy felt young once more, glowingly young. The burn of his eyes told her how much he still desired her and she was proud. His going away had always been the hardest part of their lives together, his homecoming always the best. She wished they could stay like this forever, and again she felt bitter over the years they both had lost.

He was keenly aware of the dark look that crossed her face. "What's wrong, my princess?" he asked.

She avoided his eyes. "I've made a decision," she said firmly.

"Oh? What decision? Am I to lose my head?"

Her eyes flashed. "I'm serious, Elias. I've been mulling this over for a long time, now, and I've decided: When the Fleet sails next, it will have a new captain."

Elias's own eyes darkened. "We've discussed that before, Stacy. Your part is here in Rhonnda. Mine is—"

"Yours is where I say!"

There was hurt on his face. "Is this an Empire directive? Am I to bow before you and say, 'As you will, my princess'?"

His words stung, and she showed it with tears in the corners of her eyes. "I'm doing this for us, Elias—for both of us. Can't you see that? How long must we give our lives to others? When is there to be a life for us? Oh, Elias, remember the plans we used to make? Our dreams? That simple life we hoped for?"

He sighed and looked away. "It was you who accepted this office, Stacy, not me. It's far too late to change things now. Maybe in years to come . . ." The words trailed off wistfully.

Stacy knew he didn't believe them. "In years to come, it will be too late!" she flared, letting all her pent-up anger at the world rise to the surface. "We're still young, Elias. Let's enjoy our lives together now, while we still can."

He looked at her with growing surprise. Never before had she seemed so embittered, so determined to alter their chosen courses. It left him shaken and bewildered.

"What is it, Stacy?" he asked. She had begun to cry and he leaned forward to take her in his arms.

She pulled away and looked at him sharply. "I want to be a wife," she said. "I want to be a mother."

"And you will, Stacy. Just give it a bit more time."

A bitter smile crossed her lips. "How long must I wait, Elias? I saw the children playing today in the garden and I wanted to cry. Where are *my* children, Fleet Commander? Where are *our* children? Where is the life together we promised each other?"

Elias sighed and closed his eyes. "We sacrificed it for Rhonnda," he replied at last, with a hint of the same bitterness in his own voice.

Stacy dried her eyes and shook her head. "No more, Elias. I mean it. I want you here beside me. My mind is firm. There are other captains who can replace you as commander—young men eager for the chance. The Fleet will manage without you. I need you more than they do."

He tried to hide his troubled thoughts. She made it all sound so easy, so simple a deed; but they both knew better. The world was at a crucial turning point. Events and circumstances made his leaving his post all but an impossibility. Somehow he would have to convince her of that.

"Can we discuss a few matters?" he asked.

She nodded dryly. "I want us to talk—but you won't change my mind."

"It's something too important to dismiss."

Stacy met his eyes evenly and frowned. "Official Empire matters, I suppose?" He nodded, and she said, "Can't it wait until morning? Alryc's scheduled a briefing."

"I'd rather we talk now, my princess, alone. Tomorrow there'll be too many other details to get involved in. I won't bore you now with the facts of my latest voyage, but if I truly am never to leave Rhonnda again, I want you to know what I've learned."

She stared at him curiously, wondering if his news was as dark as the troubled look on his face. "All right, Captain. As usual, you win. What is it that you feel is so important?"

He smiled and took her hand. "We came across strange tidings, my princess," he said. "News came to us from the Southern Coast of a new, uncharted land—an island, we believe, perhaps as much as a thousand leagues to the west; an island said to be so rich in resources that even the ancient Satra Empire would pale by comparison."

Stacy scoffed. "And you believed such foolish sailors' talk?"

"More than talk, Stacy. We came upon a shipwreck—a mercenary ship laden with minerals headed for Kuba."

Here Stacy's eyes widened.

Elias continued: "We think the mercenaries were racing back to bring word to the Rani. They must have been caught in the terrible gales I told you about and smashed on the reefs. But, in any event, we believe that Kuban ships are already out in force to find this island anew and claim it for Sigried's empire."

The Princess tensed. She was painfully aware of what such added wealth would mean if it fell into the Rani's hands. Sigried would use every ounce of gold to raise a new army, and regain the lost land of Satra she still claimed as rightfully hers. That would mean war—total war again unleashed upon the world—the Rhonnda Empire against the Kuba Empire. There would be no winners.

"Rhonnda must find this fabled island first," she said.

Elias nodded seriously. "We cannot afford to fail. Too much is at stake. With the island in our hands, peaceful hands, we can build that second fleet you've always dreamed of, bring new prosperity to the entire world—and fulfill your goal."

Stacy sat back, breathless. Her head was swimming with the dream of her vision at last becoming reality. "Are . . . are you positive of all this? Elias, could that shipwreck possibly have been some sort of trick to lure us?"

"If it was, it was a most expensive one. Our own ships are straining with the booty we found in it." His eyes brightened. "Wait until I show you, Stacy. Jewels, emeralds, rubies like you've never seen, freshly mined silver . . . There must be an incredible wealth of minerals begging to be dug up on that island."

"And perhaps an army of barbarians waiting to cut off your heads once you reach shore," she added dryly.

He sighed. "It's worth the risk. I've been in battle before, my princess. No Rhonnda sailor leaves home without knowing the risks."

And how well she knew it, thought Stacy, recalling the long months of fear and anxiety during the years when the newly established Rhonnda Fleet set sail to explore the Seven Seas in the name of the Empire.

"We must not let Kuba find the island before us," she said flatly. "I'll command Captain Silas to leave port at once."

Elias shook his head. "Silas's ships won't be enough. Consider: We might find our ships set upon by the entire mercenary fleet Sigried has so painstakingly built—not the Kuban navy that Commander Quentin commands but the ruthless soldiers of fortune the Rani now surrounds herself with. Captain Silas and his ships wouldn't stand a chance. Every one of our sailors would meet his death in such an encounter."

Stacy's face tightened. Elias was right, she knew. The high seas of the Uncharted Lands knew no law, no common decency. Those waters were infested with pirates and brigands, the very sort of men Sigried now so openly brought under her banner.

"Then our own warships will have to sail," she said glumly.

Elias shared her concern. "As soon as possible, Stacy. We can't give Kuba any more time. Already the situation is fraught with danger. A confrontation between us is a very real possibility. But even if it comes, as long as it happens on the high sea, there's little chance of it spreading. My hope is that our own ships can smash the mercenaries once and for all. It's a battle we can't afford to lose."

"I know," Stacy agreed. "Our forces are thinly spread. Lord Blood is forced to stay in Azura until the situation calms; our western garrisons have been deployed to patrol the Satrian corridors." She squeezed her lover's hand and locked her eyes with his. "How soon can the Fleet be ready to sail?"

"We must be off within the week."

She drew back, looking aghast. "But how can we? There are so many details to be worked out—"

"Preparations have already begun, Stacy. Forgive me, but I was forced to take matters into my own hands. I spent hours at dockside giving instructions for new rigging. That's why I was so late coming to you. Those are strange waters we sail for, Stacy—dark and turbulent, with far greater risk involved than Sigried's mercenaries could ever impose."

Tears again came to Stacy's eyes as she realized that her hopes and dreams were to be dashed once more. "I see," she said ruefully. "And now you're going to tell me that you have to leave with our ships."

He kissed her softly. "I must, my princess. You know I must. Now more than ever my men need me. Rhonnda needs me. You can understand that, can't you, love?"

She threw her arms around him, clinging tightly in a desperate attempt to wash away her terrible forebodings. "Elias, please! I'm frightened for you! Stay with me. Let another go in your place."

"Who?" he asked. "Who knows those waters better than I? Who has faced Kuban mercenaries and beat them back despite overwhelming odds against us? It must be me, Stacy. Kuban galleys are no easy mark. I can't let our men down. Remember, they're fighting for us."

She looked away. "You've won your point, Captain," she said tersely. "You know I'd never risk any man's life because of my personal selfish needs."

A lump rose in his throat as he cradled her head against him. "I'll make you a vow, my princess," he whispered. "When this voyage is done and this fabled island is safely in our hands and flying Rhonnda's banners, I'll come home to you and never sail the sea again. We'll be wed and will never be parted again. I swear this, Stacy. This will be the last voyage of Captain Elias."

Stacy held her breath, not daring to believe it but wanting to with all her heart. "Do you really mean that?" she cried, eyes wide and wet, mouth open and lips trembling.

"By the Fates I swear it! You'll have those children, Stacy, princess or no. And one day you *will* give up this throne forever. We'll live the lives we always dreamed."

She squealed with happiness, threw herself over him and smothered him with kisses. And again they made love, this time until the pall of dawn broke across the sky. It was then that they finally fell asleep in each other's arms.

As a blazing crimson sun rose against the deep purple sky, the first of the ships lifted anchor and moved slowly out of harbor. Sails began to swell in the strong winds; banners fluttered and flapped. Once again the powerful Empire Fleet set sail from its home shores.

There were many long faces that morning—faces of wives and lovers and children and parents who had barely spent time with their loved ones before they were taken from them again.

The flagship lowered its colors, as it always did upon departing, and three dozen double-masted vessels followed suit. Aboard the ships were better than a thousand men—the cream of the Empire. Many hailed from lands far away, spoke in strange accents and wore foreign garb; but all now served under the maroon and blue banner and were free citizens of the Empire. Each and every man had devoted his very life to the service of the Princess and her quest for a united world. And this was her finest achievement, the forging of these diverse peoples into a single nation.

White foaming froth splashed with roaring waves against the reefs of the deepwater harbor, and merchant vessels held back as the mighty Fleet headed into open sea. Soldiers stood at attention on shore in silent salutation to their comrades-in-arms. It was the Fleet, they knew, more than anything else, that had made the Empire what it was and kept it safe from its enemies. Now once again new lands were to be sought and the banners would stand tall upon yet another foreign isle. There were many unexplored lands to the west. This mission would be only a beginning.

With a sense of loss and sorrow, the Empire Princess watched from the citadel of the palace until the last ship was no more than a speck upon the glittering water. Then, her hair flowing freely in the breeze, she made her way back toward her court. There were many matters to settle today. Ambassadors from both the Land of the Russaks and the Western Isles were waiting patiently to air grievances over trade matters; merchants from the river cities were demanding a lower tariff on their goods; a sea captain had come to bring reports on his sighting of Kuban warships; Council ministers stood by restlessly to discuss pending agreements to refurbish Satra's depleted army.

Stacy's head swam with these many matters; but the most nagging thought in her mind was that once again Elias was gone. There was no clear reason for her discomfort—indeed, he had sailed a hundred times before and it was vitally important he claim the lost island before Sigried used it for her own vile ends—yet now, at this moment, Stacy wished she could call him back and keep him home beside her.

With a polite smile and a hidden sigh, she entered the court and took her place upon the velvet throne. Two armed women slipped from side doors and came to stand at either side of her. Their dress was Rhonnda fashion: flowing colorful skirts and decorated tunics that fell to their waists. Both women wore Satran curved daggers; both looked evenly out across the room, with feet slightly apart and heads held high. They had served the Princess half their lives, had been more friend to her than guard or companion, and would gladly give up their lives in her protection.

Stacy glanced at them, nodded and smiled. Then she turned her attention to those before her.

Alryc bowed and gestured for the first guest to speak. It was the ambassador from Russak. With his head shaven and small gold rings in his ears, he looked a strange sight to those of more cultured lands. But his grievance was a fair one, and she dealt with him on equal terms. The matter was promptly concluded.

The Western Isles emissary came next, and following him, the merchants. She was pleased to see that all was going so smoothly and quickly and had at last begun to relax, even to banter back and forth with her ministers. Her ill feelings were unfounded, she thought: Life was once again in its proper perspective.

The sea captain was next. He bowed low in a grand sweeping gesture that impressed her and reminded her in some ways of Elias. The mariner even had the same ruggedly handsome face, the same short beard. He was a few years younger, but they could have passed for brothers, and that amused her. She wondered just who he was.

"Captain Assad," said the man, as if reading her mind.

For a moment she looked startled, then she leaned back and smiled. "Ah, yes, Captain, I know your name. Years ago you were a privateer in the Kuban fleet."

Assad looked embarrassed. "That . . . er . . . was long ago, my princess. For three years now I've sailed under your banner and I am a free citizen of the Empire."

"Then you *must* be trustworthy," she said with a laugh. Her mirth was shared by her ministers and Alryc. Privateers were known for anything but their loyalty. "I am told you have news of Kuban warships; is that right?" she asked after the laughter had died.

He nodded and flashed a wide grin. "Better than that, my princess. I carry a document bearing the seal of the Kuban First Minister." He reached into the pocket of his sailor's tunic and withdrew a small rolled piece of writing paper. Eyes lowered, he handed it to her.

Stacy opened it with careful deliberation and scanned the lines with furrowed brows. "How did you come by this, Assad?"

"From a Kuban defector, my lady. The man bought his way to freedom with it. I understood its importance and cut short my own voyage to bring it back to you."

She looked coldly at Alryc. "Have you seen this?"

The mystic nodded. "My eyes and your own are the only ones, except for Assad, of course."

She frowned and looked into the sailor's face. "Do you believe what the paper says?"

The captain shrugged. "How can I say, my princess? This matter is of a higher level than I can deal with. But the document is not forged, I assure you. If I had suspected the man who brought it to me, I would have had him killed."

"Clear the court," said Stacy darkly. "Alryc, you stay. I want to go over this with you alone."

A clap of the hands from her court minister and everyone left. With hands that had begun to tremble she crushed the paper and clutched it in her fist. Her face was visibly paled now, her eyes smoldering with dark fires.

"A ruse!" she cried. "Our fleet sails to this lost island because of carefully planned deceit!"

The stargazer tensed; then his eyes narrowed and his silver brows furrowed sharply down. "To what end would the Kubans wish to see the Fleet sail far from our shore? Do they plot an attack upon Rhonnda itself? This matter makes no sense, my princess. The Rani would never dare attack our shores! Even without the Fleet our army—"

"Then why? To what purpose? But no matter, Alryc. I'm going to send a ship after them and bring Elias home at once."

Alryc's eyes cautioned against it. "This document could have two edges, Stacy. Suppose the Kuban fleet truly does seek out this island themselves. What better way to assure they find it first than by having our fleet recalled home? It would give them free rein to comb the Western Sea."

"Then this document was planted to deceive us, to make us believe the island doesn't exit. They want us to think they will attack us, so we'll have to recall our ships."

"That is my first opinion, my princess, yes. They wish freedom to find the isle themselves."

She stared at him with worry. "And your second opinion?"

"That the document is real, that this faraway place does *not* exist and that tales of it were given to our captains purposely to send our ships far from home."

She bristled with anger. There was a plot afoot somewhere that made no sense at all. Sigried would never attack Rhonnda, Fleet or no Fleet. Nor would she even dare to wage war in nearby Satra. If the letter was of genuine origin, just what could be gained by having the Fleet so far away?

"Do we call back our ships or not, Alryc? We cannot waste time. By tomorrow they'll be on a course unknown to us and we'll never find them in time."

"We must let Elias sail," said the mystic flatly. "We cannot take the risk of letting this island be found by others. If there is treachery about, we shall have to deal with it ourselves."

"Your counsel is wise, Alryc. Indeed, this document is a two-edged blade. The Rani tries to frighten us and we will not shiver. We've managed without our fleet before. And if Kuba plans war, we'll be prepared for it."

Alryc looked away, a deep scowl across his lined face; his concern knitting shadows below his eyes.

"What is it?" she asked, seeing his obvious anxiety.

"I have an ill feeling, my princess. I can't explain. 'Tis as if the sun suddenly grew dark before my eyes and a winter wind began to blow. . . ."

"Speak your mind, stargazer! Don't hold back on me now!"

He shuddered involuntarily. "Kuba plans no war, Stacy; of this I am certain. None of her armies will touch foot on Empire soil."

"Then what?"

"I know not. Who can say what vile treachery lies within that cruel beauty across the sea? But this much my visions clearly see: Sigried laughs at our peril."

Stacy was confused, angry and frightened. "Is . . . is the peril to come soon? Are we to—"

He sighed. "I shall have to read the stars. Tonight I will try to unlock Sigried's black secret." His face muscles tightened. "I fear for you, Stacy. The only target the Rani seeks is you yourself. You know that."

Stacy scoffed. "Me? Siggy would slit my throat if she could; but how? Who can she send to get close enough to kill me? You are wrong, Alryc. It's not in her plan."

He shook his head. "It *is* you, my princess; but what you say is also true: She can never get at you here. Therefore, there must be a plot to bring you to her."

"To Kuba?" Her eyes flashed. "Impossible! No power of heaven could force me to go to that dark city."

"I pray to the Fates you are right," he said glumly, "but I know Sigried's black heart—"

The Princess laughed bitterly. "I know it better. Don't forget, it was my dagger that plunged into her flesh."

"And for that she will never rest until revenge is taken," he countered. "But look! The sky begins to dim and the first stars glitter. Forgive me, my princess, but I must leave you. My reading awaits and the night is short."

It was a dark dream, filled with dread and despair. Stacy awoke with terror in her eyes. The night was silent, the winds calm. Only the gentle sounds of the surf broke the quiet. She took a series of deep breaths and closed her eyes. Her hands were still shaking, her forehead drenched in perspiration.

The images of the nightmare danced before her: the world of total dark, the flaming eyes staring at her like some hideous beast of Hel. Frozen, she had tried to run but couldn't. The eyes had burned brighter, a hoarse laugh rising all around her. She had put her hands to her ears to block out the sound, but the taunting laugh had become all the louder. Then the eyes had become larger; she had felt herself being swept down into a bottomless pit, arms flailing wildly, desperately trying to stop the fall. Deeper and deeper she had fallen. The laughing had become cries; the eyes had loomed nearer. Then she had screamed and opened her eyes.

She sat up on the edge of the bed now and lit a small candle. Long shadows bounded across the room. The flame sputtered before settling into a soft glow. Outside, a sky filled with ten thousand stars twinkled down at her. She glanced at the moon and smiled; the nightmare had passed.

But what of its meaning? That it came on the night of Elias's departure disturbed her greatly; that it came only hours after receiving the captured Kuban document frightened her more.

She threw her satin robe over her shoulders and hurried out of her rooms and along the wide corridor that led up to the towers. Startled female guards, all bearing Satrian scimitars and curved daggers, stared as she passed them without so much as a glance, her sandals slapping hollowly against the stone floor.

Glowing globes were suspended from the ceiling at even spaces, and as she passed each one, her face grew dim with shadows. The path to the tower rooms of Alryc took her up a narrow flight of winding iron steps. The way was dark, lit only by an occasional small torch, and chilled from the night breezes. It took a long while to reach the landing, where she at last knocked loudly against the arched wooden door.

Slowly the heavy door creaked open. Alryc, his mouth agape, stared at her, then flung the door open wide.

"M-my lady!" he stammered. "What has happened?"

She dismissed his question with a wave of her hand, went over to a sideboard and poured herself a cup of sweet Newfoundland wine. She took a long draught, closed her eyes and let its tingling warmth begin to run through her. Then she slumped down into a great Satrian cushion placed beside a low table.

Alryc stared, saying nothing.

At last Stacy looked up at him. "Were you sleeping? Did I wake you?"

"No, Princess. I was in my observatory, completing my charts."

Stacy stood up and reached out for his hand. "I had a terrible dream, Alryc—a vision of warning, I think. Haunting eyes followed me. . . ."

He listened as she recounted the nightmare, then led her by the hand from his rooms to his observatory.

It had been some time since she was here last and the effect of it all was dazzling. The room, oval in shape, had a concave-glass dome that gave perfect clarity to the vast array of stars and constellations above. Black night poured like velvet; the moon hung low and bright. On a small worktable were his instruments and pens and sheets of sheepskin on which he had plotted his lines. Only a tiny candle burned, giving barely enough light for him to chart; starlight provided the rest.

Awed by the sky around her, Stacy gazed out at the milky clusters of the constellations. In years past, how often she had come here to the solitude of Alryc's observatory, to try vainly to glean the hidden secrets that were woven in the magical patterns of the universe.

"Shall I read your stars for you, Princess?" Alryc stood beside her with concern in his eyes.

She smiled and shook her head. "Finish the readings you began," she told him. "It was foolish of me to have come here like this. It was only a nightmare."

The astronomer scoffed. "Dreams are a mirror of reality, Stacy. Who should know that better than you? It was right that you came. Let me read—"

Again she refused. "Finish what you began, but permit me to stay: I want to feel Starglow upon me."

He beckoned for her to sit upon the large velvet cushion. "Do you wish to read?"

She looked at him, puzzled. "Me? I cannot read the sky. Would that I could; but how?"

Bending over, he blew out the single candle. The room was washed in the totality of night. The weight of the stars pressed down. For a moment it frightened her. She felt their enormity; she was but a mortal, insignificant. At length she looked away.

"Hold your gaze firm, my lady," said Alryc with a whisper. "Do not run; never run. Let Starwarmth flow over and through you. Let the patterns come to life."

"I dare not," she said uneasily. "I would not tempt the heavens."

"The sky sparkles for all to see, Stacy. Lift your eyes and but allow the stars to speak."

Hesitantly she did as he asked; but still she feared their wrath. She was no mystic, no stargazer, merely one knowledgeable in some of their ways. "Will . . . will they show me the future?" she asked, frightened.

Alryc narrowed his eyes and stared up at Orion. "The stars will speak of what they will, my lady. Accept what they say. Let history and the present come before you. Ask not more than they will give."

She let herself be guided onto the cushion, feeling his hand holding hers tightly. His voice gentle and calming, he whispered softly for her to concentrate upon the constellation and let her mind run free.

The first sensation of Starwarmth came quickly; the heavens began to whirl. Alryc's voice was gone; so was the hand that held hers. Colors began to take shape and form. There was a vortex, a long tunnel to which she felt compellingly pulled. For an instant she drew back, then permitted herself to let go, to let loose the bonds of earth and allow her mind to be swept away into the very universe.

The black sky began somehow to brighten, first to a dull purple, then to a deep crimson and scarlet. Hues of blue and green melded at the edges of her vision and streaks of bright yellow and flaming gold trickled down in ever-widening stripes. She sat breathless. The colors enchanted her, entranced her. Was this Alryc's own magic upon her? she wondered. Or was this truly the heavens accepting her eyes and her mind and opening themselves to her? It was a journey like none she had ever known before, and she would no longer draw back from it.

At last the colors began to take shape. With amazement she watched, unwilling and unable to speak of what she was seeing. She saw the earth in its infancy. Burning volcanos spewed lava across vast oceans; flames licked viciously everywhere. Slowly, as if countless aeons had passed, the lands began to cool. White-hot lava turned to dark-brown fires that smoldered and simmered. Suddenly the sky began to darken. The familiar roll of distant thunder rumbled from far away, and then began the downpour. The whole world trembled with the thunder; flashes of lightning lit up a pallid, bleak sky. Stacy saw rivers form and once-empty canyons now swell with racing tides. There were currents surging across the hot lands and joining with the sea. The world was tossed in furious frenzy. Then the rain stopped.

Again the colors of her panorama changed. The sky was blue, the sun gold. Green grasses grew over the valleys and hills, and trees and shrubs filled the once-barren plains. Even the deserts sprang with life. She knew she had just witnessed the birth of the earth.

Birds soared in the air; on land a thousand different creatures raised their heads. A million years passed in moments. The animals gave way to man; strange cities arose. The oceans filled with ships whose flags she could not recognize. The sands of time raced ahead. The cities grew larger, taller. Spires and steeples that dwarfed those of Rhonnda sprang up everywhere. A wondrous age, she thought; if only it did not all move before her eyes so swiftly. She stared at the sight of what must have been incredible civilizations. The cities were peopled by tens of thousands heaped upon tens of thousands. All around was throbbing life. Generations passed in a single breath, centuries. Life became more confused. She could no longer grasp the strange sights she was seeing.

Bright light burst everywhere, blinding her. She felt thrown back, heaved and tossed about like a child's toy. Had the sun exploded? She tried to scream but no sound came. Then, as quickly as the blinding light had come, it was gone. A dim glow burned across the horizon. The lands had been scorched, she saw; the cities had turned to rubble. Nothing remained. The earth was dark and grim. There were no sounds. No grasses swayed in the breeze; no sweet waters ran from the rivers. The world was empty. And she cried. She knew then that she had seen the Cataclysm—that mysterious and terrible event that had erased the civilizations of the Old Time forever and replaced them with the age known to all as the Dark Time, when men cowered in fear and forgot all they had ever learned.

Rains came again, as they had in the beginning. With fear and curiosity, Stacy pulled her thoughts back together and watched the stars unfold the continuing tale. The grasses returned, and the trees. The world became filled with dark forests. The last ruins of the Old Time turned to dust. The world was different. Men hid in the shadows of the forests and the mountains. For a thousand years and more the Dark Time lasted until the first civilizations began to flourish. She knew these men to be her ancestors, knew this to be the foundation of the empire they were forging. The Fates had given them all a second chance. She knew they must take hold firmly and not lose it; there would never be a third.

The images faded; the swirls of colors came and were gone. Once more the Empire Princess found herself staring up at the constellation Orion, its stars twinkling before her eyes. The journey across countless millennia had taken only minutes.

Alryc leaned over and touched her face softly, bringing her out of her hypnotic trance.

Looking at him, she smiled and wiped the perspiration from her face. "Did you see?" she asked feebly.

He shrugged. "I saw nothing, Princess. Tonight the stars spoke only to you. What did they show?"

"I saw the world, Alryc, from the beginning. I saw the Old Time. . . ." Her voice became shaky and she looked away from his stare. "And I saw the Cataclysm."

The stargazer nodded darkly. "Then you know. You have witnessed the destruction of the world and the Dark Time that followed."

"Yes," she replied, "but I also saw the Rebirth! I saw our ancestors come out from the Dark Time."

"Did you see the future?"

It took her a long moment to realize that everything she had witnessed had happened long ago; there was no sign of what was yet to be, and now that began to disturb her. "I saw only the past," she said. "I fear the stars deny to me what is yet to come."

"Destiny can never be denied," he said.

"You are holding something back from me, Alryc. What is it?"

Relighting the candle, he sat beside her and handed her a goblet of wine. "I have finished my own reading," he said darkly, "and the answers I find bear out my worst fears. There is indeed treachery against you. The signs are clearly there. And although the culprit's name has not been given, I know it can only be Sigried."

"What is the future, then?"

He sighed deeply. "The stars are clouded. That dangers exist, there is no doubt; but as to what path they will lead, I cannot say. The Rani will strike at your person, not directly but by using another, I think."

Stacy's eyes darkened. *Sigried wishes to get at me,* she thought. *That much we know—that much we have always known—yet not through me directly; through another. Who? Elias? That would do little for her cause.* "I am determined to deal with this, Alryc. Tomorrow I will call back that mercenary captain, Assad. He knew the Rani years ago. As he was formerly in her service, I am sure there must be more he could tell."

The astronomer looked glum. "I pray we can trust him, Stacy. We have no way of knowing if he does not serve here as a spy. He would not be the first."

Stacy laughed bitterly. "Nor the last. But why be so despondent? We've dealt with her deceit before—and worse."

"We must beware of assassins," he said.

Stacy grinned. "I'm ahead of you, Alryc. My bodyguards are already alerted. The palace is crawling with our agents."

The image of the rugged forest girls with their crossbows and daggers at the ready relieved some of Alryc's tension. Those women were sworn to protect the Princess with their lives. Each had had occasion to prove her worthiness in the past. The captain of the Guard, fiery Melinda, had trained them well. For the present, Stacy was protected.

"And what of Mara?" he asked.

"Wolves, Alryc; guards also. If these assassins would dare to harm her—or, for that matter, any of the palace children—I'd—"

"Have no fear, my lady. It will never happen. Even the Rani would never contemplate such a bold move against you. She knows the price you'd exact if she tried." His soothing words belied the genuine concern in his eyes. "Nevertheless," he went on, "you must be careful. Promise me you'll stay well guarded until this whole matter is concluded."

She stood on her toes and kissed him lightly on the cheek. "I will. Don't be concerned. I haven't survived all these years to lose my life to an assassin's blade now." She smiled. "Far too many of my dreams are yet unfulfilled."

It was midmorning when Mara returned from her ride. She passed through the black gate and, kicking gently with her heels, led the stallion toward the stables. It was a quiet morning, with few sounds to be heard from the sleepy city below. The sight of a resting wolf beneath the shade of a hickory tree made the horse uneasy. Mara calmed him with gentle strokes and eased him along the bridal path. She had been riding since she could walk and was good with horses.

Since dawn she had been gone, out alone in the rugged Free Land foothills. The sun had been warm, the breezes strong. The feel of the wind through her hair and against her body had exhilarated her, made her feel fresh and alive. It was good to leave the palace grounds like this, to be free and on her own. Usually she would ride with a bodyguard beside her, but not this morning. She had been restless these past weeks, feeling an urgent need to be alone. Somehow the palace grounds, large as they were, made her feel confined. She yearned to be rid of them, to wander aimlessly as the wind and find release from her unsettled mind.

It was because she was now becoming a woman, Melinda had told her. Girls her age were always restless, needing to wander off by themselves and discover the world around them and learn to develop lives of their own. Mara had listened intently as Melinda told her these things; she always did. She loved her like an older sister and was grateful for her advice and reassurances. So close had they become, sometimes it seemed hard for Mara to remember that, above all, Melinda was the Princess's best friend and confidante and had been since even before she took the throne. Melinda was devoted to Stacy; it was she who had developed the small ring of forest girls who protected her. Each girl was highly trained and skilled, each renowned for her ability with both crossbow and dagger. Anastasia's enemies often claimed that were it not for the wolves and her bodyguard, the Empire armies would never have achieved the successes it had.

Mara dismounted to rest under the leafy shade of a tall oak. She heard children's laughter in the distance and realized that it came from the rock garden just beyond her sight. Far off to her left, the silhouettes of several soldiers marched in slow procession along the high wall, keeping a careful eye on the roads and approaches to the main gate. From their sides hung long bejeweled scimitars, telling her that these men were Satrian and probably recruited by Lord Blood. They were stern-faced and rugged, these men from Satra, and if anyone had the idea of slipping undetected into the palace grounds, she knew full well their ability to catch him. Apart from the Rhonnda Cavalry, Satrian soldiers were the cream of the Empire army.

As Mara rested, she became aware of the lumbering soldier who approached her from the direction of the stables. He was a dark, broad-shouldered man with cunning eyes and hard features. She knew him to be yet another who had been recruited from across the sea—not from Satra, though; more the type from Kreel.

"You should not have been riding out alone, my lady," he said gruffly.

"Are you going to tell?"

He laughed. "No, my lady; merely escort you to the stable. Come."

She brushed some loose grass from her tunic; her dark hair swirled. The soldier gestured for her to follow. A few minutes later she had put her stallion in his stall and was about to head back to the garden when the soldier boldly took her sleeve.

"I . . . er . . . have a favor I would ask you, young princess."

Mara's eyes narrowed.

"One of the mares in the servants' stables has gone lame," he told her, "and I thought perhaps I could get you to have a look."

It was a strange request, Mara thought. "Why don't you send for a physician to tend her?"

"The poor animal belongs to a friend of mine, my lady. I know your skill with horses, and I wondered if I could get you to look at her first."

It was an honest request, she knew, and after all, the soldier had done her a favor by not reporting that she had been out alone. Taking a look at the injured horse was the least she could do in return.

"All right, Dimitri, show me the way."

He grinned broadly and led her by the arm onto the narrow path under the arch, past the hedges and toward the row of low tiny stables. There was no activity about at all. At first Mara thought this odd, but then, recalling that the heat was oppressive at this time of day, she assured herself that the stableboys would be inside seeking shade.

When they reached the stables, Dimitri led her to the last stable in the row. He held the doors wide and she stepped inside. The air was dank and musty; it took long seconds for her eyes to adjust to the dim light. The horses snorted restlessly as she came toward them.

"Which stall, Dimitri?" she asked, peering about uneasily.

"The one at the end, my lady: the chestnut mare."

She nodded and made her way to the stall. The horse seemed frightened of her. She soothed her with soft whispers, stroking her mane, and examined her legs. "I can't find anything wrong, Dimitri. Are you sure this is the right one?"

Slowly he came in beside her. Her eyes missed the slow movement of his hand to his side. With a sudden jerking motion, he drew a dagger and pushed her to the ground.

Mara looked up, startled. "What—"

The knife flickered before her. She froze, breathless.

"One move from you, Mara, and I'll cut that pretty neck of yours!"

Her mouth gaped. "Are you mad? What do you think you're doing?"

His eyes glowered and his mouth turned down in a grimace. "I'm taking you on a small trip, Mara."

"You're insane!"

The back of his hand smashed against her face, knocking her backward. "I told you to be quiet!"

Trembling, she watched as he gave a low whistle. Seconds later two men, swarthy and grim, appeared from the shadows.

"Bind her," whispered Dimitri.

She jumped up and kicked Dimitri in the groin. He stumbled. As he did, she tried to push past the others. A swift kick brought her down again, face first in mud. She tried to get up again and felt heavy boots pressing down on her back.

"Let me go!" she cried. "You'll never get away with this! My aunt will have you—"

A hand squeezed around her throat, then pulled her hair. Dimitri stared at her with cold, malevolent eyes. His face still twisted with pain from her kick. "I should kill you for what you just did," he wheezed, "but I have orders to follow."

"Orders?"

He smirked. "You'll learn about them soon enough. I'm not to harm a pretty hair on your head." As he spoke, she could feel one of the other men tying her hands tightly with cord. Dimitri grinned and turned her over on her back. She lay there too frightened to move. One of the men was holding a drawn shortsword above her abdomen. She squirmed as Dimitri's stubby fingers ran up and down her body, caressing her.

"You swine!" She spit in his face.

In rage he squeezed her throat. "So you can't stand my touch, eh?"

She felt her mind go dim as she was about to pass out. Just then he let go and she gasped for air.

"We haven't much time," said one of the other men.

Dimitri nodded. "Gag her, and make it tight: I don't want a single squeal out of her."

The man complied, stuffing her mouth with a handkerchief and then tying it with thin cord. Dimitri smiled at Mara as he pulled her up roughly. "We'll get to know each other later," he said. "You can be sure of that." Then he pushed her from the stall.

"We'll drug her at the dock."

Her eyes widened; she realized now what they intended. Wildly she kicked again, but this time Dimitri easily sidestepped her.

"Not twice, my precious," he taunted, twisting her arm painfully. Another shove sent her beside the entrance.

One of the men peered carefully outside. There was

no one. "The way seems clear," he told Dimitri. "No Satrians or wolves."

The dragoon nodded glumly. "Good. We'll walk slowly to the bridge."

Mara's mind raced. The bridge! That could mean only one thing: Their escape would be achieved through the old unused tunnels. Under the bridge was an entrance to the old sewer system—a virtual labyrinth that twisted and wound down to the city. Once inside that dark maze, they would never be found; she would be at their mercy. But what could she do? Bound as she was, there was little chance of getting away. Her only hope was to be seen by one of the prowling wolves. At this distance even the soldiers atop the walls could never spot her.

"Move!" hissed Dimitri.

She stepped out into the sunlight and let her eyes scan carefully about. It was a long walk to the bridge, she knew, and in that time she would have to come up with something.

"Don't delude yourself," said Dimitri, again as if reading her mind. "No one will be looking for you. My agents have seen to that."

Mara shuddered as he spoke. She did not know what he meant, but something inside assured her he was telling the truth.

It was as if all Hel had been unleashed. A sweeping fire encompassed the trees and hedges, sending up huge clouds of black billowing smoke. Alarm bells sounded; soldiers ran frantically down from the parapet toward the rock garden. The children screamed as the fire circled the garden. Several forest girls managed to fight their way through the blaze to their sides.

The palace was in a panic. Stacy blindly pushed past the throng of soldiers trying in vain to reach the garden. All around, the cries of the children filled her ears. She raced on. A thundering flame shot before her eyes, sending her reeling back. Soldiers were clamoring to move through it.

Someone pulled Stacy back as she tried to battle through again. "You cannot help, Princess," came the deep voice of Alryc.

She looked about, fear whitening her face. "The children!" she cried. "We've got to save them!"

The screams grew louder, more frantic.

Alryc held her back firmly. "We'll do what we can. But you must get back from here: The fire's spreading."

"Let me go! I've got to help!"

The stargazer shielded them both with his cloak as fanning flames swept toward them. "No, Stacy. You can't—"

"I can and I will! Let me go! I command it!"

Again Alryc refused. He swept her up and drew her quickly away from the fire. A handful of forest girls came racing out from the flames, each carrying a child. The children's faces were blackened, their bodies seared and scorched. Daring soldiers plowed their way through. Stacy saw one scream as a massive burning branch fell upon him.

"More water!" shouted someone from behind.

Stunned by the sight and the sounds, the Princess numbly watched as horse-drawn water wagons roared through the gates.

More children were brought out by the last of the soldiers in the garden. A strong breeze was pushing the fire across the hill and to the walls of the palace itself. Stacy realized that the last rescue effort had been made, leaving no hope of getting out those who were still trapped among the savage leaping flames. She cried out in anguish. These were the children of her friends, her trusted advisors and ministers. She realized what terrible grief would be wrought on the Rhonnda palace.

The screams intensified as the fanning flames engulfed them all. The pleas for help faded, then ended. Soon no sound save that of the fire itself could be heard. Fifteen children had been in the garden; seven had been rescued.

Strong, bitter winds swept through the court. Outside, the roll of thunder crashed with shattering violence. The downpour put quick end to the flames, leaving the scorched grounds to smolder, the black, lifeless trees to stand bleak and deadened, a gruesome reminder of what had happened.

Throughout the palace and the city, there was a fearful silence. The streets were deserted, the bazaars and marketplaces empty. The time for mourning had begun.

Stacy sat upon her throne in the darkened chamber. Her head was bowed low, her hands covering her pale, drawn face. Tears of bitterness flowed from sunken and hollowed eyes. She raised her arms toward the black sky and cried out in anger against the Fates. "Why have you turned against me?" she wept aloud, her voice cracking with every word. "Why have you taken out your anger upon me by striking those who were innocent?"

The fall of rain was her only reply. She shivered uncontrollably. Gladly would she have flung herself from the highest tower in the Empire if that had been what the Fates had demanded. Eagerly would she have faced the fires of Hel itself had the heavens so ordained. But no, they had seen fit to punish her in the worst way possible—through the deaths of others: the children and her beloved Mara. No voice came from within to reassure her and bring her inner calm; only emptiness; only the splash of rain against the portico.

"Where are you now, Elias?" she wailed. She was in deeper misery than she had ever known, and the one she loved the most was not there to comfort her, to share her pain.

Mara was dead and Elias was gone away, perhaps never to return from those strange, cruel waters. Stacy fought to control her trembling, knowing that, as always, she was forced to bear her burdens alone.

Outside the chamber, her friends stood in stony silence. The Princess had refused to let them come to her. From their places, they could plainly hear her mournful cries, but there was nothing to be done. Both Alryc and Melinda stared blankly, their faces long and sullen. It was to their hands that the safety of the palace children had been entrusted, and they felt wholly responsible for the disaster that had befallen Rhonnda.

Melinda sighed sorrowfully. If only she had been in personal charge and not tending to other duties, perhaps this could have been averted. The Princess had given her the authority. It was she herself who was to blame. Only she had let the Princess down.

Alryc tortured himself with the very same feelings. He stood in dim shadows, hands clasped behind his back, tears rolling from his old, wizened eyes. He too believed he had failed the Princess.

Lightning flashed; a clap of thunder muffled the sobs from within the chamber. Fast footsteps clattered against the stone floor as a dark figure strode quickly toward the Princess's throne room.

Alryc turned and eyed the man. The face became clear. It was Assad, the sea captain. "What are you doing here?" said Alryc. "No one can see the Princess today."

Assad looked at the stargazer intensely. *"I* must," he whispered. "I have urgent news."

Melinda faced him, her eyes flashing wetly. "Give your news to me," she hissed. "Princess Anastasia cannot see you."

Assad shook his head firmly. "This is news for her ears alone, my lady. Please let me pass."

Melinda, beset with grief and rage, drew her curved dagger. "No one enters the court today, Captain," she told him, waving the blade menacingly.

Assad drew back a pace, fully aware that the forest girl was prepared to use her weapon if he refused to comply. "The fire was purposely set," he said, blurting out the frightful truth.

Melinda and Alryc exchanged horrified glances.

"Set by mercenary agents from Kuba."

Melinda's hand went to her mouth and she gasped in disbelief. "What? How do you know this? Speak!"

Assad drew them both close and in a low, urgent voice explained all he had learned.

"Stacy must be told!" cried Alryc after the tale was done.

Melinda nodded and sighed. "Yes, she must. But which of us has the courage to go in and tell her?"

Sitting in the shadows, Stacy was hardly aware as the three unwelcome visitors inched their way together into the chamber. She sat with her back to the door, staring at the night, frightened, abused, a lost child herself.

"My princess," whispered Assad boldly as he bowed before the throne.

Stacy turned and faced him with the saddest eyes he had ever seen. He choked with the thought of the news he carried.

"What . . . what do you want?" she said, too drained and weary to speak loudly. "I asked to be left alone."

Assad rose, Melinda and Alryc at his side. "Please forgive this intrusion," the sea captain said, "but I have news that must be told."

Stacy closed her eyes and nodded painfully. "Speak your news quickly," she rasped, "then be gone."

Assad reached inside his tunic and withdrew a small piece of writing paper. "Maralisa has been kidnaped," he said.

Stacy's eyes grew wide. She leaned forward with a look of total horror. "What are you saying? Mara is dead, engulfed by the flames!"

"No, my princess," he replied. "The fire was not an accident, as we believed. It was purposely set by unknown spies within the palace to serve as a ruse so that Mara could be whisked away while our attentions were diverted."

The Empire Princess gasped. "No" she cried, "it cannot be true!"

"It is," said Melinda. "These ruthless men, whoever they were, purposely let the palace children be murdered so that their scheme could be completed."

"Our security forces are not yet certain of all the circumstances," Assad told her in a quick, steady voice, "but it seems that Mara had not been within the palace grounds all morning. She had slipped away to go riding. Five stable hands were found murdered. We think the spies somehow led her away from the stable when she returned."

Stacy felt her head swim. "But how do you know she was away from the palace this morning?" she asked anxiously.

"A sentry at the gate saw her. She returned before noon, just before the fires began." Assad handed her the paper with a trembling hand.

Stacy took it and opened the folded page. A small lock of hair fell to her lap—Mara's hair. She read the note aloud: " 'You will not find Maralisa, try as hard as you may. The ransom for her life will be high if you want her brought home in safety.' " She looked up incredulously. "Is that *all*? What ransom do they ask? When will they contact us again?"

Assad shrugged and grimaced. "We don't know. This

note was found beside the quay. Already our soldiers are combing the docks and back alleys."

"You'll not find the young princess there!" barked Alryc.

Assad turned. "My lord?"

Alryc looked at the Princess, eyes aflame. "I see it all now!" he boomed, his voice echoing across the halls. "The plot becomes clear!"

Stacy was perplexed. "What plot?"

"Sigried," hissed the stargazer. "Only the Rani could be behind such a foul deed. The truth shines as brightly as the North Star."

Melinda's eyes glimmered with rekindled fury. "Not even the Rani would dare such a thing!"

Alryc peered down at her. "No? Then why has our fleet been sent on its errand—a fool's errand from which it will never return?"

Stacy's mouth gaped. She swallowed hard. "What's happened?" she cried. "Tell me!"

Assad glanced painfully at Melinda, realizing that this further news would perhaps grieve the Princess the most. "As you suspected, the voyage of the Fleet was a carefully planned ruse. Lord Blood learned of it weeks ago in Azura and dispatched a ship to Rhonnda to warn you; but brigands lay in waiting and the ship was attacked en route."

Stacy waited breathlessly, her heart sinking with every word, her instincts preparing her for the worst. "Go on," she whispered.

"The waters to which the Fleet sails are more dangerous than any man realized. The southern winds blow upon a turbulent sea. At this time of year the ocean becomes a maelstrom of havoc. Our ships will enter those waters at the worst possible time; the dangerous shoals will smash every vessel. They will be stranded and founder until they sink. The mysterious island will never be reached."

Stacy's hand rose to her horrified face. "Elias must be warned!" she shouted. "They must be stopped before it's too late!"

There were tears in Assad's eyes as he shook his head. "It's already too late. By now the fair trade winds will have taken them a hundred leagues from Rhonnda. We have no way of reaching him in time." He put his arm out toward the Princess, staring at her through grieved eyes. "We must . . . we must consider the Fleet to be lost. Only a miracle can save it."

Stacy slumped back in shock and tears came in a flood. "What's to be done?" she cried, her head buried in her hands. "I begged him not to go, begged him—"

"Would that I could trade places to bring him back to you, my princess," said the mercenary sea captain sincerely.

Melinda cast a long burning look at Alryc. "So now we know," she hissed. "The Rani thinks she can now sail her ships across the Seven Seas with impunity. The bitch! Who but Sigried could have conceived such a plot against us?"

Stacy lifted her head and dried her red, watery eyes. "Sigried must truly believe she can conquer the world."

"Az'i!" spat Melinda contemptuously. "In a pig's eye! Listen to me, Stacy. Recall Blood from Azura at once, bring our forces home, and unleash your wolf army from the Satrian mountains. Let them tear down the very gates of Kuba!"

"No!" barked Alryc, keeping a cooler head, as always, even in the face of such adversity. He looked at the Princess pleadingly. "We must not commit the Empire to such a war. It would plunge the world back into the Dark Time. It's what Sigried wants, don't you see? She would gloat over the destruction."

Melinda laughed bitterly. "Then should we stand by while the Rani claims the seas for her own? Stacy, I implore you: Act at once! Give the word—now!" She clenched her fist. "Let us smash Kuba once and for all!"

Stacy gazed from the one advisor to the other, weighing what each had said. She sighed and fixed her eyes on Melinda. "Alryc is right," she said after a time. "I will not let the world turn again to savagery."

"Even if Rhonnda must pay with her very being?" Melinda countered.

Stacy next turned to Alryc. "Melinda is right on one point," she said: "Siggy must be dealt with, but not on her terms; on mine."

Mystery was mixed with the urgency of her voice. Alryc seemed puzzled.

The Princess forced a thin smile and said, "Tell me, Alryc, what does the Rani hope to achieve by having Mara taken like this? To what purpose and intent?"

"Is it not clear, my lady? Sigried has no need for the girl at all. Mara means nothing to her or her schemes—nothing."

"Then why?"

Alryc's face tightened into a dour mask and his eyes slitted catlike. "It's you the Rani wants, only you, and she hopes to lure you to Kuba to save Mara."

"Sigried must be mad!" snapped Melinda. "What fools does she take us for? Dare she dream that the Princess would go to her vile city for any reason?"

Stacy waved her hand and leaned back on her throne. Her hands clutched tightly at the leather armrests. "I think perhaps I understand what you said better than Melinda does," she told the astronomer. "Your reading foretold that Siggy would try to get at me through another and she has succeeded. First she made certain that Elias and our fleet were lost and doomed and then she hatched her plot. Mara is the bait, and if I want her back, I'll have to bite."

Alryc nodded glumly. "Exactly. What better way to hurt you than through those you love the most? She knows you will do anything to save the girl."

Melinda looked from one to the other, aghast. "But we can't even be sure Mara is still alive," she protested. "A lock of hair and a mysterious message mean nothing. The Rani's agents could have killed her long ago."

Stacy shook an imperious finger. "I think not, Melinda. Mara is too valuable a pawn in the Rani's little game. She will need her to use against me. Siggy has burned with hatred for years, and as long as I sit on the Rhonnda throne, she'll never rest easy. Mara will be used to get at me."

"Remember the ransom note," added Alryc. "It says that the cost for Mara's life will be high. What higher price than the Empire Princess herself?"

"*Az'i!*" flared Melinda. She looked at Stacy incredulously. "Don't tell me that you're seriously thinking of going to Kuba to fall into this obvious trap?"

Stacy looked at her friend sharply. "Trust me, Melinda. If I am to go, it will not be as Siggy expects."

"Stacy, no!" cried the forest girl. "There would be no exchange of you for Mara. The Rani will keep you both prisoner." Tears streamed down her soft cheeks. "I beg you, my princess: Unleash your wolves; take Kuba now while we still can!"

Stacy's eyes focused on the soft curl of hair. She picked it up and held it against her breast. "Siggy knows me too well, I'm afraid," she sighed. "She knows I cannot let Mara be held her prisoner. Mark my words: In days to come, a letter will arrive from Kuba and Sigried will at last admit to her role in this plot. I'll be asked to sail for Kuba—"

"To find the Rani's fleet waiting for you," Assad interjected. "You'd be captured long before you even reached her shores."

Stacy looked at him curiously. "Perhaps not, Captain. If I am forced into her game, it will be as I said: on my terms, not hers."

A pained expression lingered on Alryc's lined face.

"Let me go to Kuba in your stead," he asked. "Let me be the one to repay the Rani for these injustices against you."

The Princess smiled warmly, but her mind was resolved. "You and I have traveled many roads together, Alryc," she said softly. "But in this adventure only I can play the decisive role." She glanced at Melinda. "You have both been my closest friends. You would both give your own lives gladly to save mine if you could. It's more than I would ask, though. I love you both too much. Only I can repay the crimes done to me. The Fates will it so."

"Then what will you do, my princess?" asked Alryc feebly.

Stacy smiled a strange smile. "Leave me," she whispered. "Please go now, all of you. I need to be alone with my grief."

They all bowed and sadly turned away from the crying Princess. Their hearts ached for her, but they would do as she asked: leave her to reflect and ponder the turn in her fate; let her alone decide what must be done.

Of them all, only Alryc had an inkling of what the Princess was going to do. The very thought of it, though, only added to his concern for her. Again she would take everything upon her own shoulders and boldly meet her destiny head on, without care or concern for herself, to selflessly risk her own life so that her loved one might be spared.

No, the stars had not lied to him. Fate could not be altered, try though mortals might. Stacy had known this all along. He had been a fool for ever believing otherwise. And he suddenly realized that for good or ill, this new adventure upon which the Princess was prepared to embark would change the course of the world forever.

Stacy watched them leave with a sad smile. It was

good to have companions such as these. Indeed had the Fates blessed her. Elias was all but gone, she knew, but for Mara there was still a chance. Whatever the cost, the girl could not be made to suffer because of the blind feud she and Sigried had waged for so long.

Again Stacy cried. Elias would never be her husband now, she was sure; never would she have the children she so desperately wanted. All that was behind. She must put such thoughts away forever. Maybe it was better this way: It would give her a clear path for the difficult roads ahead. *Bury the past. Think of no personal future.*

Now she would live with one purpose and one purpose only: to free Mara and repay Sigried. Apart from that, Stacy knew, her life was to be an empty shell, lonely and despairing without the man she loved. Like creeping spiders, the web of intrigue had been drawn around her. The vile poisons of hate had spread into her veins. One day, if she survived the tasks she faced, she might be able to rebuild upon those bitter ashes and memories, but not now; there was no room for such feeling. She knew she had to be every bit as cold and calculating as the enemy she faced; yes, even as cruel, if she must. Sigried had to be met on her own terms.

"I begged you not to leave, Elias!" she sobbed. And her face lifted to the heavens. *Sweet Fara, if it's not already too late, make him hear my plea. Make him turn around and come safely home. Do this for me and my own life I'll willingly give. I am crushed, forever broken. Let me die if you will, but let Mara and Elias live.*

It was this dim spark burning in her heart that kept her going. Without it she knew she would never be able to face the dangers ahead.

It did not take long for the awaited letter to arrive, merely the time it took a swift ship to ply the Newfoundland Sea and deliver it. The days in between had passed slowly and painfully for Stacy. There was not much time for her to formulate her plan; she was forced to overlook small details and rely on the will of the Fates to bring her through. Until the arrival of the letter from Kuba, no one, not even Alryc, had been told what she would do. But now that it was here, there was no time to lose in implementing it. So it was with great courage and determination that she called Alryc and Melinda to meet with her.

Sitting on a great wicker chair, her legs crossed, her face turned to the warm sun, Stacy put the sealed letter beside her and waited for her friends' arrival. She was dressed in a soft-yellow loose tunic with thin stripes of silver at the edges, a slim copper band holding back her long flowing hair. The time of bitter tears was behind. The damage had been done. Now was the time for action, and no force on earth could stop her from taking it.

Alryc walked up from the winding path behind the stone wall of twirling ivy. He reached the portico from behind the spouting fountain and paused briefly to sip from its cool water. The heat was intolerable; he had yet to understand Stacy's love of the sun. Sitting under a shady sycamore by a cool brook was how he spent such days.

Melinda came from the opposite direction, from the palace gates. Somber, large eyes downcast, she walked along the rows of berry bushes. Thick grass covered the lawns; off in the distance she could see several workmen busily pruning weeds from the flower beds.

She clutched unconsciously at the hilt of her dagger as she reached the portico. Stacy smiled in greeting and gestured for her to sit on the small slat bench beneath the ivy wall and help herself to a goblet of crystal water recently brought from the Western Isles. Melinda took the drink gratefully.

Alryc sat beside her but refused a drink, his eyes fastened on the sealed letter. He had expected the Princess to be in a rage now that it was here. Once again, though, she had surprised him. Instead, she sat calm and collected, bathing in the sun and acting as though nothing had happened.

Stacy caught his stare and smiled. She reached down, picked up the letter and held it gently in her hands. "The messenger delivered it about an hour ago," she said evenly.

Melinda was unable to contain her anxiety. "What does it say?"

Stacy laughed caustically. "Needless to say, it's not quite what we expected; but let me read it to you."

They both leaned forward nervously.

"Siggy deserves a lot of credit for this," said Stacy. "She writes in a way that leaves no reason for our army to march. You'll both see what I mean." And then she began to read:

" 'My dear sister upon the throne: How fortunate that circumstances have at last allowed me reason to write to you personally. It was a grievous shock to me when news reached my court that your lovely niece had been abducted by foul mercenaries. Such bandits are the scourge of the world. My own captains informed me when this very brigand ship dared to enter our territorial waters. Naturally I immediately dispatched warships to seize the vessel. The Fates were with us both, dear sister. The brigand ship fell with little fight. At my instruction, your niece was brought to me at once. Although she was badly shaken by this terrible ordeal, I am pleased to say that she is uninjured in any way. She is a lovely young woman, Anastasia. It would have been a great shame had harm come to her.

'I understand that her abductors had planned to take her somewhere in the land of Kreel, where such privateers flock from justice. Thank the heavens my ships were able to stop them in time. Now Mara waits only to go back to her home in Rhonnda-by-the-Sea, and I trust she will be able to leave soon.' "

Here Stacy paused to let the first half of the letter sink in.

Melinda looked up with disbelief. "Privateers from Kreel? Is it possible, Stacy? Perhaps the Rani really did not have a hand in this matter."

Alryc shook his head. "Sigried is cunning, like an Azuran Helcat. The letter is not yet done. When it is, I fear we'll see just how shrewdly she operates."

Stacy smiled and began to read again: " 'Alas, dearest sister, I cannot yet allow Mara to sail. The season of summer squalls is upon Kuban waters and such a journey would be far too hazardous for a passenger as important as she. I have implored Mara to stay with us for a while and learn more of our land and customs. She seems content to do so. So, with your permission, Anastasia, which I beg, I ask that you permit her to spend this added time with us. But lest you believe my motives are ill against her, I implore that you yourself come to Kuba as a guest of our hospitality. We have not seen each other for how many years now, dear sister. I know that your arrival in my city would be a cause of great joy and celebration for all concerned. There are so many matters of mutual interest for us to discuss. Our enemies have kept us separated for much too long.

'Come to Kuba, Stacy. Let our lands be forged together in peace. But, as a sign of your own goodwill, I ask that you come only with the single ship that carries you. The sight of your fleet would not sit well with my reckless allies. Unlike myself, they do not trust you. They fear you would do Kuba harm. I know otherwise.

'I trust this letter will have reached you in the way intended and that you will leave for our lands at the earliest moment. It is a pity that Captain Elias cannot join you, but I have heard of his latest voyage and realize that he will be gone from Rhonnda for quite some time. My own ships will stand by on constant alert to greet you. You will be given full escort with honor. Let not the time fly: Mara counts on your arrival. Your sister, Sigried.' "

Melinda fumed, her eyes flashing. "The Kuban bitch!"

"So there you have it," said Stacy dryly. "An invitation into the Rani's arms, with full escort."

"To her dungeons, you mean!" snapped Alryc. "The Rani blends words of honey with a viper's poison. She hides her threats carefully and lures you as a spider entices a fly."

Stacy leaned forward with her chin in her hands. "I know; but she knows I can't let Mara rot in her cells. I'll have to go."

Melinda looked away, tears in her eyes. "Please, Stacy," she pleaded, "don't do this thing. Let me send for Blood. Even without the Fleet we can poise a massive force. Our soldiers in Satra can march by land. We can cross the Thunder Plain in days—"

"And let them fall into the hands of Sigried's army?" Stacy shook her head and laughed bitterly. "No, Melinda: You're letting your heart rule your head. The Rani expects as much of us. Her galleys would smash our boats like kindling without the Fleet beside us."

"Then we'll wait for Elias to return. We'll sail to Kuba and burn every port in her empire. We'll march on Kuba itself and turn her jeweled city into cinders!"

Alryc's face grew glum. He sighed deeply. "No, Melinda, the Princess is right: Empire forces must not converge on Kuba. It would be begging for Mara's death. Worse, it would commit us to total war. The years we so painstakingly spent forging peace would be torn asunder beneath the banners and blades of destruction. Thousands of lives would be lost."

Tears streamed down Melinda's face. "Then to keep the peace we lose our princess. Is it worth the price? I love Mara as if she were my own"—here she lowered her head and her eyes, unable to meet the looks of her companions—"but I love Rhonnda more."

Stacy felt her own tears rise. "I know how you feel," she whispered; "but Mara cannot be punished for my deeds."

"So you walk into her trap knowingly? There'll be no exchange, Stacy. A blind beggar in the streets of Sytherna could see as much. Once you're in Kuba, Sigried will have you both and you'll both suffer for it."

"I've thought of that. I've turned every possibility over in my mind. I can't sit still and let Mara be kept in Kuban dungeons. Sigried knows me too well for that. One way or another, I must go."

"And wittingly the fly steps into the web," mumbled Alryc sourly.

Stacy's eyes smoldered with rebellion. "Not quite!"

His brows rose; his face tightened. He knew that Stacy's plan was about to be unfolded.

"Sigried expects me to sail into her water openly," she said. "That I will never do."

Melinda was puzzled. "Then how will you reach her shores?"

The Princess folded her arms. "From the east—from Kreel."

Alryc gulped. Those waters were dark and unknown. Kreel was a land of strange peoples and stranger customs. They recognized neither the maroon and blue flags of Rhonnda nor the gold and black of Kuba. They were a race apart, living amid arid deserts and grim mountains. Sailors who dared touch their shores were lucky to come back alive, and the tales they told could make the stoutest of men shudder.

"You can't be serious, Stacy," he stammered. "First off, those waters are infested with pirates. If they knew that Princess Anastasia were to come—"

Stacy's eyes darkened. "Anastasia will *not* come."

"My lady?"

She leaned forward and spoke so low her voice was barely audible. "No one must know that I have left the palace. I intend to take the guise of a Satrian noblewoman seeking shelter in their land. With fortune on my side, I will cross the plains and mountains of Kreel and enter Kuba boldly on my own. My disguise will fool even the Rani, I promise you. And once I reach Kuba..."

The words had no need to be spoken. Both Melinda and Alryc understood full well. Many years ago, Stacy could have taken Sigried's life, but her distaste for murder allowed the Rani to live. It was one of the few mistakes she had ever made. Now she would correct it.

Melinda winced at the thought. "What disguise will you take?"

The Princess smiled. "In the folklore of Satra, there are many tales spoken of the Lady Kesa."

The stargazer nodded. "I know them well. She was a highborn noble forced to flee to save her life."

"And she encountered many adventures in the years before she returned. The name fits well, Alryc, don't you think? I will leave here as Kesa and use that name until Mara is safe. No one in Kreel knows my face. Few in Kuba have ever seen it. Satra is a second home to me; I will not be lost in their ways. I can easily play the role."

" 'Tis a dangerous journey you embark upon, Stacy. Are you sure this is the only way?"

The Princess's eyes were resolute.

"Elias would not allow you to do this if he were here," offered Melinda.

"But he's not, is he? He sails across some accursed unknown sea!"

"And you sail upon a worse one!" Alryc's face was distraught with worry. "No man knows what is to be found in Kreel. I fear you would leap from the pot into the fire. Sailors avoid those waters like a plague."

"I have found one who knows the way and who has agreed to take me."

"Who?"

Stacy smiled. "Assad, the mercenary. Remember, he once served the Kuban fleet. He knows the way as well as any man alive."

"How can one know the Uncharted Lands? And how can you even be certain you can trust one such as he? A mercenary dances only to the tune of gold in his pockets."

"He will be well rewarded for his efforts. Besides, he assures me that Kreel's mystery is more the fable of frightened men than a reality."

Alryc scoffed, "How does he know? Has he been to Kreel?"

Stacy had to admit that he hadn't.

"Ah, so you see!" Melinda chimed in, almost triumphantly.

The Princess sighed and leaned back. "There is nothing that will change my mind, my friends. The decision has been made. The Lady Kesa will sail tonight."

Alryc put his head in his hands.

"Is there no one to go with you?" asked Melinda.

"I have sent for Cicero."

Both companions smiled at the name. The old mountain wolf was a cagey beast and would protect Stacy with his life. In her youth, she and he had been close, Stacy often spending long days in his dens and among the packs. This was not the first time Cicero had been called to aid her in her efforts, the last time being only a few months ago, in the grim hills of Azura. Cicero was a warrior and a general in his own right, leading his hordes of fierce hunters to fight in her name. They knew that, with Cicero about, Lady Kesa would be in good company.

Still, Alryc knew, one wolf would not be enough. "I will come also," he said solemnly.

"And I," declared Melinda.

Stacy looked at them, exasperated.

"We are as firm as you," said Melinda. "Mara is as important to us as to you. We let her down once, but never again. Besides, you'll have need of my dagger—"

"And my star-reading," added Alryc. "Rhonnda will manage very well without us while we're gone. What say you, Princess?"

Stacy frowned. She had not planned on it; yet slowly that frown turned to a full smile as she recalled earlier adventures they had all seen together. "Very well, then: the four of us." She licked her lips mischievously. "We'll turn Kuba on its head," she said, laughing.

"And dunk Sigried's in the bargain," rejoined Melinda.

A sparkle returned to Stacy's eyes and her cheeks regained some of their former glow. "When we return, we'll have quite a tale to tell."

"If the Fleet does return, Elias will sulk like a school brat." Melinda beamed.

But Stacy's smile faded. If only that were true. *Fara above! Let it be so!*

"Enough of this gaiety, then," she said. "The time is almost at hand. Assad's ship is ready and waiting for our arrival at the quay. With the moon tide we'll be gone and the first journey of Lady Kesa will begin. I only hope it will be the last."

PART TWO

TO THE DARK SHORES OF KREEL

The sky was dark; a dull overcast obliterated the stars. Assad stood stern-faced and silent on the prow of his boat as the four passengers quietly climbed the gangplank and came aboard. First came the red wolf, Cicero, his beady eyes aflame, his long curved fangs bared. Next came Melinda; dressed in a silver tunic that tapered above her knees, her dark hair flowing wild in the salty breeze, she kept her hand firmly on the hilt of her dagger. Third came the mysterious passenger known only as Lady Kesa. She wore a Satrian sari, dark maroon, and a long black cloak. Her face was covered up to her eyes with a thin veil, also Satrian fashion, and above it her dark eyes brooded. Around her waist, too, was a dagger—a silver dagger. It reflected the harbor lights brightly and sent off a dazzling display of color.

Lady Kesa nodded briefly to Assad. The captain was about to bow before her, then checked himself in time, recalling that for this voyage she was not to be known as the Empire Princess.

Last came the mystic, Alryc of the Blue Fires. The crew stared up at the giant but shied away from the glare of his deep, cold eyes. In his right hand he carried his staff; in his left, a small bag of instruments.

Assad gazed down at the shimmering water. A strong easterly wind was beginning to blow. Hands on hips, he gave the order for the plank to be lifted and the ropes to be untied. The chain of the anchor groaned as it lifted under the bow. Ready hands heaved and hauled it aboard, dripping shells and weeds and black mud.

"Prepare to sail!" called Assad.

The crew grappled expertly at the halyards; the flaxen sails unfurled. Wind spilled through them and with a rush they swelled eagerly into the night. Slowly the ship slipped from harbor.

Stacy and the others stood at the aftcastle rail and stared with sad thoughts as the lights of Rhonnda glowed and flickered before them. Rhonnda-by-the-Sea, the city of lights. Stacy stared at the dancing, glowing globes of the harbor, indigo and flaming orange, watching them till they grew dim with distance. Soon everything became blurred—dark silhouettes set against a starless night. Only the sharp lines of the palace remained intact. She saw the lights still burning in the towers, the glow of torches lighting up the long gray walls of stone. It was hard to leave home at any time, she knew, but all the harder when you knew you might never see it again.

Recognizing her feelings, Alryc put his arm around her. Stacy forced a smile, but her heart was far heavier than the astronomer realized. She knew and understood that even if the wastelands of Kreel were successfully passed and the gates of Sigried's city opened before them, the chances of their escaping with Mara were remote at best. And Stacy thought on the part of her plan that she had not confided to the others: She would let them flee with the young princess and stay behind herself. Killing the Rani would not be easy, but she was confident she could do it; however, it would surely cost her her own life in return. Once inside the Kuban palace walls, escape would be impossible. Neither she nor Sigried would live.

As Rhonnda slipped completely from sight, the small band prepared to go to their quarters below.

"How long will it take to reach Kreel's coast?" Melinda asked before they left.

Assad shrugged and scratched at his chin. "With good weather," he drawled, "less than ten days; with bad, fourteen. And if we should fall prey to coastal pirates, never."

The blue banner of Satra flapped gently in the breeze. Above, the sky was rich and deep, set off by a brilliant blazing summer sun. The halfway mark had been reached in the small hours before dawn. Assad was pleased. The weather had been about as good as he could ask—brisk, clear days with gusty winds at every tack. At this rate the tall, rugged Kreel mountains would be appearing on the horizon in a scant three days' time.

Still he was uneasy. Such mild weather would bring with it increasing chances of pirate ships. He shuddered at the thought. Years before, while still an honest merchant in the employ of Kuba, he had once encountered those black flags on the high seas. The battle had been furious, even with a powerful Kuban galley as escort. The brigand ships had swept down upon his own like vultures, fire and arrows pouring down like rain. Battering rams had torn at his hull, and frenzied nomadic barbarians had climbed his ropes like roaches, screaming strange war cries and wielding long curved swords. He had barely escaped with his life; most of his crew had not. Uneasily he prayed that his luck would still hold and that the ship that was a speck on the horizon now was merely a Kuban merchant hurrying through these waters as fast as possible.

As he stood with his hands gripping the edge of the prow rail, his knuckles white, he was barely aware of the Princess beside him. He turned his eyes from the sea and faced her with a forced smile.

"What is it, Captain Assad?" she asked.

"So you've seen it, too?"

Stacy nodded gloomily. "So has Alryc. What do you make of it?"

"A Kuban ship, I hope."

Taken aback, she stared at him.

"Don't misunderstand," he said. "The last thing I want to encounter is a Kuban warship. They'd love to get their hands on me. I'm still considered something of a traitor in their eyes. But a brigand ship is worse. They'll fight us to the death." His eyes darkened for a moment. "And they won't spare the women, either."

Stacy scowled. She pushed back strands of blowing hair from her face. "Is there any way we can avoid them? They seem to be still some leagues away."

"I doubt it, my prince—, er, Lady Kesa. If we've seen them, they've probably already seen us. If she's a merchant, she'll run like blazes to get away. A Kuban galley will dog us slowly, hovering about until she decides whether or not we're a threat. A pirate will tear down our throats. We'd need ten more sails to outrun her."

"Not very encouraging, is it?"

Assad was surprised at her cool demeanor. It was difficult for him to grasp that this woman was far more than she seemed, that she was used to wars and violence and could use that glittering dagger at her waist as well as any man who ever lived.

Just then there was a call from the sailor perched atop the crow's nest. "She's triple-sailed, Captain! Full war rigging!"

Assad cursed. "Is she a Kuban warship?"

The lad shrugged and strained his eyes to see. "Can't tell yet, sir, but there's something emblazoned on her mainsail, a dark— It's a black dragon!"

Assad kicked angrily with his boot. Now there was no doubt. "Better get below, Lady Kesa."

From behind came the growl of a wolf. Assad turned,

startled, to see Cicero arching his back, his fangs bared. The Princess gave a low snarling sound, then three successive quick barks. Cicero wagged his tail and drew behind the bulwark.

Assad stared dumbly. This was the first time he had ever heard Anastasia speak as a wolf. It was more than a little disconcerting.

Stacy smiled, aware of his uneasiness. Assad, like many foreigners, was not used to Rhonnda ways. He could never know how it was in the Newfoundland forests, where men and wolves depended on each other for mutual survival. "I'll stay above," she said.

"But, Lady Kesa, they're coming to fight!"

Stacy threw back her head. "Captain Assad, I've sailed with the Empire Fleet more times than I care to remember. I've faced the Russaks and the Azurans, even the cold, calculating *samuri* warriors of the Long Continent. I'll not hide from a handful of brigands."

There was a fatalistic tone in her voice, and he saw that she could not be deterred. "Very well, my lady. This is a small ship; I can use every extra hand I can get."

"Good. I'm sure Melinda can give some of your lads a lesson or two in how to use a crossbow."

He wiped his mouth with his hand. The thought of the pirates truly did frighten him; yet he was also a little eager to see if these women would live up to their reputations. "Take a position by the aftcastle," he told her. "I'll have crossbows brought to you both."

"Make mine a long bow, Captain, and short-shafted arrows; they're much better at close range."

Assad shook his head in disbelief as she turned to go, the red wolf at her side. If they lived through this fight, he mused, he would indeed have a tale to tell.

The brigand ship bore down swiftly. Her sails were gold and yellow, the black dragon shimmering in the sun. Stacy could see white froth pushed aside as the prow of the pirate ship cut boldly through the waters. It would be only minutes until the first arrows were loosed. The pirate ship was easily twice as big as Assad's scrawny Satrian boat. Long, sharp battering rams gleamed from either side of the prow, ready to tear at the hull. Stacy saw the frantic scramble of shirtless men taking up strong positions all along the port side of the ship, raising both bows and axes.

At her side Melinda toyed with her crossbow, adjusting the winch, drawing back the taut string with her finger. With most weapons she was an expert and had been ever since she was old enough to hunt in the forests, but the crossbow was like no other; she excelled in its use.

Alryc crouched low, his massive frame still providing a large target. His eyes were too old and weary to be of much use with bows. Years ago he had begun to compensate for this failing by using his great strength behind the weight of a flashing longsword. The moment the pirates came close enough to reach, his blade would lash out with untold fury. He was not a man of war and never had been. Still, there were times when a fight could not be avoided and scoundrels must be taught a lesson. He did not need the stars to tell him that this was one of those times.

At the edge of the group stood Cicero, proud and tall, a snarl upon his lips. As a hunter and a lord of wolves, war and battle was something he had lived with throughout his life. No stranger to violence, he fought at his best when at Stacy's side. His only regret now was that there were no other hunters at his side to share in the fight.

At the bridge, Assad locked his gaze with that of the pirate leader, a broad, sinewy man with long, unkempt hair reaching to his shoulders. There was a look of hate and contempt in his eyes. His beard was flecked with gray, and harsh lines around his mouth told of his many years sailing the high seas in quest of plunder and rape.

Assad had to chuckle: Once he too had considered joining such a band as this. The life of a mercenary was a hard one: You were always selling your soul and your blade to the highest bidder. Many a young man had considered privateering as a way to gain riches and women with a single thrust of the sword. And now he himself might be on the receiving end of such a thrust.

The mercenary watched uneasily as the pirate ship began to turn at a slight angle. The rams gleamed; he could see black smoke rise from small oil fires as the brigands began to light their arrows. The Princess had paid him a pretty penny—in advance—to make this journey, and now he would do his best to ensure that he lived to spend it. For an instant he thought of the pretty tavern girls of Rhonnda and the soft, nubile women of Satra. If he were to share their company again, his wits would have to be far sharper than those of his adversary; but then Assad the mercenary was no fool.

"Raise your bows!" he shouted.

And all along the side of the ship, from the forecastle to the aftcastle, his tough Northland sailors held their bows close and ready, fingers on the hair triggers. The cabin boys had brought up their own pots of flaming oil and the first points had already been lit. Assad smiled grimly and looked to the Princess and her companions. The small group stood bold and defiant in the face of overwhelming odds.

"All right, lads," he cried, "let's teach these ruffians a lesson! They'll soon learn not to fool with men of the North!"

And a great cheer went up as the battle began.

Arrows sang on both sides, flaming darts striking against beam and plank alike. Sails smoldered, then burst into flame. The pirate ship freed the first of her catapults. With a rasping growl, the throwing arm sprang up and released a huge fiery rock toward the bulwark of the Rhonnda ship. It fell with a powerful splash over the far side, the flames snuffing out as it sank into the sea.

Bare seconds later another oil-doused rock came whistling through the air. This time it crashed onto the mainsail, which collapsed in a melee of burning canvas and wood. Two sailors screamed as shattered burning timber fell above their heads.

"Now!" cried Assad. His own catapult sprang up like a leopard, the rock smashing onto the pirates' forebridge. Three ax-wielding pirates were thrown into the air like rags, disappearing helplessly over the side into the pounding waves.

The air rang with war cries on both sides. Arrows fell like rain; again the mercenary's catapult roared. The hull of the pirate ship was badly torn; flooding water slammed forward; the ship tilted and began to founder.

"We've sunk her!" Assad shouted gleefully.

Stacy beamed. The ship had fallen quicker than even Elias could have hoped. Truly Assad was a master of his trade; if not, the most blessed man the Fates had ever graced.

But this jubilation was short-lived. At that very moment, another pirate vessel came sailing in from the starboard side, this one every bit as large and awesome as the one just dispatched.

The mercenary ship tried to dodge her, but there was not enough time. The pirates howled and screamed at the sight of their sister ship and her drowning crew. Now the real battle began in earnest. The hostile ship drew in her oars and furled her golden sails. The sides of both ships grated against each other; the pirates tossed ropes and grappling hooks. The first group swung up high on the ropes, their legs wrapping round the twine, their bodies swinging forward. Several fell at once, the victims of flaming Satrian arrows.

Stacy drew an oil-dripping dart and swiftly loaded her bow. The string drawn, she took good aim and released it. An unearthly scream erupted from a brute of a man about to plant firm feet on Empire wood. He staggered back, dropped his dagger from between his teeth and fell over the side, body aflame.

Melinda's crossbow sang a deadly song; her arrow caught a black-bearded pirate with a swinging ax in the side of his head, the tip piercing through his skull and protruding out the other side. Bits of gray brain smeared with blood splattered those near him. Slowly he fell forward, a look of crazed shock on his face.

Cicero leaped high, knocking down two more attackers. His fangs quickly sank into the throat of one; Alryc's blade removed the head of the other. The fast reflexes of Assad's own hand and dagger were all that saved Alryc from the thrust of yet another frenzied pirate. Assad's knife plunged deep between the man's shoulder blades and Stacy's silver dagger did the rest, thrusting with lightning speed up through his gut. The attacker sagged as she withdrew, then crumpled at her feet.

Alryc clenched his fists and grinned gratefully at the two who had just saved his life; then he lunged at the charging group of pirates ahead, swinging his longsword above his head. The sight of this giant of a man coming at them with a blade they could barely hold sent them into a panic. Frozen in their tracks, they were ripe game as Stacy and Melinda let loose another volley. Two died instantly; a third felt the rush of Alryc's sword; a fourth fell to the hot arrow of a Satrian sailor. The fifth, in his fear, dropped his weapon, turned to run and tried vainly to make it over the side. He slipped on blood, and as he tumbled, he felt the sharp bite of Cicero's fangs sink into his throat.

Smoke burned Stacy's eyes. She saw another sail go up in great tongues of lusty flame, flickering upward and igniting the sail above. The heat became unbearable, reminding her of that terrible day in the rock garden, and she felt her stomach tie in knots. More pirates landed on the deck; combat became hand to hand. Swords clashed; sparks flew as metal clanged on metal. Stacy dropped her bow and put her faith in her dagger. Lashing and plunging, she dropped two more brigands where they stood before she felt something hot strike her, a pirate arrow tearing through her shoulder, knocking her off balance. All at once Melinda and Alryc were at her side, shielding her, protecting her. The cut was not deep, merely a flesh wound. She pleaded with her companions to leave her, to let her stand again, but they refused. They stood firm beside her and fought with all the more ferocity. The struggle had not ended—not by a long shot.

Satrian and mercenary sailors fell by the score, but each one took at least two pirates with him. The stench of burning flesh was nauseating; fallen decapitated bodies were strewn across the deck.

Someone's lunge caught Assad off balance. A blade slashed at his arm and he fell bleeding. His curses went unheard amid the screams of dying men. His ship was lost, he knew; so was his life, for surely the pirates would make him pay bitterly for his savage resistance. The only regret he had was that he would be remembered as the man who had brought the Empire Princess to her death, and such infamy was more than he could bear.

Stacy woke with a start. The pain in her shoulder threw her back against the mat on the floor. Her eyes tightened with tears; she bit her lips against the pain. The soothing hand of Melinda was soon on her brow and Stacy managed to open her eyes and look about.

They were in a dark cabin, she saw, one that reeked of sweat and urine.

"Rest easy, my lady," came the voice of Alryc.

She strained to turn her head and saw the mystic sitting behind her, knees up, arms wrapped despondently around them, his face long and glum. Beside him, his shoulder covered with hasty bandages, lay the restless form of Assad, face white and lips pressed together tightly.

"What . . . where are we?"

"In the hold of the pirate ship," whispered Melinda.

From off in the corner, beneath the shadows, Cicero growled.

Stacy smiled at the sound, filled with thanks that the red wolf had not been slain. "Are there any other survivors?" she asked, afraid to hear the answer.

Alryc, pushing a shock of silver hair from his eyes, shook his head. "None, Lady Kesa. Those who did not fall in battle were put to death. Our new hosts allowed the passengers and the captain to live—at least for a while. They seem to think they can hold us for ransom."

Stacy grimaced. She knew what that would mean. If no ransom was forthcoming, they would all probably be sold as slaves. It would be worse, though, if they were to find out who she was.

"Have no fear," said Alryc, reading her mind. "I've told their captain that the household of Lady Kesa will pay dearly to save her life."

Stacy nodded. "And did you tell our hosts who must be contacted?"

The mystic smiled wryly. "The lords of Satra. It will take some time for the message to be delivered."

The Princess breathed a sigh of relief. She should have known that Alryc would not let her down. "Lords of Satra" was a code carefully devised by Melinda. If the pirates did send word to Satra, her allies there would immediately know she was in danger. Not only would ransom be paid; a cohort of Satrian soldiers would be waiting to see that proper justice was meted out.

"Have you been told just where this ship heads until our payment is made?"

Alryc frowned. "The Southern Coast, I fear."

Stacy sighed and forced herself to sit up. The ship was going far from both Kreelian and Kuban waters. The chances of her true mission being accomplished grew dimmer with every league the ship sailed.

As the group sat, downcast and not speaking, the door to the cabin opened and in walked a brawny, hawk-nosed man with a short red beard and a small gold earring in each ear. He wore a loose tunic, Kuban style, with a hanging belt and a bejeweled Satrian dagger dangling from it. At his side stood a short, stocky man with a wide grin and an ugly face. The grin exposed rotting teeth; the lips were chapped and sore from scurvy.

"Well, well," rasped the first man, "I see that our lady has finally awoken."

His companion grunted and fingered the hilt of his scimitar. "We are told you are a lady of Satra. Is that right?"

The Princess nodded slowly. "My name is Lady Kesa, of the Glowing Mist country. Do you know it?"

The man with the red beard rubbed at his chin. "The Satrian nobility interests me not," he said bluntly. "But if you indeed come from a family of wealth, as this giant claims, I think that we can come to terms."

"The terms must ensure not only my safety but also that of my companions," she replied calmly.

The man threw back his head and laughed. Then he winked at his companion. "Some bitch, this one, eh? Already she makes demands of us. Oh, she's an aristocrat, all right. I can see that plain as the ugly nose on your face."

Again the second man grunted.

"Tell me, Lady Kesa, where were you bound in these waters? Surely not to Kuba?"

"To Kreel, Captain."

The pirates glanced at each other.

"And what would bring you to a strange land such as that?"

"Urgent business," she answered truthfully. "You see, my family once had holdings at the Kreelian port."

The captain leaned over her. She could feel his hot breath on her face and it made her want to vomit.

"Don't lie to me, you aristocratic whore! No one from your part of the world has holdings in Kreel. No one! Now, tell me the truth and make it brief. My mate here has less patience than I and he's eager to have his way with you, if you know what I mean."

She swallowed hard, knowing all too well what he meant. "All right, then, I'll tell you the truth: We sailed for Kreel to hire a mercenary. A family matter, one of honor."

The captain winked as if he shared some secret with her. "I see. Some despicable noble has robbed your sister of her virtue, eh?"

Stacy glared harshly. "Something like that, yes."

The pirate straightened up again and wiped at his nose with his sleeve. "A pity your voyage had to be disrupted, then. I'll wager your sister's looks are fashioned after your own."

His companion leered and snickered.

Alryc fumed. "Touch one finger upon my lady and I'll have your head!"

"Your tongue is too lose, giant! It would give me great joy to toss you to the sharks."

"My ransom is for my companions also, Captain," said Stacy quickly.

The red-bearded pirate spat on the floor and stared

at Alryc. "We've a long voyage ahead of us, giant," he warned coldly. "Mind your manners." Then he smiled at Stacy and Melinda. His gold earrings glimmered in the dim light. "Tend to your servant's manners, Lady Kesa," he said. Then he spun on his heels and strode from the cabin, his lackey behind him.

The moment the door had shut and their footsteps became distant, Assad lifted himself on his elbows.

Melinda looked at him with surprise. "I thought you were unconscious," she said.

Assad put his finger to his lips. "I know that brigand," he told them with a grim look. "He's a clever devil. Years ago we sailed together in the Rani's service."

"And he didn't recognize you?" said Stacy.

"I trust not. If he did, there'll be more to pay than we realize. I sailed with the Kuban fleet to capture him after he became a renegade; but somehow he eluded us after we caught his companions. He swore an oath to have his vengeance. I shudder to think what he'll do to us all if he finds out who I am."

Stacy sighed. They were in enough trouble already without having this added burden placed upon them. But Assad had served her well. It was clear that he was as trustworthy and loyal as any of her captains. She must do all she could to protect him from the pirate's wrath.

Before she could speak, the door opened again and a small wisp of a man entered, carrying an iron pot filled with slushing dark slime. "Your supper," he cackled, placing the pot in the center of the room and withdrawing quickly.

Melinda put her finger in it and tasted it. She pulled a face and spit. "Is *this* all we'll get until we reach the Southern Coast?" she grumbled.

Assad nodded and frowned. "Afraid so, Melinda. Cuisine aboard brigand ships is known to be lacking."

Cicero crawled over, sniffed at it and growled. Even he could not bear it. And if a wolf refused to eat, you knew it was bad.

Stacy dunked her hand inside the pot and withdrew a small piece of greenish meat. She forced a bite, chewing slowly.

The others looked at her with horror. "My lady!"

She shrugged with a wan smile. "It's this or starve, my friends, and it's a long voyage to the pirate cove."

Knowing she was right, Alryc also took a piece and chewed glumly. This new fate was a bitter pill indeed, but still they would have to swallow it. Soon everyone, including Cicero, had forced himself to eat.

After they had finished, they once more sat with long faces, pondering the destiny that faced them.

It was Stacy who broke the silence. "Assad, you know these waters. Just how far are we from the nearest shore?"

The mercenary thought for a while. "Too far to swim," he mumbled bitterly. "Even if we were given opportunity to escape and take their longboat, I doubt we could row ourselves to shore. The currents here are treacherous."

"Besides," said Alryc, "we don't even have any weapons."

Melinda smiled slyly. From beneath her skirt she withdrew Stacy's silver dagger. The blade gleamed.

"How did you get it?" asked the Princess, eyes wide with delight.

"In the confusion of the battle I hid it. They took all other weapons, including my own knife. This one I managed to keep well away from their eyes." She handed the dagger over.

Stacy took it gratefully. It felt good in her hand. She ran her finger against the razor-sharp edge, then quickly hid it under her sari. "At least we're not *totally* helpless," she said.

Assad shook his head. "There must be fifty pirates aboard, Lady Kesa. There are five of us. I'm afraid it won't be of much help. We can't even see where we are."

"Not so!" blurted Alryc. He turned toward the wall and scratched at the aging timbers. Between two beams a thin needle of light appeared. "Our window to the world!" he said triumphantly.

Stacy and the mercenary went to see. It was not much of a window, merely the slimmest slit between the boards, but it provided a decent view of the water on the starboard side.

"Are there any islands we might pass?" asked Stacy.

The mercenary glanced at her. "It depends on the course our friend here decides to take. If he's looking for further booty, he'll stay fairly close to Kreel's shore. There'll be many Kuban vessels about at this time of year. But if he feels we're enough prize, he'll head for open sea and we'll be doomed."

Alryc strained at his window and tried to get a fix on their position by the azimuth of the setting sun. His trained eyes had no trouble gauging a rough position as the ship moved on her course.

"We're traveling on an easterly tack," he said, "a true east."

Assad grinned. "Are you certain?"

The astronomer looked injured. "I have studied the skies since before your birth, young sea captain. I know of what I speak."

"Then we might just be in luck," replied the mercenary.

Alryc eyed him oddly. "Oh? How so? You know of an island close by?"

"An island? No, but something just as good. An easterly course will take us straight into the Kuban shipping lanes—and with it the chance of being sighted by a warship."

Stacy groaned. What could happen next? she wondered. They were all caught between the devil and the deep blue sea. The pirates would put them in chains and hold them for ransom. The Kuban ship, if she came, would probably burn this ship and send them all to fiery deaths. Either way, her hope of freeing Mara was lost. Everyone, it seemed, shared her thoughts—everyone but Assad, that is. He was grinning like a fool, and she wondered what he had to be so happy about.

The night was long and uneventful. Restlessly the five captives tossed and turned and tried to sleep. The waters became rougher, great cross swells tossing the brigand ship like a cork. Frothing waves smashed against the sides, and the ship dipped and rose furiously as she cut through them. The wind began to shift, and the vessel was forced to trim sail and tack a few degrees off her former course. A storm was brewing, Alryc knew as he sat awake beside his little window, gazing up at the menacing sky. The squall would pass over quickly, but until it did, they would be in for a severe pounding.

The rains came swiftly. The ship rocked and moaned; creaking wood sounded as though it would give way to the tumultuous waves. Alryc could hear faint calls from the sailors on deck as they followed new commands and tried to keep the ship on even keel.

Melinda vomited. Not used to such weather at sea, she crawled into a corner of the cabin, hugging her knees to herself. Her head throbbed. Ashamed of herself, she buried her head and prayed to the Fates for this misery to stop.

Poor Cicero found himself in a similar situation. Often he had sailed with the Empire Fleet in quest of glory; yet the shock of such weather was more than he could take. Rolled up in a ball, his bushy tail beating wildly against the floor, he forced his eyes closed and shivered as the thunder crashed overhead and the lightning roared. As the ship rolled, he slid from side to side, moaning and calling on Fara, the goddess of all forest Dwellers, to protect him from nature's terrible wrath.

By the first light of dawn, the squall had passed. Thick clouds broke swiftly apart, giving way to a deepening-blue sky. The strong winds were replaced by gentle breezes. The waters beneath them stirred gently now, the waves placid and smooth. Used to the anger of the sea, Stacy, Assad and Alryc were all soon awake and eager to find what this new day would bring.

It came sooner than they expected.

On the horizon, Alryc saw the sails, a huge canvas of yellow and gold. The new ship was immense, yet sleek and fast. Its prow was long; on the bowsprit was a great wooden carving of some ancient Kuban icon. Without speaking, he gestured for the Princess and the mercenary to come have a look.

Stacy shuddered. Her eyes focused on the flags the ship flew. There was no mistaking the black and gold: imperial flags, she knew, belonging to a Kuban galley.

"The warship's seen us," growled Alryc. "See? Already she turns."

"And our hosts know it," added Stacy, feeling the pirate ship hastily shift position so that she could run with the wind.

"Can the pirates outrace the galley?"

"Not a chance," replied Assad. "We carry only half her sail. That warship may be big, but she doesn't lumber. She'll be on us like a wolf after a buck."

The astronomer sighed. "Then all is lost. We're as good as sunk."

"Perhaps not, my stargazing friend. The galley will fight, to be sure; but she may not want to sink us so fast. Remember, pirate vessels usually carry great booty. That Kuban captain will want it for the glory of his

Rani. Sigried's ordered no ships to be sunk until everything is taken."

Stacy gulped. "They'll board us?"

Assad nodded. "Of course. Why not? I'd do the same."

"Then they'll capture us, too," cried the Princess, "and we'll be delivered right into Sigried's arms!"

"What makes you think they'll know who you are, my lady? You fooled the pirates. Surely no Kuban sailor will recognize you. All we need do is stick to our stories. You, Lady Kesa, of the Glowing Mist lands of Satra, were taken by pirates on your way to Kreel."

"You expect them to believe that?" said Alryc with a scowl. "Satra is an Empire ally. That means an enemy of Kuba. You don't really believe they'll let us go?"

"I don't know," he replied honestly, "but I'd rather take my chances aboard a Kuban galley than a tub like this."

"He's right, you know," said Melinda. "They'll bear no hatred for Lady Kesa of Satra. With luck, they might even drop us at Kreel."

"And without it, they'll see through my disguise and we'll all be hauled into Sigried's palace."

"Then we'd better pray fast," said Alryc, glancing through the slit in the side. "They're almost upon us!"

The galley's rams gleamed in the morning sun, sharp iron ready to rip the hull of the brigand ship to shreds. Arrows began to fly again; right before Alryc's eyes came a pirate hurtling to the waters below. Screams rose all around, and they could smell smoke from burning sails.

The rams hit with shattering force. There was a deadly crunching sound from behind, and the ship instantly began to tilt on her side. Flames bolted around them as fire arrows made short work of the hull.

"We've got to get out of here!" cried Assad. He

bolted to the door and grappled with the frightened sailor standing guard in the corridor.

"Let's move!" shouted Stacy.

Cicero leaped to the aid of the mercenary while Alryc and Melinda fought their way up the narrow steps. The hatch from above banged open. In the doorway stood the red-bearded captain, his face blackened from the smoke, blood from an arrow wound oozing from his shoulder. Venomous hate glazed his frenzied eyes. He gestured with his sword.

"Thought you'd get away, eh? Well, we'll die together, I promise you that!"

Like a madman he bounded down the steps. Melinda ducked the thrust of his blade. Alryc crouched low and, springing like a leopard, knocked the pirate flat on the floor. Stacy whirled and drew her silver dagger. The blade flashed and plunged deep into the pirate's gut.

With glassy eyes he stared at her. "Who are you?" he rasped, blood curdling from the side of his mouth. "Who are you *really?*"

She stood over him defiantly, the dagger dripping with his blood. "They call me Anastasia."

His mouth gaped and his eyes grew wide with disbelief. In his hands he had held the Empire Princess herself—the greatest prize any privateer had ever captured—and now it was lost. He reached out to touch her with trembling fingers. "I could have bought a kingdom for your ransom," he managed to whisper.

"That and more, Captain—that and more."

And with a look of sorrow for what might have been, he breathed his last breath and died.

"The fire's raging everywhere!" called Melinda frantically. "We'll have to jump overboard."

"Well, we bloody well can't do it standing here," retorted Assad. "Quick! To the deck!"

Under the sun, terrible fighting raged. Tunic-clad sailors of the Kuban galley were rampaging over the deck, dealing strong blows to the remaining survivors of the sinking ship. The mainmast was a fiery torrent of flame leaping high up into the sky. Collapsing, it tumbled across the deck, wreaking havoc on combatants below. Stacy and her band barely dodged it in time. They ran to what was left of the bridge and looked down into the calm turquoise waters.

"Jump!" yelled Assad, ripping off his shirt.

Tense and frightened, the others made ready also.

"Stand as you are—all of you!"

They turned, to stare glumly into the stern, smoke-blackened face of the galley captain. He was tall and young and sported no beard, only a small mustache. His eyes were gray and steely under furrowed brows.

Alryc stepped boldly forward and spoke in the drawling Satrian accent: "Fates above! Bless you, sir: You've saved our lives!"

The galley captain cocked his head and called for his aides to surround them. "And who, pray tell, are you? How came you aboard this ship?"

Alryc bowed graciously. "A long tale, Captain, but the ship burns around us! May we not tell our story on safer ground?"

The captain grimaced, then nodded. "We'll get you off here safely enough, my large friend, but your story had better be good if you don't want to find yourselves in a Kuban dungeon."

Alryc gulped. "I'm certain it won't come to that, but please, at least for the sake of the women, let us fly from this raging pit of Hel!"

Within half an hour all were safely aboard the galley. Stacy and her companions were brought directly to the spacious quarters of the captain. His rooms were large, larger than she had ever seen before on a ship. Strewn across his desk were a multitude of charts and instruments. On one wall hung a huge black and gold

Kuban banner, emblazoned at the center with the image of a tiger. A small purple velvet banner hung from the wall opposite. Stacy realized that this banner was the crest of the captain's own title, whatever that was.

Three grim Kuban soldiers stood at the open door as the prisoners anxiously waited for the captain's arrival. From the large recessed windows they could see the pirate ship slowly dropping beneath the waves. Smoldering planks and timbers, still burning, bobbed upon the gentle waves. Then the sea took the ship and all her crew into its belly.

As heavy footsteps made their way along the wide passage, the soldiers stood stiffly at attention, saluting smartly, Kuban fashion, with their hands spread across their chests and heads bowed low. The captain paid them scant attention, focusing instead on these curious guests. His face had been washed, Stacy saw, and his clothes changed. He now looked far younger than before, certainly not more than twenty-five, and she wondered how one so young had come to command such a fine ship as this. And it was a fine ship, she had to admit. If nothing else, Sigried certainly knew how to adorn her vessels with luxury while still keeping them fit and in fighting trim.

The young captain brushed aside a shock of dark, unruly hair from his forehead; then, hands behind his back, he carefully studied the faces of his guests. Being a gentleman, he bade them all sit on his chairs and divan before he began his questioning. A snap of his fingers brought an aide running with a pitcher of dark wine and a goblet for each. Stacy took hers with a pleasant "Thank you" and the others did the same. Cicero lay at her feet and snarled.

The captain leaned against the edge of his desk. He took a few small sips, put the goblet down and drummed the desk top with his fingers. "Now," he said at last, looking at Alryc, "you were about to tell me just who you are."

"I am Lady Kesa of Satra," said Stacy boldly before Alryc could reply.

"Oh?" The captain raised his brows. "Of what part of Satra? I am familiar with many of those lands."

Wondering if he was telling the truth, she replied, "Glowing Mist country. If you know Satra, then you'll recognize my accent."

He nodded politely. "I do. That accent is similar to that of Rhonnda, isn't it?"

Her heart missed a beat. Was he toying with her? Did he know? "Some say so," she said with a smile; then, shrugging: "Others don't. But I'm not the one to say. I've never been to Rhonnda-by-the-Sea."

The captain fidgeted slightly and shifted his weight. "I see. And who are your companions, Lady Kesa?"

"Servants, Captain."

"And the wolf? I didn't know Satrians kept wolves as pets."

Cicero growled at the insult.

"He was brought to me as a child," said Stacy with a calm but firm tone. "And he doesn't like being called a pet."

The Kuban commander smiled. "I can see that, Lady Kesa, but never mind. Please be good enough to tell me how you came to be aboard that pirate vessel. We've been trailing that red-bearded devil for months. I was sure he'd slip us again, as he always does."

"It's our fortune that this time he didn't, Captain. Our story is a sad one. We were bound for the Spice Island, near Kreel, when our ship was set upon by his—"

"His ship was alone? That is curious, Lady Kesa. Usually that devil sailed with another brigand at his side."

Here was a tricky statement, Stacy knew. If she said

that the other ship had been sunk, the captain would know that her own ship had been prepared for fighting and was not just a peaceful merchant vessel, as she would have him believe. She would have to answer carefully and hope that she would be believed.

"You're right," she said. "There *were* two ships. The first took aboard our goods and our crew—probably to sell them as slaves on the Southern Coast, I should think. After our own ship was sunk, this one took only us to hold for ransom. I think our red-bearded pirate thought my ransom worth more than our goods."

The young commander smiled grimly. "Then you were most fortunate. That brigand rarely thought human life worth the bother of keeping. He must have valued you highly."

"He would have made my lady his whore," said Alryc. "That is why he let us live so long."

The captain eyed both Stacy and Melinda appreciatively. Both women were more than a little attractive, and it did make sense that the pirate would have at least some value for them, aristocrats or no.

"Do you know who I am?" he asked, now changing the direction of the conversation.

"I know that this is a Kuban warship," said Stacy, "and I know you to be her commanding officer."

He bowed his head politely. "Lord Quentin, my lady, at your service."

Quentin! Stacy blinked. Few in Rhonnda had not heard of the daring Kuban commander. Beloved and trusted by Sigried like few others, he would prove no fool. His youth was surprising, even his manner; but she knew that behind it lay a cunning mind and a heart loyal only to the Rani. If Quentin suspected her merely of being from Rhonnda, let alone of being the Empire Princess, he would spare no haste in delivering her directly to Kuba's dungeons.

"Your eyes betray your thoughts," he told her dryly.

Stacy tilted her head and locked her eyes with his. "Oh?"

"You seemed frightened by the name."

"Not frightened, my lord—respectful. Everyone in the Empire knows of your courage and deeds."

Quentin laughed. "You flatter me. Respect is the last thing I would expect from your empire. I wonder if your princess would say the same."

Again Stacy wondered if he was toying with her. If he know her true identity, why didn't he just come out and say it? "I think Princess Anastasia would be the first to acknowledge what I've just said," she answered with flashing eyes and a coy smile.

"I wonder, but no matter. Tell me, Lady Kesa, have you ever seen the Empire Princess? Face to face, I mean."

"Yes, my lord—once. Anastasia often comes to Satra. As you know, she has many friends there. But only a single time did she come to my own land, Glowing Mist. We met only briefly."

"Is she as beautiful as they say? As pretty as you, for example?"

The question threw her off guard. She blushed. "I . . . er . . . cannot answer that, my lord. Such a question is better asked of a man."

Quentin smiled warmly. "Is it true she snarls like a wolf, can actually *change* into a wolf?"

Stacy laughed and relaxed in her seat. "Is that what they say at the court of Kuba?"

He shrugged. "Some say it—usually fleeing soldiers and scoundrels who need an excuse for their failures upon the battlefield."

"Then you know it isn't true, Captain. The Princess is just a woman."

"*Just* a woman?" He laughed loudly. "No, Lady Kesa, now I think *you* do your princess an injustice." He then looked at her companions.

"What will you do with us?" came the voice of Melinda.

Quentin's smile disappeared. He glanced from one to the other. "Well, I can't very well drop you off in the sea. No matter what you might hear in Satra, Kuba is not a land of savages. We are civilized, you know."

"I'm sure of that," said Stacy firmly. "Then what *will* you do?"

His face was blank now, as if he himself had not decided. "My orders have been carried out. These waters have been cleared. Now I sail back for Kuba and the palace of my Rani. I'll bring you there. You should be able to find some passage on another ship to take you either back to Satra or to the Spice Island, whichever you prefer."

Stacy smiled at him. "That is kind of you, Lord Quentin, but that would rob us of valued time. We've lost far too much already. Can't you take us to the Spice Island yourself?"

He sighed. "Would that I could, Lady Kesa, but you should know better. If I did, I might encounter Empire ships, and I don't seek a confrontation. Unlike Empire captains, I don't prey on innocent vessels."

Stacy winced. "I always thought it quite the reverse, my lord," she said. "I think I could be the richest woman in the world had I all the booty Kuban mercenaries have stolen from Satra."

Quentin's eyes smoldered. "I'm not a mercenary, Lady Kesa. My ship flies Kuban flags proudly, with honor."

Stacy was about to speak, then thought better of it. No point would be served by inflaming him, especially since up to now he had treated them so gently. Still, she was certain that his kind treatment concealed more purpose than he was revealing.

"We argue for nothing," said Quentin. "Policy of state is neither my domain or your own. I think that when you reach Kuba you'll begin to see that people are people, whether from your empire or mine."

"Wisely spoken for one so young, my lord. Alas, we really cannot afford the time. My family's fortunes dwindle even as we speak, and I must get to Spice Island to correct the deficit."

"I am sorry, Lady Kesa, truly I am, but I can't take you to your destination."

"I understand, you have your duty. But tell me: We are near the shores of Kreel, are we not?"

He looked puzzled. "Yes. What of it?"

"Then drop us there."

"What? In Kreel? Lady Kesa, those lands are dangerous and hardly known!" He was shocked.

"But Kreel's port can be reached by road. From there we can reach the Spice Island quickly."

He shook his head slowly and ruefully, in truth thinking more about their safety than anything else.

"It would be a great favor, Lord Quentin, and it won't delay you in reaching your home."

"Did I save you from renegades merely to deliver you into the hands of strange and mysterious souls who have yet to come out of their own Dark Time?"

"We'll be safe in Kreel, I assure you."

He laughed caustically. "What? Two men, two women and one wolf?"

Stacy pressed on, undeterred. "We can pay you—"

"I saved you not for gold, my lady, but for my honor as a gentleman."

"Then as a gentleman, do as I ask, I implore you, my lord. Let the Fates govern our destinies."

Quentin had to agree that no man can set for himself a path different from that which the Fates had chosen; yet it was still with great misgivings that he pondered her request. "The port of Kreel is still some distance away," he said at last. "Will you seek the known road and stick to it, never once leaving its path?"

"My word on that, Lord Quentin. The road is known to be safe, at least as far as the port. Not once shall we step from it."

He stood up, took her hand and kissed it softly. "Then may the Fates protect both you and yours, Lady Kesa. I pray that I have done the right thing in letting you go."

Stacy smiled, her eyes flashing brightly. "You have, young captain. It is more than my own life you have just saved. There is much more at stake."

He looked at her oddly for a moment, as though wondering what was behind her words. Then, shrugging it off, he said, "Perhaps someday we'll meet again, Lady Kesa of Glowing Mist. I pray we do. And perhaps someday you'll come to Kuba after all."

"I just might do that, Captain," she answered gently. "And when I do, even your Rani will know of it."

Quentin stood alone on the bridge of his ship, watching as his longboat rowed Lady Kesa and her companions to the dark, gloomy shores of Kreel. As always, there were grim mists covering the shoreline like a gray blanket. In the distance he could make out the rugged peaks of the strange and forbidding Kreel Mountains. He knew that somewhere beyond them his own lands of Kuba began, but few, if any, had ever made that journey to tell just what lay between. He felt more at ease, though, when he reminded himself that Lady Kesa and her companions were headed in the opposite direction, toward the known, safe lands around the port.

They were a strange lot, this Lady Kesa and her friends, and something told him it was wrong to let them go. He shrugged this feeling off, though, and waved forlornly as his longboat slipped into the mist, gone from sight. What destiny awaited them he did not know, but somehow he felt that he had not seen the last of her, that Lady Kesa would someday play a role in his life.

He prayed that this role would be a happy one.

The horn from the Kuban galley blasted three times in a shrill good-bye to her departed passengers. Stacy stood in the evening shadows, peering out toward the sea. The mists covered everything; she could see nothing. Grimly she shivered and pulled her cloak tightly around her shoulders. Alryc and the others sat resting on the coarse sands of the beach, trying to forget the happenings of the past few days.

How ironic, thought Stacy, as she stood apart from her companions and contemplated the tasks ahead, that it had been one of Sigried's own ships that had saved them, bringing hope back into her plan for saving Mara. It could only have been an act of the Fates that had brought young Quentin's ship to their aid and caused him, against his better judgment, to set them down here upon these feared and largely unknown shores. Stacy was grateful to Quentin; indeed she had grown fond of the young man in those few hours they had shared each other's company. She hoped the day would not come when she would find herself in conflict with him. Strong-willed, even as was her beloved Elias, the young man would surely give his life to save his Rani, and Stacy knew that she would be forced to kill him— assuming he did not kill her first, that is.

"Which way now, my lady?"

She turned from her thoughts to see Alryc, his face masked in eerie gray shadows, standing beside her.

"To the mountain lands," she replied. "To Kuba."

The astronomer fondled the shortsword Quentin had given him with which to protect Lady Kesa. "There's no point in starting our journey before daylight," he said. "Better that we build a fire and make our first night as comfortable as possible."

The Princess nodded. "All right, but let's get away from the beach. We can find better shelter in those trees on that hill. Maybe we can even catch a rabbit for supper."

Alryc grinned. He looked over at Melinda, who was sitting lazily with the small bow Quentin had presented to her. "Then let's get on with it," he said cheerily, trying to lift their spirits.

Tired and apprehensive, they picked up their supplies and trod across the cold sands, up to the rolling, fog-shrouded hills. It was a bleak landscape: The winds whistled in strange tunes, rustling through dark leaves, the hills were filled with sharp and jagged stones that tore at the soles of their boots. No birds sang; no frogs croaked from the many bogs and mires that dotted the scape. The trees leaned precariously from the hillsides, boughs twisting in fearsome shapes. Even the grass, so rich and pure in Rhonnda and Satra, seemed sickly and bleak here.

"This place is as good as any," muttered Alryc, throwing his cloak down across a patch of soil between a scattering of withered willow trees.

"This country frightens me," admitted Assad. The mercenary's eyes darted fearfully about as he sat uneasily against the trunk of a squat tree.

Melinda rested beside him, stretching her legs out between the twisting roots. "It's creepy," she admitted, "but really no worse than a lot of other lands I've visited."

Assad laughed warmly. In their short days together he had come to have a warm liking for this unusual forest girl. "Hello, what's this?" he said.

A great brown hare dashed from behind a dark bush and scampered toward the thickets. Melinda's bow flew to her hands; she drew an arrow and let it fly. The hare tumbled dead in a heap.

"Looks like we'll have a good supper after all," she said with a wink as she ran to fetch her prey.

Astounded at her speed and agility, Assad watched her come back, full of smiles. The poor hare hung limply over her shoulder.

"And what are you staring at?" she demanded. "I've provided our food; the least you can do is cook it!"

Assad laughed good-naturedly and began to gather up dried sticks for the fire. Alryc and Stacy helped.

"You don't have to do this, my lady," Assad said.

Stacy's eyes flashed merrily. "You really don't know me very well, do you, Captain? I grew up in forests like this. Hunting and cooking are my way of life."

He looked at her strangely but admiringly. "I get the feeling you like this sort of thing."

She laughed. "Would you believe it if I told you that I'd gladly trade the Empire throne for a small cottage in the valley of my birth?"

"And give up all your glory and fame, not to mention a thousand nobles to bow at your feet?"

"All that and more, Captain Assad, all that and more. The only empire I yearn for is that of my family and my own home—and, of course, a few good storytelling wolves to keep me company."

Cicero growled knowingly. Like Stacy, he also missed those days of years gone by, when they ran free and wild through the heather and the grasses with only the wind to watch.

Under the circumstances, it was a most pleasant meal. Nearby was a tiny spring with fresh, clear water. The hare proved more of a meal than it looked, giving everyone his fill. Despite the mist, the air was pleasant and warm; they could even catch a glimpse of stars peeking from behind the haze. This made Alryc feel more at ease. As long as the stars were about, he knew the Fates stood watching and they were protected.

After the meal was done, they sat around the tiny fire and pondered the difficulties ahead.

"As I gauge the sky," said Alryc, "I'd set our route right between those two great peaks up there." He pointed off toward two dark, slumbering mountains. "Once past there, we should reach the Arid Lands. Then it's straight onto the Kuban plains and to the city itself."

Assad drew a deep breath. "That's quite a distance, my friend. If we had horses . . ."

"Wait a moment," said Stacy. "Our plans didn't call for you to come with us. Why, you don't even know why we're going to Kuba."

The mercenary sat back, tugging gently at his ear. "I suppose I don't, Lady Kesa, but what matter? It's clear to me that danger is involved, and I know you'll have use of my sword."

"I don't know," the Princess said honestly. "Too many hands can spoil our plot. I thought perhaps you'd want to go your own way, find the road to Kreel's port. You'd have no trouble finding a ship to bring you home."

"You shame me, good lady! I am in your service now. Do you think I'd desert you and your friends so that I might be cozy and warm in some barmaid's bed?"

"You actually *want* to come with us?" asked Alryc. "The roads ahead are filled with danger—and not danger just in Kreel." His dour face tensed.

"I would be honored if you'd take me with you," Assad admitted. "But if you refuse to have me, then of course I'll reconsider."

"It's not that we don't want you, Captain," said Stacy. "You see, the real danger will begin only at the finish of our journey, not at the start. The chances are you'll never come home alive."

"Maybe we should tell him our mission," said Melinda. "He's proved a friend. We know we can trust him." She smiled kindly into his eyes, and the mercenary beamed.

Stacy glanced at Alryc, who nodded approval. Cicero, did likewise. "All right, then. Listen carefully, Captain: I'll not repeat this." She drew closer to him and spoke in whispers: "My niece, Mara, has been kidnaped. That much you know. What you don't know is that it's the Rani herself who has done the deed. She holds Mara in exchange for myself. That's why we travel in disguise."

"And you go to the Kuban palace to free her?"

"Exactly, but also to kill Sigried. That much I've vowed to the heavens, even if it costs me my life."

Assad whistled. He scratched his head disconcertedly. This was truly far more of an adventure than he had bargained for. No wonder it was all being done in such secrecy!

Melinda held her breath. "Do you still want to come?"

A broad smile crossed his face. "I do. And it's good for you that I do. I once sailed for the Rani, don't forget. I know the Kuban palace well. You'll have need of my services."

Stacy appeared to consider again. Then: "Agreed, Captain." She held out her hand. "Now you're one of us. Now we are five instead of four."

Assad took her hand and laughed. "And such five fools the gods have never seen!"

The morning sun burned off the mists. All at once this gloomy land seemed bright and fair. Luster returned to the grasses; colorful wild flowers were scattered the length and breadth of the hills. It was a crisp day, a day good for walking. After a breakfast of cold hare, they set off to follow the route Alryc had pointed out.

For a while they crossed through thickets filled with

tall oaks and rows of thorn and thistle bushes. The winds blew a bit more chilly and they covered their faces with veils and scarves. At the crest of a high hill it became possible to see the wide winding river that twisted its way into the mountains. Very gradually, it seemed, its brown banks blended and meshed into the mass of forests looming on each side. They still had not seen a single home or farm or any other sign of human life; only an occasional track of a bear or of some great prowling cat broke the soil. Stacy wondered if they would ever see people again. In this barren land even the sight of a barbarian would have been welcome.

Under the shade of leafy trees, they paused for the noon meal. Assad, with Melinda at his side, had no trouble setting a trap, which snared another hare almost immediately. Part they ate right away; the rest they saved for later. Days were growing short this time of summer, and they were eager to put as much distance between them and the sea as possible before the second night, with its ghastly mists, began.

All afternoon they pressed on, up sharply angled slopes and ridges, then down again, into hollows and peaceful dales. Here life stirred again: small lizards and rabbits, even the tracks of deer were found in abundance. But it was strange, Stacy mused: This was the first time in her life she had been in a forest where there were no birds to sing.

Slowly, very slowly, the sun began to wane against the horizon. They could literally see a wave of gloomy gray fog from the mountains begin to move down over their heads. It was a depressing sight. Going on much farther would be futile, yet there were no good grounds nearby upon which to rest, no streams from which to drink. They decided to keep going, at least till dusk.

Night closed in all around. Odd sounds filled their ears, causing them to peer constantly over their shoulders, seeking their source. They moved on for at least an hour after dark, still searching for a place to camp. At the top of a hillock Alryc stopped, gaping out into the blackness.

"Do you see something?" asked Stacy.

"Look there, my lady," he said, pointing out into the fog. "It looks like a light—a fire, perhaps."

Stacy stared. There did seem to be a faint glow from the distance, a speck of blurred orange light. She shuddered at the thought of where it might be coming from.

"Shall we try to reach it?"

She bit pensively at her lip. "We *should* try," she answered. "Maybe it's a farmhouse. Sooner or later we'd have to come across one. They could give us directions; water, too. Perhaps they'll sell us some food."

The thought of food other than hare was enough to persuade them! Without further discussion, they moved on slowly down the hill, coming upon a dark and inhospitable-looking open dryland. The light glowed brighter, higher, as if coming either from the top of a hill or from some tall window.

"I like this not," muttered Assad.

"Nor I," chimed in Melinda. "Let's sleep right here. In the morning this place might not look so frightening to us."

Stacy scoffed, "Don't be silly, Melinda. So far we've walked and walked and walked and there's been nothing to attack or harm us. It's only the mist that makes us tremble. My vote is to continue on."

"And mine, too," said Alryc. "We must overcome this false despair."

Cicero concurred with a soft growl. He put his nose to the earth and led the way. Stacy was next, Alryc third. Assad and Melinda were close behind but still apprehensive.

A sudden gust of cold wind swept around them.

As it did, some of the fog was cleared away. There before them, some five hundred meters distant, stood what appeared to be a tall, gloomy castle atop a small hillock, surrounded by clusters of thick trees. Upon its high stone walls, Stacy counted three towers, grouped so as to shadow one another. All windows were dark save for a dim orange glow in the highest tower.

Alryc shivered and tightened his cloak. "A forbidding place at best," he mumbled. "But at least we now know these lands are inhabited."

Melinda drew back a pace, clutching Assad's cold hand. "Yes, but inhabited by what? I've heard horrible tales of Kreel."

"Witches and goblins?" said Stacy with a smile. "I think not, but there's only one way to find out." And with Cicero at her side, she walked brazenly ahead, leaving the others staring at the grim walls.

"Perhaps we can persuade these folk to sell us horses," said Alryc, now also starting to walk. "It would make our journey much swifter."

As if giving credence to his words, from the distant stables beside the castle came the neighing of steeds. The astronomer laughed as Melinda froze at the sound. "Come little Dragonfire," he said, using his affectionate name for her. "The Princess is right, you know: There's nothing to fear."

The forest girl looked at Assad.

He smiled lamely. "I suppose we can't let the others go on alone."

"Very well," said Melinda with a sigh. "We'll go together. But don't blame *me* . . ."

Alryc tousled her hair affectionately and they walked on side by side as the mists lifted around them. At length they came to a narrow road that twisted and wound to the top of the hill. The trees loomed larger at the sides; the wind seemed to sing a gloomy but melodious song.

Stacy paused in front of a huge arched entrance; the doors were thick oak, braced with black iron for hinges. Upon each door hung a long black knocker in the shape of a serpent. She looked over her shoulder, checking to see that the others were close. Satisfied that they were, she nervously ran her tongue across her lips and knocked twice. The sounds echoed with fierce intensity. She was taken aback.

Silent and fearful, they waited long moments for their call to be heeded. No one came.

"Maybe they didn't hear us," said Alryc.

Stacy's eyes widened. "Not hear us? That knocker makes more noise than a pride of baboons!"

"Let me try," said Assad. He took the metal in his hand and banged it. Again it sounded like rolling thunder unloosed, and this time it didn't take long for someone to hear. The shuffle of boots rang hollowly from within; a horizontal slit slid open with a clang; a pair of dark, brooding eyes stared down at them.

"Who are you?" came a harsh voice.

Stacy cleared her throat. "Weary travelers, good sir, on our way to Kuba."

"What do you want here?"

Alryc spoke, gazing directly into the eyes. "To buy food, if you can spare it—also lodgings for the night, if it pleases you."

The eyes studied him carefully. "From where have you come? Are you mountain folk?"

"No, sir. We sailed from Satra. But that's a long story. We would be pleased to recount it for you if you'll open your door."

"Very well," came the hesitant reply.

The massive doors creaked as they swung open. Stacy shaded her eyes from the light of a single candle flickering from the hallway. Before her stood a very tall man with a slight hunchback. He wore a dark robe and a small gold chain dangling from his neck. He was an ugly fellow, with a broad, flat nose and bushy brows. He wore no beard or mustache. His neck seemed as thick as a tree trunk, his shoulders as wide as those of two normal-sized men. Indeed, save for Alryc, he was undoubtedly the largest man Stacy had ever seen.

He stood aside and beckoned them to enter. "I am Riordan," he announced matter-of-factly. "Welcome to my home."

"Then you are master of this castle?" said Stacy, noting that he seemed an odd sort to be a landowner. She would have guessed him to be a servant.

"Yes, I am lord here— I and my brothers, Rhys and Regum."

"Three brothers, then," she said smilingly, trying to please his dour demeanor.

"Yes, madam, but I just told you that: Riordan, Rhys and Regum. Perchance you know our names?"

"Unfortunately, no; but then we are strangers to Kreel. Allow me to introduce ourselves. I am Lady Kesa of the Glowing Mist country. This is my companion, Mistress Melinda." The girl curtsied for him. "And these are my protectors, Assad of Fable Island and Alryc of Rhonnda. The wolf is a childhood companion. He is called Cicero."

Riordan looked them over slowly. Assad and Alryc bowed politely. "You say you head for the Kuban frontiers?"

Stacy nodded. "A long way, I know; but alas, a journey must begin at its beginning."

Her host nodded glumly, as if she had just spoken some deep words of wisdom. "Where are your horses?"

"We have none," said Alryc. "We travel on foot. But if it is your desire, we would be glad to purchase steeds from your stable. Horses of Kreel are much admired throughout the world."

For the first time, Riordan smiled. "You have come at an opportune time," he said. "My brothers and I were just about to dine. Please come and join us."

"Delighted," said Stacy.

Melinda wanted to object. She felt that the quicker they were gone from this gloomy place the better, food or no food. A sharp glance from Alryc stopped her from speaking. She buttoned her lip and hoped for the best as their host led the way up a long row of winding wooden steps.

The floors creaked and the whole place looked as though it had not been dusted in years. The walls were filled with cracks that allowed hints of wind to enter.

"This way, if you please," said Riordan, gesturing for them to walk down a long, dim corridor.

Melinda shook her head ruefully, noting giant cobwebs in the corners of the high ceiling. At one point Cicero snarled at the sight of a small mouse scurrying from hole to hole on opposite walls. Riordan paid no heed either to the mouse or to his wolf guest.

At length he pushed open a tall, solid door and showed the way into the dining room. It was a large, drafty place. A log fire smoldered dimly across the room and long beams crisscrossed the ceiling. In the middle was a long oak table with many chairs set around it, but only two of the seats were taken. Two men, each taller and uglier than Riordan, stood up at the sight of their visitors. Each had the same features as his brother, each wore a similar dark robe and gold chain.

"These are guests come to stay for supper and the night," said Riordan, showing little emotion one way or another. In his slow way, he introduced them one by one.

The tallest of the brothers, Regum, nodded politely

and told them to sit. Stacy and Melinda did so first, then Assad, last Alryc. Cicero curled up on the floor beside Stacy, saying nothing but wagging his tail. Like Melinda, he thought little of this place.

"Bring our guests wine," said Regum to Riordan.

Riordan complied, pouring a heavy brew from a tall pitcher into small round silver goblets.

Regum held his own cup high. "Drink," he said eagerly. "Let our brew quench your thirst. You must be weary after your travels."

Stacy sipped at the wine; it was delicious. "Yes, my lord, we are tired. And we thought we'd never come upon human beings again. All we've seen these past two days are forests."

Regum laughed. It was clear that he was not only the tallest but also the oldest and therefore the true master of the castle, for when he smiled, his brothers smiled; when he put down his goblet, they put down theirs.

" 'Tis true," he lamented. "Men are few in these parts. Seldom do my brothers and I have company, but tonight we are especially blessed: Not only have we guests; they are noble ones at that. Tell me, Lady Kesa, what business has brought you to Kreel? Why had you not sailed directly to Kuba from your own port?"

From his questions, Stacy realized that he was quite ignorant of the political structure of the world. It was as if no one had ever told him that Satrian ships were unwelcome in Kuban waters, that the Rhonnda Empire and the Kuba Empire had few dealings with each other, save when Empire ships were forced to fight Kuban galleys.

"You ask a fair question, my lord. It would take hours to explain. Suffice it to say that our ship was captured by pirates in these very waters and my companions and I were held for ransom."

Regum's eyes darkened, so did those of his brothers.

"But no! It pains me, dear lady, to think that you and your gentle friends were at the mercy of brigands, yet now you are here."

"Fortune smiled kindly upon us, Lord Regum. The pirates, in turn, were set upon by a Kuban warship. They were slain, and my companions and I were freed to continue our journey. The Kuban ship dropped anchor two days' journey from here and we departed. Since then we have walked—"

"What?" Regum became agitated. " 'Walked,' did you say? But, Lady Kesa, 'tis shame that one as lovely as you should be put to such pains."

"Permit me to say, my lord," interjected Alryc, "that we hoped perhaps we might buy horses from you."

" 'Buy'? Do you insult me, sir? We do not sell. We are not traders or merchants. I will *give* you horses, all of you—my finest steeds. In the morning you can take your pick. Let it never be said that men of Kreel were unkind to strangers."

Stacy smiled at him and cast a puzzled look toward her friends. "Thank you, Lord Regum. Your offer is most generous. I can see you are a gentleman among gentlemen."

Regum beamed. " 'Tis my pleasure, dear lady. But come, finish your tale. Supper is not quite done and we have much time."

"Alas, there is little left to tell. We go to Kuba on important business, to the palace of the Rani."

The lord of the castle rubbed knowingly at his chin. "Ah, I see: You are envoys to the Rani."

"Something like that, yes," said Assad. "We bring her . . . er . . . urgent tidings from Satra."

Regum leaned forward and cocked his head as he stared at the mercenary. "Your features are not Satrian, are they? I think perhaps you are from these parts."

"No, my lord—from Fable Island, between Kuba and Satra."

"A land known for its ships!" cried Rhys, speaking for the first time.

"And for its beauty," chimed in Riordan.

"And also for its mercenaries," added Regum. "Tell me, are you a man of the sea, good sir?"

Assad nodded, choosing his words carefully so as not to betray either himself or the Princess. "I was born to the sea, my lord, and in my time I've sailed across three of the world's oceans; but now I live peacefully in Glowing Mist, serving my lady and her house."

"Have you been to Rhonnda-by-the-Sea?"

Stacy stirred, her eyes on Assad.

"Only once, Lord Regum," Assad said, "and then but for a short while."

Their host leaned back sullenly. "A pity," he rasped. "So little news of the outside world reaches this land. I had hoped to hear from you of the Empire Fleet and its famous voyages."

"I am a Rhonnda man," said Alryc proudly. "That is, until I came to Satra I was. What are the questions you would ask?"

Regum's eyes lit up. His brothers smiled. "Is it true that the Fleet has sailed upon all Seven Seas?"

"It is. Captain Elias has circumvented virtually the entire world. One by one, strange lands are brought out from their Dark Time and into the light. The Empire banner waves with pride wherever it is set."

The lord listened and agreed. "So much I have already heard. The world needs such unity. But tell me, sir, have you ever set eyes on the woman who sits upon the Rhonnda throne?"

Alryc glanced at Stacy. She shook her head slightly. "Er . . . no, my lord. Few common men have seen her."

All three brothers frowned.

"I once knew a man who claimed to have met her," said Regum.

"Oh?" said Stacy, curious. "What did he say?"

Their host shuddered. "It was a grisly description, Lady Kesa. He said that the Princess is a woman with green scaly skin and fangs like a wolf. Her gaze can make a man turn to stone."

"Bah!" growled Alryc. "Do you believe such loose talk?"

Regum shrugged. "It must be so. How else could such a woman rule so vast an empire?"

"I have heard that Anastasia is quite lovely," said Melinda, round eyes wide.

Regum looked at the forest girl with some shock. "Lady? Do you not know that the Princess is a witch, that she changes form to please the eyes of those who please her?"

Stacy smiled inwardly at the thought. It was curious to hear how men in foreign lands spoke of her; but talk of this kind could serve no purpose, she knew—not in the circumstances they were in. Tactfully changing the subject, she said, "Mmmmm, your wine is delicious, Lord Regum—perhaps the best I've ever had. Is it local?"

The ploy worked: Regum beamed. "Made from our very own vineyards, Lady Kesa. I thank you for your compliment. But please, have some more."

Riordan jumped up and hastily poured for them all.

"A toast, then," said Rhys. He held his goblet high. "Good fortune to our guests—"

"And a pleasant journey to Kuba," added Regum.

They all took a long draught, smiled and exchanged pleasantries.

"I too offer a toast," said Alryc. "To our kind and gracious hosts: May your lands grow fertile and rich with each passing day."

Again everyone drank. The potent wine worked swiftly. Soon the atmosphere was more that of longtime friends than of passing strangers meeting in the night.

From the kitchen came three servants, each carrying

a tray laden with steaming broth and potatoes and a pot of boiling stew.

"Ah, at last," said Regum jovially, indicating for the servants to serve his guests first. Upon hot, fine plates supper was served. Even Cicero was given a heaping portion, and like the others, he ate eagerly, savoring every morsel. The food was strangely spiced, crunchy to the taste. Feeling that such exotic spicing was not to be wasted, Stacy made a mental note to ask Regum for the recipe.

Hungry as they were, each had second helpings of the delicious stew, except for Alryc and Cicero, who had three. Then, for a while after they had finished, everyone sat back and glowed in the warmth of the room.

Alryc rubbed his stomach and smiled contentedly. "Excellent, Lord Regum. I enjoyed your meal thoroughly."

"It was the spicing that set it apart from lesser fare," said Assad, leaning back and sipping his wine.

"And those crunchy beans," added Melinda. "What are they?"

Before Regum could answer, a servant hurried in with a tray of tiny yellow pastries.

"Ah, dessert has come. Help yourselves, my friends."

Stacy chewed one slowly and smiled at her host. "Like all your food, sir, this too is excellent."

"I shall have my servants prepare some for your journey."

"Most kind of you, my lord," said Melinda, who was also enjoying the pastry. "It will be more than welcome on the long roads ahead. What are the ingredients? Someday I may have a husband who will need pleasing."

Regum laughed and looked over at Riordan. "Tell them your secret, brother," he said with a wink.

Riordan grinned wildly. "An easy recipe, Mistress Melinda. First we mix flour with salt, cut in shortening and sprinkle with water. Then we mold it into balls and flatten—"

"Surely there's more here than that," said Stacy.

"Yes, Lady Kesa: dry-roasted insects."

The Princess stopped chewing immediately.

Alryc, who was about to have another pastry, put it slowly down on his plate.

"Insects, you say?" asked Melinda, trying to keep a calm composure.

"Indeed yes," said Riordan, laughing. "We spread them alive and fresh, then bake for an hour. Flies are abundant in summer, so we make great use of them, too; but my brothers prefer crawling creatures."

Alryc grimaced; Regum noticed and shot him an angered look.

"Ants are too common, except, of course, for red ones, which I find in the hills," Riordan went on, "and when we really want a treat, we serve roaches. There are dozens of varieties in these lands, you see, and—"

Melinda put her hand to her mouth and gagged.

Riordan was oblivious. "We take special delight in preparing them. First we freeze them in ice, then serve them in ice cubes with our water."

"You eat them *raw?*" asked Assad, feeling a bit sickened as his stomach curdled.

"Oh, yes; they're better raw. Would you like me to bring you a plate? You can watch them squirm before you eat them."

The mercenary waved his hand. "Er . . . thank you, but no."

"Our fare is no longer to your liking, sir?" cried Regum, his eyes widened and wild.

"It is not to your palate?" chimed in Rhys.

Stacy could see that her hosts were becoming inflamed. It was clear that her companions' disapproval was being taken as an insult. "Forgive us, good lords.

We are foreigners. We know little of the food in these parts."

Regum's eyes smoldered darkly. "Then you also disapprove?"

Stacy opened her mouth, but before she could reply, Alryc said, "None of us has ever eaten such things before."

"'Things'?" cried Rhys. "You call our delicacies *'things'*? This is outrageous, sir!"

"They offend our names!' responded Riordan.

"You misunderstand," said Stacy. "We mean no ill against you—"

"Yet you eat our mealworm stew—"

"Mealworm?" cried Melinda. "You mean those beans I was so fond of?"

"And lice potatoes," Riordan told her.

The forest girl became as white as a sheet. When the lord spoke of insect broth and curdled worms, it was all she could do to keep from vomiting. Assad stood and helped her up from the table.

"Where are you going?" demanded Regum.

"For a bit of fresh air, my lord. The lady is ill."

"Ill? Ill, you say? Our food has made her *ill?*"

"This is an insult!" bellowed Riordan.

Tempers began to flare all around. Rhys rose to his full height, and Stacy was astounded to see that he towered over Alryc. Then Regum stood—and he was bigger yet!

"We have been shamed!" Regum roared.

"Disgraced!" cried Rhys, pounding a fist.

Stacy stood, flustered. Cicero leaped up and growled at her side.

Alryc's hand slid to his sword. He was reluctant to use it against these strange brothers, because up until moments ago they had truly been kind hosts; but now things had taken a darker turn. He saw that a variety of weapons hung from the wall opposite—long sabers, flat-pointed axes, stout shortswords—and he knew that the frenzied brothers would not be reluctant in using them. "Let us leave you in peace," he told them. "We seek no fight."

Regum looked astounded. "You seek no fight? Indeed you are strange folk. Gentlemen always fight after supper. It is our custom to draw first blood." And with that, all three brothers bolted for the wall and drew their favorite weapons.

"Quick! To the hallway!" shouted Assad as he flung open the dining-room door. Stacy raced out with Cicero at her side, Melinda on her heels. Riordan, wielding his ax above his head, gave chase. Assad drew his sword menacingly, but Riordan paid no attention. His eyes were frenzied. Assad ducked the ax as it came down and thrust the hilt of his weapon into Riordan's stomach. The lord arched back, sprawling to the floor, his ax sliding to the far end of the room. Alryc's sword flashed, stopping the thrust of Regum's blade; sparks flew. Then, with his boot, he pushed the lord back a few paces and made a hasty retreat from the room, Assad on his heels.

"The stairs!" cried Stacy, leading the way. She drew her silver dagger and waited for the others to reach her. Then, helter-skelter, they bounded down the steps as though the Devil himself were on their trail.

The brothers, however, were not so easily defeated. Rhys came charging down the stairs, wielding a saber in one hand and a long sharpened dagger in the other. Regum, back on his feet, was racing behind him, eyes blazing.

An ax sailed past, inches from Alryc's head. He looked over his shoulder and saw the brothers coming, leaping and bounding. His attention was diverted by Melinda's scream. Ahead, on the landing, stood five servants, each armed and prepared to stop the guests from leaving. Cicero jumped high, his forceful weight knocking over three. Assad pushed past the fourth, his fist knocking out the man's front teeth as he did so. The man spit blood, and then Alryc's blow to his windpipe sent him reeling across the room. The fifth servant cowered and shivered. He too was knocked aside, not by Stacy or her companions but by Regum, who had now reached the landing and was determined to stop them from reaching the door.

"Get out first!" called Assad. "Alryc and I will hold them back!"

With all her energy, Stacy swung the heavy doors open and dashed into the safety of the night. Melinda whirled as a dagger whistled past her head and stuck in the wood. She pulled it out to use, but Assad shoved her through the doorway, then ducked as another knife came sailing after them.

"They're crazy!" he said to Alryc.

The astronomer nodded grimly, but there was no time for words, for just at that moment Rhys joined his brother at the bottom of the stairs, flashing his weapon in front of him.

"Aha!" cackled Rhys. "So we have our fight after all!" Crazed, he swung his blade.

Alryc blunted the downward thrust and grappled with Rhys. "Very well, then! If a fight cannot be avoided, let's make it a good one!"

The swords clanged together as the two men fought with reckless abandon. Assad halted Rhys's parry, then thrust at Regum. "I'll hold them all off, Alryc! Flee while you can!"

"We came together; we leave together!" With a powerful shove, Alryc sent Rhys stumbling into his brother. In that moment's space, both he and Assad ran into the night. Stacy and Melinda, Cicero beside them, stood in the shadows along the path.

"What about the horses?" called Assad.

"Horses? Are you insane? They won't give us horses!"

Assad laughed. "All right; then we'll take them!"

Alryc looked aghast as Assad and Stacy made for the stables. The mares began to whinny and stamp their feet. "Hurry!" he shouted. "The brothers are running down the path!"

But, worse than that, on the towers servants had begun to take up positions as archers. Their bows sang a grim song; short-shafted crossbow arrows danced all about.

Suddenly the stable gates banged open. Stacy came charging down the trail on a fine black mare, her dagger glittering in the darkness. She blocked the path and held the brothers at bay, oblivious to the arrows falling on either side. Assad, still afoot, came running with three more horses. Expertly, Melinda jumped into the saddle of the first, took hold of her crossbow, slung it into firing position and loosed her dart. A savage scream quickly followed, and from the tower a servant hurtled to the ground. Assad gaped. Her aim, even in the dead of night, had been perfect. She winked and laughed, reloading. Alryc climbed atop his steed; Assad did the same.

"Are we ready?" called Stacy, still fending off the brothers.

"All set, my lady! Let's move!"

She kicked hard with her boot and the horse reared; the brothers drew back in fear of the animal. Then, turning, she galloped down the path to catch up with the others, Cicero running at her side. The arrows still came, but fewer and fewer. She could hear Regum cursing at her at the top of his lungs and his brothers joining in; then soon she could hear nothing at all. The castle once again disappeared into the fog, and the travelers found themselves upon the same ground they had stood on only hours before.

Beside a dark brook they watered the horses and rested, too weary to go on.

"Do you think they'll follow us?" asked Assad.

Stacy frowned. "Not a chance. We taught them a lesson, I think."

Alryc, who was sitting glumly against a tree, his bare feet soaking in the brook, suddenly laughed. "And they taught us a lesson, too, don't forget."

"Indeed?" said the Princess.

"Of course. The next time we're invited for supper, I'll remember to ask before I eat. Remember: One man's wine is another man's vinegar."

At that they all laughed and settled down for the night. Their first adventure on the dark shores of Kreel was one they would never forget.

Quiet fell throughout the Temple. All eyes lowered as the light dimmed and the flickering candles sent shadows dancing down from the domed ceiling. The skylight glowed with a thousand dazzling stars, reflecting the tiny flames in the glowing globes suspended from the ceiling. The curtains at the long recessed windows swayed in the breeze. All was quiet save for the tinkling of the ever-present Temple bells. They were lulling in their song, yet also provocative. They hinted at the ritual dance to come.

Slowly the altar began to glow in a soft rainbow of color. The pilgrims who came to see the dance gaped at the splendid sights and sounds. Hands crossed over their breasts in respect, they were immersed in the strange world around them.

Only once each year would the Kuban Temple be opened to pilgrims; only once each year did the priestesses perform the rites. This was that day; but more that, this was the day when the Rani herself would dance, and eagerly the thousand souls jammed tightly into the hall waited patiently, hearts throbbing with anticipation, for her appearance.

The roots of this day could be traced back a thousand

years, even as Kuba burned darkly in its lost days. Always there had been a Rani to dance, to bring Kuba's plea directly to the Fates. Many former Ranis had chanted and danced in dizzying display, but none throughout Kuba's proud history had commanded the devotion or the desire that Sigried stirred. Through her, the pilgrims knew, Kuba would one day take its rightful place; through her would be achieved the greatness once known in ancient days. Beloved in her land, even as Anastasia was in Rhonnda, Sigried used her wile and her charms cunningly. The crowd had come meek and passive; by the time she had finished, they—men and women alike—would be whipped into a frenzy of desire and belief. And like children she would mold them, shape them, and her will would once again be done.

The wind song of the bells began to fade. As it did, a slow, melodic rhythm grew from somewhere distant. A soft drone murmured; a drum sounded dimly. Rainbow lights intensified, all colors of the spectrum seeming to sway in time with the music, crimson shadows replacing those of purple and blue. A yellow globe began to burn, illuminating the center of the altar floor. The icons at either side loomed larger than life. Their stone faces seemed to come alive, jeweled eyes sparkling with cruel lust. The pilgrims held their breath, staring hypnotically into the light. Coals in a recessed hearth glowed. The stage was set.

Sigried emerged from the darkness behind the vibrating rainbow. Slowly, eyes downcast, she wound her way toward the altar. She was stunningly beautiful. She wore a yellow dress, cut low, with black and gold stripes at the sides. In the dim setting, her skin glowed golden, like her hair. Gold bracelets adorned her wrists, tinkling against each other as she swayed, her arms above her head. Her long yellow hair tossed in waves, like the sea, as she raised her head, eyes closed, and began to sing in a soft chant. Her song was strange, recalling languages long dead; but it mattered not what the words meant. The pilgrims watched her part her lips seductively to the gods and trembled as her hips started to sway. Feet apart but firm on the tiled floor, she lifted the jewel-studded diadem from her head and shook her hair wild and free. It fell over her breasts, down below her shoulders. Her silhouette revealed a perfect shape, that of a woman who truly was the envy of every other in the world. Her legs were long, her calves well rounded; they blended tauntingly against a flat stomach and soft, curved hips. Her waist was small, her firm breasts trembled erotically with her every breath. Around her slim neck she wore a thin black velvet band.

At length she opened her wide, ice-blue eyes and gazed about the room. A servant bowed lithely before her, and she handed over the diadem. Then the haunting music began to rise.

Sigried bent gracefully down to sweep up from the floor the waiting dark shawl, the magic shawl of the priestess. She spun on her heels, tightening the brilliant garment around her shoulders. Then, as if submissive to an unseen lover, she bowed her head, let her hair cover her face and held out her arms. Her fingers beckoned, calling mutely like those of a mysterious siren. Then she raised her chin and parted her lips. Her golden body began to quiver, faster and faster; her skin glistened with perspiration. She ran her hands along her thighs, up her waist, and gently lifted her breasts.

Now she began to spin again, wildly, savagely. The drums beat faster. She pulled the magic shawl from her shoulders, swinging it tauntingly with one hand, as if calling back her unseen lover to her bed. Her breasts heaved; a shoulder strap fell down her arm. Sigried threw her head back and laughed, eyes flashing with fire and desire. Her back arched, her hips pounding with the rhythm. The wet dress began to cling to her perfect body. Aware of her beauty, she taunted her lover, drew back and held out her arms. She turned, dress flaring, arms behind her back. Once more she quivered, excitedly, her whole body vibrating.

Suddenly the colors began to change. Where the dark crimson flames had been were now soft indigo shadows. The music slowed, then faded to a whisper. Once again there came the wind song of the bells, Siggy danced slower, more provocatively. The swirling colors matched her eyes. She stared, pupils dilating, breathing heavily. Then, turning left, she moved her arms like snakes. Turning right, she pretended to groan in the pleasure of her god's lovemaking.

The pilgrims had never seen anything like this. Even in their wildest expectations they had not thought the Rani a woman such as this.

Desire rose to an unbearable pitch. Siggy quivered tauntingly again, her dress rising, her legs emerging fully. On her face was a look of passion, her lips full and dark as wine. Gasps came from the audience as she slipped both shoulder straps down. The dress fell to the floor. All light died save that of the stars. The Rani was naked now but bathed in black shadows. Men strained their necks and their eyes. She slipped slowly backward, darted between shadows and reappeared dimly with her face pressed close to the stone icon. She squirmed in its arms as the god made love to her. She panted and sighed and moaned. Her hips thrust slowly, forcefully, her breasts dancing with a life of their own. Her body seethed with need of her lover. She and the god were intertwined, were one.

And so the pilgrims watched and believed. She was more than mortal woman, more than flesh and blood. For her they would throw away their lives; for but a single glance at her perfect body in the light, they would commit any act, any crime. All they saw was her silhouette, hard against the icon, but it was enough. Each man felt that this dance was for him; each dreamed of being called out and brought to her palace to spend but a single night in her arms.

The magic shawl hung limply from her hand. The heaving slowed, then stopped. She had given herself to her god and had pleased him. Humbly, still in slow rhythm, she parted from the icon and slipped the shawl over her shoulders. It hung long and low, covering most of her body. The pilgrims could almost reach out and touch her now, feel her wet skin, scent the perfumes. Her shoulders hunched slightly, she smiled at the darkened crowd. All were transfixed, their eyes locked with hers. The women in the crowd felt their own bodies tremble, felt their own desire to dance and make love rise. The men wet their lips, breathing laboriously.

Sigried had stirred them as no other could.

The music died. The wind song of the bells lingered. The Rani swayed again, moving ever back into the shadows. Her silhouette lingered for a while; then suddenly it was gone. Small flames burned again and the rainbow light returned. All was as it had been—the altar, the icons, the glowing globe—but the Rani was gone. The ritual dance was done.

Alone in her resplendent bedroom, Sigried sat relaxed upon the side of her massive bed, running a thick brush through her hair. It had been a long, tiresome day, but she had enjoyed it, this opportunity to play the role of priestess again. This year the crowd had been especially pleased. She had sensed it, as any woman could. She reveled in the memory of the burning looks upon their faces, the almost fanatic wish to throw away their lives in her service. On rare occasions she had chosen a pilgrim from such a crowd, brought him to the palace and rewarded him with position and honor for his deeds. Rarer yet, she had once or twice, on a whim, taken such a man to her bed. This had almost become legend, she knew. Each year they flocked from all over

Kuba to see her dance; but behind the ritual, she knew, was their hidden hope that perhaps one would again be chosen from among them.

She held up a small hand mirror, anxiously seeking the first lines of age. There were none. Her skin was flawless, as it had been when she was twenty. With a smile she threw back her hair and tossed the mirror and brush to the carpeted floor. She felt restless; not tense—things were going too well for that—but just slightly ill at ease. Was it because she would soon be face to face with Anastasia again? She asked herself if Stacy would still look the same. It had been a long time since they had last seen each other. Would Stacy's skin be as flawless as her own? Would Stacy still be an attraction to men's eyes?

The Rani frowned. She knew Stacy would. Things came easy to that bitch; they always had. While Sigried had had to build Kuba from virtual ashes, Anastasia had been delivered her own throne on a platter—a throne she didn't even want! While Siggy strove and cajoled for her few pitiful allies, Stacy's flocked to her like whimpering children.

Children, thought Siggy bitterly.

It was here that she hated the Princess most. The Rani had no husband—never had. There was no Elias in her life, no daring and courageous captain to fulfill her dreams and aspirations; only vultures—witless soldiers and ambitious politicians. They used her, she knew, but what matter? She used them, too, and not just to comfort her in her bed. She needed their skills and abilities more than she was willing to tell. Kuba was hard-pressed; Empire lands were springing up on every side. Matters could not continue like this indefinitely.

Once, years before, she had secretly sent for the famous Lord Blood and offered him anything to forsake his princess and her banner. She had offered him everything she had, including herself and half her empire.

She had hoped that Blood would accept. And why not? Years before, he had loved Anastasia, would have done anything for her, but she had spurned him and taken Elias instead. Yet Blood had remained loyal. Siggy seethed at the memory of her encounter with the dashing soldier. He had laughed at her. Laughed! She had wanted to have his head removed right there and then, but she had let him go, let him depart in peace and secrecy, as he had come. And then she had wept— alone, in the solitude of her bedroom. No one could see; no one could hear. Blood was a man she could have loved.

The bitch has a man while I'm alone!

Siggy sighed softly, wiping the memory from her thoughts. But it had smoldered for so long it was hard to erase. Jealousy, hatred, whatever it truly was, she had harbored it and nurtured it over nineteen years. At last fortunes were changing. It was in her palace now that the lovely Mara was kept, and she intended to keep it that way.

No regrets, Stacy. Whatever the outcome, no regrets.

A soft knock interrupted her thoughts.

"Enter."

A short, plump woman slipped inside and bowed. "The dragoon, Dimitri, wishes to speak with you, Rani."

Siggy frowned. What did he want now? She'd shared her bed with him enough already. Now he was becoming tiresome. Still, he had kept his promise and had brought Mara. She would at least have to see what he wanted. "Tell him to wait. I'll join him presently."

"Very good, my Rani."

Hastily she threw on her velvet robe, pushed back her hair and walked from the bedchamber to the greeting room. There, with his back to her, Dimitri stood gazing out the window at the domes and steeples of the city. It was a dark, gloomy night, but his erect stance told her that for some reason he was happy.

"You wanted to see me?"

He turned around, startled. "You walk like a cat, Sigried." He grinned. "I didn't hear you enter."

She looked at him blankly. "You weren't supposed to. Now, what is it?"

He walked forward, took her hand in his and kissed it softly.

She pulled away, showing distaste. "Don't dawdle over me, Dimitri. What are you here for?"

The dragoon disregarded her annoyance and slumped lazily down onto her cushioned divan. "Just to give you some news, my lady. A merchant vessel that's been across the sea just came into harbor. The latest news from Rhonnda is that Princess Anastasia has decided to go into seclusion for an undetermined time. Rhonnda's council carries on in her absence."

Sigried could not contain a smile. "Seclusion, my foot! She's bitten, Dimitri! She's left Rhonnda to come here!"

He grinned foolishly. "Do roses bloom in summer?"

She clapped her hands. "Then we've really won! I can't believe it! All ships will be alerted to look for her vessel."

"And give her a royal escort." He slid his finger across his neck. "Why not let your young cousin bring her back in chains?"

The Rani's eyes darkened; she glared at her visitor. "Quentin does not know of this little venture of ours, Dimitri, nor will he. Is that understood?"

The mercenary looked surprised. "All right, Siggy."

She bristled at his using her familiar name. "I sent Quentin away from here purposely, Dimitri. My young cousin would not approve of our tactics, and I don't want him to know anything of it until it's done with."

"I see," replied the dragoon, rubbing at his chin. "I wondered why you sent him out chasing pirates instead of facing down the Empire Fleet."

"Oh, he'll face the Fleet, all right, but not now—later. You'll find him to be a match for any sea captain."

Dimitri's brows rose. "Even for Elias?"

"Even Elias. Quentin's got all of his assets plus youth. For once we're going to face down Anastasia's ships, and this time we'll be the ones on top."

"They'll fight all the harder to free the Princess," he cautioned.

Siggy smirked. "Let me worry about those matters, Dimitri. I thank you for coming to bring me this news. Now, if you'll excuse me..."

He looked at her awkwardly, sensing that he was being rudely dismissed. "Will I see you tomorrow?" he asked haltingly.

"Perhaps, perhaps not; we'll see then. Right now I'm tired. It's been a long day for me."

"I saw you dance," he said, frowning as he stared at the floor.

The Rani cocked her head and brushed aside her hair. "You were in the Temple?"

"I was. I donned a pilgrim's robe and came with the procession."

"How dare you!" she flared. "That was sacrilege. You know it's forbidden for foreigners to watch the priestess."

"I didn't. I came to see you."

He sounded like a youthful lover lost in jealousy, and she scorned him for it. "Were you pleased with what you saw?" she asked acidly.

His face darkened; he shied away from her stare. "I didn't like the way you threw yourself—"

"And who are you to make demands of me, mercenary?" She stood with her hands on her hips, her head thrown back. Contempt crossed her lips. "You forget your place here, Dimitri. You haven't won the right to sit beside my throne *yet*. And sharing my bed at my pleasure doesn't give you the right to question my actions." Deep fires kindled in her ice-blue eyes.

He crossed his arms over his chest and bowed his head.

She scowled at the sight of him humbled before her. *A spineless eunuch,* she thought. *I need a man like Elias.* And again she cursed Stacy for her good fortune.

Without speaking, Dimitri backtracked slowly from the room.

Siggy turned away in quiet disgust. *Just who does he think he is?* she asked herself. *A man like that deserves no better than a slut from the brothels.* She'd remember one day to send him back there.

PART THREE

ON THE ROAD TO KUBA

All through the day Stacy and her companions rode through the rugged lands of Kreel. Their path took them across grassy plains and up the slopes of gentle hills thick with trees and shrubs. At one point they saw another castle loom loftily in the distance, but with the memory of the three brothers still fresh in their minds, they decided to avoid it.

The mountain pass that would lead to the Kuban frontier was still far from sight, although the hazy broad mountains themselves were clear on the horizon. The lands they rode through now were high with dark grass and filled with wild flowers. There were old, lofty trees whose boughs and trunks swayed low above them, and long, twisting streams that forked and rambled across the dark hills. In many ways these parts reminded Stacy very much of home—not Rhonnda, of course, but the sweet and peaceful valley near the forest where she was born.

The burdens she carried weighed down all the heavier as her thoughts wandered back to those days lost. It was a simple time: There were no seas to cross, no dim, distant lands to conquer. Her friends were the wolves and the birds; she knew no enemies.

What madness had taken her from those things to sail the ocean and begin a life of such adventure? The fires of youth had been strong. She had yearned to seek out and solve the mysteries of the world, and no one had been able to deter her from it—no one.

It was her destiny, Alryc had said. Written across the stars by the finger of the Fates themselves—glory and fame, the crown of an empire; the envy of every woman and man—but he had never spoken of the loneliness that came with the crown, nor the loss of the simple pleasures of life that others took for granted. To be a princess was to be a slave.

Again Stacy resolved to give up her throne—leave it all behind forever and return to what she had been long ago. She was well aware that many would mock her for it, this throwing away of so much; but the idle chatter of fools would not be considered. Few, if any, could have worn her shoes any better.

In the shade of a row of chestnut trees the band stopped their journey and set up camp for the night. Assad and Melinda set out to seek supper, while Alryc gathered wood for the fire and cleared the ground of rocks and fallen boughs. As he did so, Stacy sat against a tree and stared blankly out toward the menacing mountains that would take them to the Kuban frontier. It was Cicero, intelligently seeing through her façade of calm, who first noted her bitter mirth. With his bushy red tail wagging, his sleek fur glistening in the setting sun, he nuzzled close to her and ran a wet tongue across her face. A hunter of few words, he wasted no time in small chatter.

"You're troubled, Khalea? Why? Our journey goes well." His snout snuggled nearer.

With a warm smile and the hint of a tear in her deep eyes, Stacy ran her fingers through his fur and hugged him close. "This place, Cicero; doesn't it remind you of home?"

Cicero was a mountain wolf, not of the forest; his lands were wild and rugged; but he knew of the Princess's valley and the endless forest of which she spoke. "You are sad, Khalea. I see it in your eyes, even as I feel Aleya, the wind. Is it home you crave?"

She nodded feebly and wrinkled her nose as a wolf does when trying to keep from crying.

Cicero, sighing, slumped closer to her, his tail beating back and forth in a slow rhythm against her tunic. He could easily sympathize with her and more readily understand her feelings than men. Khalea was no mere woman who had befriended wolves but a huntress in her own right. And the title of huntress was never given, only earned. Years ago Stacy had proved herself to the pack and become one of them. So deep were her roots among wolves that many no longer even thought of her as a woman. She was of the forest and all the Dwellers that lived wtihin it. The throne of men was a meaningless token—and Cicero was seeing just an inkling of the grief it had brought.

"You *will* go home one day," he growled in a whisper.

"Do you . . . do you really think so?"

"Do the spring rains follow the winter snows, Khalea? Does the setting sun kiss the rising moon at evening?"

Stacy sniffed and looked at him through the curtain of her hair. "I want to go home, Cicero—more than anything. I have dreamed of little else for all these years."

"And that dream will come true. Fara, the goddess who rules over all Dwellers, will make it so. She will watch over and protect you, Khalea, as she always has."

The Princess gave a wan smile. "Even when we reach Kuba?"

He nodded. "Even then. Mara will be saved, and we'll all go home together."

A happy whistle from the crest of the hill broke them from their thoughts. Melinda, crossbow in hand, was signaling for them all to look. Behind her, a long shadow in the evening light, came Assad carrying a small buck over his shoulders.

"A feast tonight!" he called merrily. "And thank Melinda. I never saw such fine shooting!"

"Well, bring it here!" called Alryc, striking flints under the dry kindling.

Small finger-flames leaped up and danced. Assad skinned the deer and skewered the choicest cuts. Everyone watched hungrily as the red meat dripped tasty juices. Stacy's dark mood faded; she realized she was as hungry as the others. Eagerly they ate, savoring every bite. It was a fitting meal after a long day's ride, and each hoped that every day might be equally rewarded.

The horses, tied to trees at the edge of the camp, suddenly became restless. Cicero leaped to his feet, ears drawn back, and began to snarl.

"What is it?" whispered Stacy.

"Shhh. Listen," said Melinda.

There was a dull sound of grass being trampled, then the snap of a twig. Assad drew his blade.

Alryc's night eyes glowered toward the dancing shadows. "Who goes there?" he demanded.

No answer.

"I repeat: Who goes there? Speak swiftly or my sword will answer for you!"

Just then a dark silhouette moved out from the shadows. Firelight glowed dimly against a hard, scruffy-looking face—the face of a man with dark, shifty eyes half hidden in the shadow of the hood of his dirty robe. He hunched slightly, his mouth gaping at the fire and the leftover meat.

Cicero crouched low, as if poised to strike.

"Hush," said Melinda. Her eyes showed pity for the bedraggled man. "Are you hungry?"

He nodded eagerly.

"Will you sit by our fire?" Melinda gestured politely.

Again he nodded.

"Can't you speak, man?" bellowed Alryc.

The guest shuddered and hugged himself as if for protection.

Stacy stood, her eyes telling Alryc to let the man be. "You need not speak to us if you don't wish."

The man smiled, exposing a mouth full of rotted black stumps for teeth. Stacy handed him a chunk of meat and bade him sit down in a comfortable spot. Mouth drooling, he ate the fare swiftly, like a beast. Melinda drew some fresh water and handed him a cup. The man, wiping his fingers on his robe, slobbered the water down. Then, with a grin, again showing his lack of teeth, he belched loudly.

"You are welcome to sit beside our fire for a while," said Stacy, overlooking his lack of manners.

Melinda nodded. "The mists are closing in. You won't be able to continue your travels anyway."

The man rubbed his hands by the fire happily and nodded, still not uttering a word.

For a long while he sat like that, away from the others, staring dumbly into the flames. At length Stacy said, "I mean no offense, sir, but tell me: Do you not speak because you are a mute?"

Here the man's eyes lowered and he began to whimper like a child.

Stacy reached over and put her hand on his shoulder. "Never mind," she said softly. "I understand."

The tenderness of her words brought him to tears again, but this time he didn't look away. His sad eyes stared into hers, seeking her warmth and understanding.

"Were you born mute?" she asked.

He shook his head violently.

"No?" said Assad, suddenly interested. "You mean that someone—"

The stranger nodded.

Stacy shuddered. What kind of savage would tear a man's tongue from his throat? She wondered if such terrible crimes were common in Kreel.

"Was this done to you as punishment?" asked Melinda.

He stared blankly.

"Did you commit some crime? Had you taken a life or hurt someone?"

Again he shook his head violently. Stacy glanced at Melinda; but the forest girl seemed to be as puzzled as she. Then, to her surprise, the man shot out his arm and pointed his finger wildly in the direction of the fog-shrouded mountains. As he gesticulated, his mouth strained to form words. None came.

"I think he's trying to tell us something," observed Assad.

The poor lout began tugging at Stacy's sleeve. She looked him in the eye. "Was my friend right? Are you trying to tell us something?"

"Something about the mountains?" asked Melinda.

Another nod.

"Can you write it for us?" asked Alryc.

Their guest frowned, shrugged and made a gesture that told them he could neither read nor write.

Stacy sighed. How were they ever to find out what his message was?

Tugging at her sleeve again, the man tried to draw a picture in the dirt. Melinda leaned over to watch. It was something like a man, but she wasn't sure. The face had no eyes.

"Is that the man who tore out your tongue?" asked the forest girl.

He indicated that it was, with a mournful sigh.

"A man without eyes in his head?"

Stacy had no idea what to make of this. "Without eyes? What do you mean?"

The guest closed his eyes and covered them with his hands.

"Blind!" cried Assad. "He's telling us that a blind man did it!"

The mute clapped his hands gleefully. He began to draw another picture, now excited and eager to tell his tale.

"Slow down, my friend," said Stacy. "You're going too fast for us. Let's reconstruct what we know. You're saying that somewhere in the mountains is a man—a blind man—and he did this to you."

The mute nodded and pointed to each of his hosts.

"And he'll do it to us?" offered Melinda.

A sour nod followed next. He began to pretend to count on his fingers.

Alryc's face darkened. He alone grasped what this meant. "He's saying that the blind man has done this to many people."

"But how?" cried Melinda.

The mute stood in imitation of his foe. He pretended to heave a mighty sword, catch and bind someone, then drag him off. Stacy saw that he was trying to tell a frightening story of what had happened not only to him but to many others as well. After a while the mute sat back; his tale was done. Now it was up to his hosts to put the pieces together.

Assad sat back, scratching his head.

Stacy, still somewhat confused, tried to puzzle it out by speaking aloud. "On the road to the mountains, we'll come across him. Is that right?"

The mute nodded.

"He preys on travelers? I see. And if we take that road, he'll come after us. Is that your warning, my friend?"

The look on the mute's sorrowful face told her that it was.

"My guess is that he's some sort of bandit," said the Princess after some consideration. "He robs, sometimes kidnaps, then cuts out the tongues of his victims so they'll never be able to speak of what happened."

"But how so, my lady?" Alryc said. "The man is blind! Surely a blind man cannot do all those things."

"Then our friend must be mistaken," said Assad confidently. "The bandit *can* see. Perhaps he pretends to be blind."

The mute shook his head, his eyes imploring Stacy to believe him.

"There are strange works about in Kreel," said Melinda darkly, "if a blind man can actually *see* to catch his victims."

The mute pointed to the mountains, shaking his head again.

"He's telling us not to take the mountain road, I think," said Stacy.

"Not take the mountain road?" said Alryc incredulously. "But, my lady, how are we to reach our destination?"

With a sigh the Princess turned to the bedraggled stranger. "Tell me, friend: Is there another road that can take us to the Kuban frontier?"

He shook his head firmly.

"That settles it, then," said the Princess. "We have no choice. We cannot turn back. If that's the only road to Kuba, we'll have to take it—and take our chances on running into this blind brigand."

There was fear in the mute's eyes as Stacy spoke; more than fear—terror.

"We must go on," she told him honestly. "Our work is not yet done. But I thank you for your warning. We'll be very careful."

"Will one blind scoundrel thwart plans that even a host of pirates failed to stop?" Alryc's question needed no answer. "Besides, we are five and not so dim-witted that we should fall easily into the fiend's clutches."

The mute hung his head, shaking it from side to side. It was obvious to him that no matter how much he beseeched his new-found friends, they would not heed his warning.

Stacy smiled warmly at him. "Don't be so downcast

and glum, good friend. We'll travel swiftly and close together. We'll be safe enough."

His eyes pleaded for them not to go; but Stacy was firm. They had come too far to be stopped now. The mute saw this; sighing, he thanked them for their food and hospitality and made ready to leave.

"Won't you sleep this night beside our fire?" asked a concerned Melinda.

Looking evenly at her, the pitiful man refused.

"Then where will you go?"

A forlorn gaze was her only response, and as strangely as he had come, the mute disappeared into mist and grim shadows.

The group sat unspeaking, looking out into the moonless night.

"I think it would be better if we took our minds off this strange business and tried to get some sleep," Alryc told them all as he lay back with his hands behind his head. Cicero concurred and rolled up into a ball beside the Princess.

"I doubt I'll sleep a wink," said Melinda.

"Better to face a host of crazed Regums," said Assad, "than to come to grips with a blind man who can see. Kreel makes my flesh crawl. It always has. You never know what's lurking about in these strange parts."

"Bah!" said Alryc with a scowl. "You've all let the mute upset you. If we do run into this unusual fellow, I'm certain we'll find there's a logical explanation."

Assad laughed bitterly. "Only one problem, good astronomer: It'll be difficult for us to convey this 'logical explanation' without the benefit of our tongues. I don't think I'd like to spend the rest of my life drawing meaningless pictures in the sand."

Dawn crept slowly across the eastern horizon. Stacy stirred at the feeling of fingertips running gently along the side of her mouth. Opening her eyes, she stared up into Alryc's worried face. Behind him she saw a curtain of thick clouds rumbling down from the mountains. She sat up, cleared her sleepy eyes and rubbed at her stiff neck. Distant thunder clapped menacingly and she frowned. Bad weather would make the ride through the pass all the more difficult to complete in a single day.

Hardly a word was spoken that morning as the band gathered their packs and watered and saddled the restless horses. Alryc scrounged up a few herbs and roots and, boiling them, prepared a lackluster broth for breakfast. It was not much of a meal, but at least it was warm. Then off again they rode, on a sharply slanted upward path that led across the ridge to the mountain pass.

Alryc, cloak swirling behind in the wind, took the lead. Looming cliffs pressed close on either side. More than once the horses were startled by the growls of strange mountain cats from dens high among the ridges. Occasionally Cicero would return their cries with one of his own, telling these Dwellers to stand aside, that it was not mere men who crossed their lands but friends of wolves. And the wrath of wolves was something no Dweller wished to incur.

Under towering black-gray clouds they inched their way carefully along the treacherous path. The wind began to howl; rain began pouring down. The band covered their heads with their cloaks and rode on in gloomy silence. Once, when lightning lit the black sky with flashing silver, Stacy's horse reared in terror. She jerked her head around and brought her scraping down against the boulders, running her hand along her soaked mane, and soothing her with soft words. Alryc came to her side, but Stacy shook her head, declining his help. Wiping the driving rain from his eyes, the stargazer nodded, turned his horse and started back up the path.

By midday it became apparent that to continue was futile. It had taken all morning to gain little more than a single league. At this rate it would be a week before they came out of the mountains.

High to their left, atop a craggy ridge, Cicero caught sight of a small grassy knoll well covered with trees and shrubs. In the sheer walls of rock behind it was a small cave—not very wide, not very deep, but it was shelter. And right now, exhausted as they were, drenched to the bone, it was shelter they wanted more than anything else.

Slowly, painstakingly, they made their way up the higher ground, carefully negotiating the slippery earth. Clomping over moss and mud and thistle bushes that stung painfully at the horses' flanks, they at last reached the ridge. The cover of the trees provided instant shelter. Assad led the horses to feed in the wet grass while Stacy, Melinda and Alryc cleared the cave of stones and broken boughs. Cicero, quicker than a fox despite being twice the size, caught sight of an unsuspecting hare feeding at the edge of a warren and snapped its neck before the animal could blink. Happily the red wolf loped over to the cave, his prize dangling wetly between his powerful jaws.

The fire was started and wet cloaks hung on a branch to dry. The hare turned on a skewer above the flames. Stacy hummed softly, sprinkling it with small pinches of salt found in the pouch of her saddlebag. Sweet juices dripped from the roasting body, causing the flames to hiss and sizzle.

While they ate, the rain outside began to taper off and for an instant the glow of hazy sunlight appeared from behind a break in the clouds. With the rain all but gone, a warm fire taking the chill out of their weary bones and a hot meal to fortify them, the world no longer seemed as bleak as it had an hour or two ago.

"No point in going on today," said Alryc after they had eaten.

"I agree," said the Princess. "We'll be safe enough

here in our cave, and with luck, by tomorrow night we'll be well away from the mountains." But even as she spoke she was uneasy. It was nothing she could put her finger on, nothing of substance, just a gnawing feeling that this warm cave wasn't as homey as it seemed. A glum darkness insisted on prowling at the edges of her mind—a dire warning from somewhere that she must be careful and not tarry too long in this place. Things in Kreel were never quite what they seemed.

She awoke just as the sun had set and the mists had begun to rise. Looking about uneasily, she saw that her companions were all in deep, restful slumber. Cicero lay curled at her feet, his ears twitching. Alryc rested beside the mouth of the cave, his head on his chest, snoring lightly. Melinda's hand touched Assad's as each lay peacefully near the glowing embers.

There was no purpose in waking them. Better for her to go back to sleep herself and start the journey afresh in the morning. Yet, despite the peaceful scene all around, she was still uneasy.

Standing now, she reached down and stroked Cicero's back. He opened a lazy eye, growled like a contented cub and quickly fell back into slumber.

She walked to the mouth of the cave, stood beside the entrance and let the wind run through her hair. *Fara's kingdom! How long has it been since I've had a bath—a real bath?* With a shrug and a sigh, she stepped out of the cave to tend to the horses. All four were standing calmly beneath the trees, shifting occasionally in their sleep.

A faint sound, like the snap of a twig, caught her attention. It came from her left, somewhere behind the trees. The fogs had settled completely, though, and she could not see a thing. She stepped lightly across the grass, her eyes peering into the mist. A chilly gust sent shivers down her back. She was about to turn and go back to the cave when the sound came again. *This time I wasn't imagining it,* she thought.

Her eyes narrowed; canine-like, she moved through the trees. Summer leaves dripped rainwater about her, splashing at her feet, catching her dress. She stood perfectly still, scanning the dim terrain around her.

An animal? she asked herself. *A big cat on the prowl?* No. Her wolf senses would have picked him up long before this. Her hand slid to her dagger. Something told her that whatever was about was far more malevolent than a cat.

Suddenly something shoved at her from behind and she fell face first to the ground. Like a huntress she sprang to her feet, her dagger lashing out. In the mist before her stood the lumbering silhouette of a man— tall, broad, sinewy. His face was bathed in darkness.

Stacy froze at the sight of the long, heavy blade he held before her eyes. "Stand and deliver!"

Her mouth gaped. "Wha—"

"Stand and deliver! Turn over all your goods—and you can start with any gold chains around your neck!"

"Abyss of Hel! You can't—"

His fist lashed out and again she sprawled to the ground. He came closer, sword pointed at her throat, and for the first time she caught a glimpse of his face. It was grim at best—lined, ragged, with a small, down-twisting mouth and a broad, flat nose that looked as though it had been broken more than once.

He pulled her up and pushed her farther into the mist, not caring if he hurt her. She reeled about to try to run, but brawny hands grabbed her and turned her. For a moment she stood frozen. His eyes! They were crimson pools awash in a sea of white. He was sightless!

The Blind Man of the Mountains!

He squeezed her wrists tighter and tighter, all the while glaring at her with those frightening eyes.

"Let me go! I'm not alone, highwayman. I give you warning: If you dare to harm me . . ."

The highwayman let go of one hand, threw back his head and roared with laughter.

Her dagger had been knocked to the ground at their feet; if only she could reach it . . . She strained to break free, but his free hand caught hers and twisted her arm. Although his eyes were blind, it seemed that his senses were so sharp he could feel her every movement, anticipate her every thought. Pain shot through her body.

"Ouch! All right, highwayman. Just let go."

He let go and she fell to the ground. His heavy boot landed firmly on her blade before she could scoop it up.

"Now, girl, where are your goods?"

"I haven't any."

Long fingers groped at her neck, searching for a chain. Then they felt her hands and wrists. "No rings, eh? No bracelets, either. You're not a very well-to-do girl, are you?"

Her mind began to race and scheme. "I . . . I have a few things in my bags."

He stood over her, hands on hips, sword glittering at his side. "Where?"

Stacy gulped. "There's a cave where I sought shelter, and a fire—"

He bellowed loudly, "You try to trick me, don't you? Gates of Kuba! You take me for a dimwit, girl! I know about your cave and I know about your fire. I even know about your friends."

Her breath came in short, sharp pants. This blind man seemed to know far too much for one who was sightless. Again her mind raced. "Your foot, good highwayman, is upon my dagger. Take it in your hands. I think you'll find it a handsome prize."

Wary of her, he kneeled down and picked up the

knife. He examined it carefully, feeling the precious stones on the hilt, running his finger along the edge of the blade.

"It's forged with a blend of silver and steel," she told him truthfully. "There's not another like it in the world."

He toyed with it a moment longer, feeling its weight and shifting it from hand to hand. "I like it. It will serve me well. And what are you doing with such a prize, I wonder?"

"I stole it from a sailor at the port of Kreel. I was going to sell it."

The highwayman snorted. He grabbed her by the hair and pushed the knife at her larynx. "Know what I'm going to do?"

Eyes wild with fear, she stammered, "Yes. Your reputation has followed you all the way to the city. You'll cut out my tongue, I suppose."

Delighted with her response, he said, " 'Tis a shame to have to take out a tongue so glib, but I have little choice, dear girl. A man in my precarious position cannot afford to let his whereabouts be known, and you've already seen much too much."

His hand suddenly began to squeeze at her mouth; he brought the dagger close, ready to thrust.

"Wait!" she gasped, eyes wide as saucers.

He scowled, eager to be done with this business. "Why should I, my dear?"

"If you spare my tongue, I can get you another silver blade."

He looked at her suspiciously. "There is no other; you told me yourself."

"Not a dagger, highwayman, a sword."

He lowered the blade and pulled at her hair. "Are you lying to me? Is there such a sword?"

She nodded. "I swear it, highwayman—a silver sword studded with rubies and emeralds, a gift of kings.

It was to be a present for the Rani of Kuba. I stole it together with the dagger."

Years of his grisly work told him to be wary of the tales his victims told to spare their tongues, yet this girl had indeed provided a jeweled dagger, so why not a sword also? He yanked her hair harder and pushed her head down toward the mud. "Where is the blade, girl? Speak! I'm a man of little patience."

"I have it buried, hidden away not far from here. It can make you a rich man, my sightless friend, but let go or you'll never get your hands on it."

He pushed her away like a rag. "Take me to where it's buried, girl. But no tricks, mind you; otherwise it'll be more than your tongue that you'll miss."

She got up, wiping mud and grass from her tunic. Her first ploy had worked; the rest, though, would not be so easy.

"Which way?" He grabbed her arm, wrenching her close to him.

"Not far, I told you. Ouch! Let go of my arm. It hurts."

"Not until we reach the spot. Now lead the way!"

Aimlessly, through the dank mist, she led him down the path from the ridge and headed toward the road below. Her mind raced furiously. How long could she keep him going? At what point would he suspect her ruse?

Grunting as they stumbled over rocks and thistles, they made their way slowly down. Stacy could tell that her captor was becoming restless, that this long hike had somewhat dulled his desire for the silver blade. Purposely feigning a fall, she threw herself against him, forcing him to hold her in his arms. He tensed at the feel of her warm, supple body. She pressed against him briefly, but long enough for the contact to take hold, and he relaxed at the touch of her softness. She wondered how long it had been since he had had a woman

—indeed, if he had ever had a woman. His grip slowly eased. *So far so good,* she thought.

"Could you let go of my arm, please?" she asked in a low voice. "It's terribly bruised."

He hesitated, then: "No tricks?"

She brushed against him again. "My word. Hold my hand instead." Before he could reply, she took hold of his large, sweaty hand and held it tightly. Abashed, he began to withdraw. "Stay close to me," she cooed. "It's just a little farther along the path."

She led the way, confident that his thoughts were becoming confused. His desire was growing steadily, she knew, and with it the dulling of his senses.

She nudged him as they approached the road. "Almost there."

His arm reached out, and his hand began to caress her shoulder.

She squirmed from his grasp. "Not now, please. Later you can take me to your hideaway."

The blind man, so fierce for so long, stood gaping like a lovesick fool. "You . . . you want to come with me?"

Stacy laughed tremulously as if with a mixture of fright and excitement. "Yes," she said softly. "You and I—together."

Bewildered at her offer, he said nothing as she led him onto the road. But were his senses fully diminished? Stacy knew she would have to find out, and now was as good a time as any. Boldly she turned and led him in a broad circle, stopping only when they had come back to the point at which they'd started. The highwayman said nothing. Her heart pounded like a drum. He had weakened; an hour ago he could have sensed even a single wrong step.

"How . . . how much farther, girl?"

"A moment more," she promised.

At the edge of the road, a place that was especially

muddy, she stopped. "It's here, but we'll have to dig: I buried it very deep."

He sighed and drew his sword, plunging it into the ground. Then, on his knees, he began to use the blade as a shovel. With each thrust the desire for the silver sword increased. Stacy, at his side, began to dig with her bare hands, counting the minutes, hoping for the first light of dawn.

The hole became almost a meter deep. The blind rogue had to strain more and more with each succeeding layer of dirt. His tunic and cloak became caked with grime and slop; his face broke out into a heavy sweat. He was not used to such tedious work. Robbing innocent victims was far easier and paid much better.

Soon he became vexed and frustrated. "Where is it, girl? Blast you! Are you certain this is the right spot?"

"This is the place," she replied in a serious voice.

"Must we dig all night?"

She put her hand on his. "No hurry. No hurry at all. Just a little bit deeper." Then she began digging again with her hands. "Ah, my hands hurt. This digging is hard without a shovel. Lend me back your silver dagger. It will make our work pass so much faster."

He grunted and shook his head. "You rest; I'll dig. It can't be very much deeper."

"But I can't allow you to toil all alone. Lend me the blade. The quicker we're done here, the quicker we can leave for your hideaway."

"I can trust you?"

"Of course. What do you take me for?"

With a frown he drew the dagger from his pocket and handed it to her. Stacy took it, making certain he noted none of her eagerness. Then bending over at his side, she went back to work. She could have killed him right then and there, she knew, could have plunged the knife deep into his spine; but a bloodsucker like him deserved no such swift death. She was not yet certain if she would kill him at all; but whatever she decided, he would never again rob or cut the tongues from innocent travelers.

The hole gaped before them, as deep as it was wide. No matter how much the highwayman strained with his long sword, he could scoop up nothing from the bottom.

"One of us will have to jump in," she said tactfully. "Shall I be the one? The treasure is close."

Lusting for the buried weapon, he shook his head. If the sword was close, *he* would be the one to find it first. "I'll go," he said gruffly. "You wait up here. And don't try to run away. Remember, I know these hills like the back of my hand. I'll track you down and kill you."

Stacy smiled. "Let me sing for you while you dig. My voice will assure you that I'm close and my songs will ease your labor."

"A good idea. Sing for me. Now help me over the side."

She helped him climb down into the hole. At first he stood chest deep, throwing mounds of dirt by hand over the side. After a while he was down so deep that only his head could be seen. Stacy took out her handkerchief and wiped his beaded brow. "Poor man—so hard you have to work." And then she went back to her song.

Morning came softly, as it always did in late summer. The sky turned a blazing crimson as the sun's first lights peeked over the mountains. Humming, Stacy lay back with her hands behind her head and exulted in the glowing warmth. Once in a while she peeked over the side to see how her captor was making out. Deeper than a grave, the highwayman did not realize that he could no longer lift himself out. For all intents and purposes, he was trapped.

At long last the sun began to bake them. He looked

up, shading his crimson eyes. "Bring me some water, girl! Fetch it from the stream."

Stacy grinned. Her eyes caught the morning shadows of horses coming down from the distant ridge. With them, bounding over the rocks, was a wolf. She waved and laughed. Her friends had come at last.

"What's the matter with you, girl? Didn't you hear me? Bring me some water!"

"Water? Water, you say? Why? I'm not thirsty."

It was at that moment that the highwayman began to panic. The realization of her trick came to him in a flood and he pounded the sides of his new cell. "You tricked me! You tramp! You bitch! You whore! I'll kill you!"

Alryc was the first to arrive. He stared down at the writhing man in the hole. "Who's your vile friend?"

Stacy shrugged. "Someone I met last night. Shall I introduce you?"

The highwayman heard the new voice and turned in its direction. "Get me out of here! Help me out! I'll pay you any price you ask. I'm not a man without means. I have great wealth—"

"Stolen from unsuspecting travelers!" hissed Stacy.

Alryc gasped. "The Blind Man of the Mountains!"

"The very same, Alryc. He thought to make me his latest victim."

Assad leaped from his mare and happily embraced the Princess. Then, hands on hips, he stared down at the raving brigand. "Ho, good sir! I see you have a problem."

"Let me out of here! Let me out, I beg you! Have mercy on a blind man."

" 'Mercy'?" mimicked Melinda. "Had you mercy on that poor beggar we met two days ago? You tore his tongue from his throat! I'll give you mercy!" She loaded and raised her bow.

Stacy stepped in front of her. "No, Melinda."

"But why? You would allow such a fiend to live?"

"If he never robs or maims again, yes."

"I swear an oath!" cried the highwayman. "Never will I turn back to my old ways. I'll give every single coin I have to charity, I swear, only let me out!" He fell to his knees and began to sob.

"Lower a rope," said the Princess.

Alryc looked at her darkly. "True, he may be forgiven his deeds, but still he must be punished."

Stacy nodded and turned her eyes away. "I know. Hand me your sword." She waited nervously as Assad and Alryc hoisted up the trembling thief. And when they saw him in the light, even they were forced to feel pity for him. Sightless, ugly, in looks as well as in character, he was really only a pitiful soul doomed to the fires of Hel for the life he had led.

"Hold out your hand," said Stacy imperiously.

He groveled before her. "Please, don't do that. Please..."

"Your hand has cut off its last tongue, my friend. The day for justice has come at last. Now hold your right hand out!"

The blade flashed swiftly. The hand toppled from the wrist and tumbled down into the hole. The thief sank to his knees and cried with pain.

Alryc, knowledgeable in the medical arts, took out bandages and newly found herbs from his saddlebag. Distastefully he tended to the wound. "You'll live, old thief, never fear."

The highwayman whimpered, "But what shall I do? I have no eyes and but one hand left to me. Where can a man like me go?"

"To the Temple," replied Stacy, "as a pilgrim. There you will find comfort and solace. Perhaps the Fates will one day even forgive you for your crimes; but I cannot. Now begone!"

With a sob and a moan, he forced himself to his

feet, his left hand clutching at the bloodied stump where his right hand used to be, and slowly shuffled down the road until he was out of sight.

For a long while the band stood in silence, still staring after him.

Melinda sighed. "Perhaps it would have been better to have let him die," she said.

"No," said the Princess reflectively. "A man must live with his deeds, no matter what they've been. The Blind Man of the Mountains is no more. In his place there comes a pilgrim, a man of devotion. Maybe one day he'll make up for the wrongs he has done. But I fear that until that happens, there'll be many roads for him to travel."

Alryc nodded at the wisdom of her words. "And we have ours. Come, the sun is high and the road through the mountains lies before us. If we leave now, we can reach the other side by dusk."

"The other side," mumbled Stacy. "Yes, at last. The Arid Lands and the Kuban frontier. The first part of our adventure is done and the most difficult lies ahead."

"Then let us begin, my lady. Onward, to Kuba! Sigried is waiting."

A gusty wind roared through the streets, whipping across the boulevards and rattling the shutters of the pastel-colored houses. The streets were empty save for an occasional beggar making his way between darkened alleys or a fast-riding Kuban soldier on his way to some unknown destination.

The night was moonless; a thin, filmy haze dulled the stars. Dim lights glowed from distant windows. Along the docks the black silhouettes of ships loomed against the sky, and the great seawall rose to block the first entrance to the harbor. As high as the tallest spire, with towers and granite fortifications running the entire length, it stood as an awesome reminder to any approaching ship that the city of Kuba was an impregnable fortress—Kuba, the Opal City, as dazzling as the jewels inlaid in the Rani's crown, as defiant as Sigried herself. She alone had molded her city, rebuilt it from its ancient ashes, and now it stood as a monument to her skill and ability. It was an impressive sight, even to an unwilling visitor.

Mara stood looking from her barred window in a tower of the Kuban palace. Directly below, in the courtyard, tiny figures of soldiers marched back and forth in silent procession. Along the palace walls, other soldiers watched from their posts in the towers—grim men, silent and tough: Sigried's crack Panthers; mercenaries; Satrian renegades; dragoons from Kreel; Kuban fanatics. The Rani protected her palace with walls of granite and men of iron. Just as they kept unwanted visitors from coming in, so did they keep Mara from getting out.

With a scowl she turned from the window and plopped herself down disconcertedly on her bed. She must get out, she knew. She must somehow escape; but how? Every inch of palace ground was covered by the eyes of the Panthers. Mara knew this all too well. From the very first night, she had watched from her window, noting their movements, timing the changing of guards at midnight and at dawn. The web was drawn too tight. Even if she could make her way from the tower, which was unlikely, how could she ever manage to make it through the gate? The soldiers would be on her like hounds.

Hounds—the word made her shudder. Just as wolves prowled the Rhonnda palace, so Siggy had her hounds, fierce animals trained to kill. Short on intelligence but not cunning, they could smell her out as quickly as any wolf could and tear her to pieces while the soldiers looked on.

There must be a way, she thought. *Even the most*

solid of walls has a crack! A crack was all she needed. The problem was how to find it.

From outside came the dull ringing of the watch bell. Midnight—another change in the guard; another night lost to her. She sighed, closed her eyes and fought back the rising tears. *I won't cry! I won't!* With all her effort she pushed her fear down and felt it knot in her stomach. Since her first moments here she had firmly resolved not to give her captors the satisfaction of seeing her tears. She must be strong. She must not let Sigried know.

She heard laughter from below—dull, coarse laughter. The deep, throaty voices reminded her of Dimitri, and that truly did frighten her. She was more afraid of the dragoon than of the Rani. After all, Sigried had not hurt her; but the mercenary had and in more ways than one. She knew what his leering stares meant and what he would do to her if Sigried ever gave him his way.

It was almost dawn. Grubby hands pushed at her, waking her from a sound sleep. Feebly she opened her eyes. Two broad-shouldered guards were standing over the bed.

"Time to get up, young *princess*," one said sarcastically.

Mara raised up on one elbow. "Wha—"

Hands yanked the quilt and pulled it off the bed. She sat up in a rush, and the guards snickered as they looked at her. She smoothed down her gown, modestly covering her breasts with her arms.

"Up," demanded the second. "The Rani is waiting."

"Now? The sun isn't even up."

A hand pulled at her sleeve. Small, intense eyes glowered. "Better you don't argue, sweetie." His grip tightened on her wrist, causing her to wince.

"Okay, okay. Give me a minute to dress."

DUNGEONS OF KUBA   163

The guard stood back, hands on hips, and laughed. She slipped off the side of the bed and reached toward the divan, where her tunic was carefully folded. "You're not going to stand here and watch me dress, are you?"

The guards glanced at each other and sneered.

Angrily Mara grabbed the tunic, pushed past them and walked behind the screen. "You worms!"

"Just make it fast, sweetie. Today's an important day."

Fuming, she slipped the tunic over her head, clasped it at the shoulder and front and tightened the belt. Fully dressed now, she slipped on her sandals and ran her brush through her hair.

"No time for that now," mumbled the taller of the two. Mara resisted as he tried to wrench the brush from her hand, and it fell hollowly against the stone floor. "We don't want to get rough, sweetie, but we're in a hurry."

She stared through slitted eyes. "What about breakfast? Don't I eat today?"

He pulled her up gruffly, disdainfully. "You eat later. Now move!" he ordered, and shoved her stumbling past the door.

They held her by the arms, guiding her down the winding ramp and to the corridor that led to the Rani's throne room. About midway down the corridor there was a long, narrow window. A shaft of bright sun slanted down, pouring over the dull surface of the stone and restoring a touch of its long-lost luster. But it was the noises from outside that caught her attention as they passed: horns blasting through the city; bells ringing from the steeples; shouts from what sounded like milling throngs. She paused for an instant and peered out. Beyond the massive seawall she could see several dozen ships making their way toward the harbor—a fleet of them. Warships, she knew. Her heart pounded in her throat. What was it the soldier had said about this being an important day?

They shoved her savagely from the window, jerking her arms.

She tore loose and kicked. "I can make it on my own, you camels! Now leave me be!"

One soldier twisted her arm hard and brought it up painfully behind her back. "Do we go quietly, sweetie, or must we get rough?"

"What's going on here?"

At the crack of the voice, the soldier let go. He and his companion stood stiffly, their heads bowed and their arms crossed over their chests. From the end of the hall a tall, youthful soldier in a regal crimson uniform and a long dark cloak stepped closer. He glowered angrily at the soldiers.

"We bring her to the Rani, my lord," said one of the men apologetically.

"Is she a criminal that you treat her like a dishrag?"

The taller soldier swallowed hard. It was clear to Mara that this noble, whoever he was, was an important man in the Kuban palace.

"No, my lord, but she—"

"Take care, guard," hissed the noble. "Never let me see you treating someone like this again."

They gulped. Mara rubbed at her wrists. She was about to thank the man, but he had spun around, cloak flaring, and was already making his way in the opposite direction.

Sunlight swept across the balcony, seeping brightly through the curtains and bathing the chamber in vivid yellows and golds. The sea breezes were brisk and cool. Sigried, unattended, sat upon her throne, all smiles. Her ships had returned, and the news they brought convinced her more than ever that Stacy would soon be in her hands.

She brushed back her long yellow hair with her hand and let it fall and toss over her breasts. The reflection from the jewels in her diadem gleamed and danced along the walls each time she moved her head. This was a wonderful morning, she mused—a glorious morning. Nothing could spoil it.

The two guards entered, bowed and stood back as Mara stepped forward toward the throne.

"That will be all," said the Rani to the soldiers. With smart turns on their heels they withdrew, leaving the young girl alone with her.

Siggy's eyes ran up and down the shapely girl's form. "Good morning, Mara. A lovely day, don't you think?"

The girl gazed up defiantly. "Is that why you had those animals arouse me from bed? To admire the weather?"

On a day like this, even this disrespectful outburst could not anger the Rani. Reaching over to the small crystal table at her side, she drew a piece of fresh fruit from the bowl. She indicated for Mara to do the same. With a quick movement the girl snatched an apple and bit into it loudly.

Sigried laughed. "You do take after your aunt, don't you? But it's too fine a morning to let you upset me. Have you seen our ships? Our fleet's come into harbor."

"I heard all the commotion, yes. Is that why I'm here now? To help you celebrate the arrival of your buccaneers?"

A faint smile played around the corners of Sigried's mouth. Everything about the young Rhonnda princess reminded her of Stacy. The two were more alike than she could ever have imagined: caustic, often crude, certainly lacking in refinement by Kuban standards, but as cunning as the wolves that fought for them.

"My ships have brought me good news, Mara—very good news. That's the reason I sent for you. I want to share it with you."

"I have no interest in stolen booty, Rani. May I return to my room?"

A twinge of impatience burned in Siggy's ice-blue eyes. She shifted into a more relaxed position, chewing slowly on a seedless grape. "It's news about your aunt, child. Are you sure you wouldn't like to hear?"

Mara's eyes widened, and Siggy smirked inwardly: How easily the girl had bitten.

"What about Stacy?"

The Rani toyed with the grapes in her hand. "My captains report that the Princess has left Rhonnda—gone into seclusion, I understand; but my spies tell me she's secretly sailed from Rhonnda and is on her way here now."

"I don't believe you. Stacy would never come here of her own free will."

"Oh?" Siggy's brows raised. "Not even to claim her niece, her successor to the Empire throne? Ah, dear Mara, how can I convince you? You saw the letter I sent."

No matter how hard the girl tried, she could not keep tears down. "Why do you hate Stacy so?"

The innocence of the question caught Siggy by surprise. "Your aunt and I play a game, Mara, and the whole world is our game board."

"She once spared your life."

Siggy winced; her eyes flashed. The memory of that painful day raced through her mind, burning like a lighted arrow. "What do you know of it, girl?"

Mara returned the hateful stare. "I know that she could have killed you but didn't."

"Ah, Mara. Yes, we fought each other once. Both of us were little older than you are now. But it was wolf tricks that brought me down. Woman to woman, she was not a match for me."

"That's not the way I heard it."

Siggy sighed. "Has your aunt told you that it was I

who spared her life when the soldiers came to seek her out? Any debt I may have owed is long repaid, dear Mara. Stacy and I both bear our scars."

The girl frowned. "So what am I here for? I'm no threat to you or to Kuba. I'm just a pawn in your game."

The analogy to chess interested the Rani. Like the Princess, she was an avid player. Picking at her grapes, she said, "You're far more to me than that. You are my key, Mara, don't you see that? With you here I shall bring down your entire empire and restore Kuba back to her rightful place."

The young girl seethed at the Rani's arrogance. "You wish! Our fleet will smash you like kindling."

"But your fleet's not here, is it? Elias is off somewhere on a fool's errand, an errand my agents sent him on. And you need a history lesson, child. While your empire was still groping at the edge of the forests, Kuba was in her height of glory, the center of the world. The wars changed that, though, and when I took my father's place on the throne, there was nothing left but a shambles. I built the new Kuba, Mara, with my own hands. I sought favors from none and gave none. My empire has not come as easily as Stacy's has. I had to struggle for my gains. Stacy was handed a crown she never even wanted, or didn't you know that? For too long I've been hidden in her shadow."

"And now?"

Siggy smiled malevolently. "Look about you, Mara: All this is mine, and it's only the beginning. Kuban galleys prepare to sail even as we speak. The Seven Seas shall be ours and ours alone. Not for myself, Mara —even I am not *that* vain—but for the glory of my land, for Kuba. The world will cower at our might. Our will and determination *cannot* be blocked, neither by your fleet nor by your princess."

And as Siggy ranted on, speaking of ancient glories and lands and banners that Mara had never heard of, the girl became intently aware of how fragile the world's new peace really was. The only thing preventing the realization of the Rani's dream was indeed the Fleet and the Princess. And Stacy, knowingly or not, to save Mara's own life, was falling right into Sigried's hands.

Now more than ever Mara was resolved to escape. She had no idea how; she only knew that she must. The Princess must not be taken: Too much was at stake, more than she had ever realized. The Kuban fleet could tear asunder in a year what had taken decades for the Empire to build. Mara could not let that happen, even if it cost her her own life.

Mara sat indecisively on the stone bench in the rock garden, the only place she was permitted to exercise. On three sides of the garden loomed high stone walls with metal spikes embedded along the top. There was no way she could scale those walls. The fourth side of the garden led to a broad walkway, which in turn led to the first gate and tower. Guards were posted everywhere; but even if she somehow managed to slip past them, there was the constant fear of the prowling hounds. At night sometimes she had heard their barks—savage, vicious. The dogs dimmed her chances much more than the soldiers ever could. Once, on a ploy, she had called to one of the hounds in the canine tongue. The reply was curt and brief. Wolves, and their allies, were unwelcome here. Fanatically loyal, these hounds could be counted upon to tear her to pieces the moment she stepped from her given bounds.

Deep in thought, she was hardly aware of the sudden shadow that blocked the sun. Looking up, she saw a man standing a few paces away. At first she tensed, believing it to be Dimitri. She narrowed her eyes. Tall, young, certainly aristocratic . . . Mara smiled in recognition. It was the young noble who had berated her guards that morning.

He returned the smile and came toward her. "I thought I recognized you," he said in a pleasant voice. "I trust that since our encounter you've been treated a bit more kindly."

She smoothed her hands over her thighs and looked at him curiously. Since when was a Kuban lord concerned about the welfare of an Empire girl? Or didn't he know who she was?

"They became quite docile after you gave them a tongue-lashing. I wanted to thank you, but you left so suddenly."

He smiled boyishly, losing that authoritarian manner she had seen earlier. "They're a surly lot, these mercenaries," he replied. "But from what I saw, you weren't helping the situation any. You should really try to be a little more tactful."

Mara frowned, then grinned. "You sound like a diplomat."

"Fates, no!" He laughed, his eyes crinkling at the corners. "It's just that your agitating them isn't going to help you any."

She looked at him thoughtfully. "You know who I am?"

The smile remained. "I do. I didn't when we first met, but since then I've been told."

"And you're not afraid to talk to me?"

He shrugged and brushed back his hair. "Why should I be?"

She sighed and looked toward the guard post. "Because I'm watched and you'll be seen. I don't want to get you into any trouble."

He dismissed the thought with a wave of his hand.

Mara met his gaze. "I mean it. You did me a favor before; I'd like to return it. You'll be reported for speaking to me."

He glanced up at the tower. The soldiers were intently watching their every move. Much to her surprise, he said, "May I sit down?"

She happily gestured for him to sit. "I'd hate to see you make enemies on account of me. You're the first gentleman I've met in Kuba and I wouldn't like to see you punished for it."

He grinned and sat down beside her.

"Do you always take such risks?" asked Mara.

"If they're worth taking, yes. And sitting here and talking to you is worth it."

She blushed and looked away. An ironic smile crossed her lips. Here was the first man in her life she somehow felt attracted to, and he was a noble of Kuba! Alryc's ears would burn.

"Are you . . . are you sure you know who I am—I mean who I *really* am?"

"You're Maralisa, the young Rhonnda princess."

"And that doesn't bother you? Our lands aren't exactly friends, you know."

"How well I know," he sighed, toying with his mustache. "But somehow I can never see pretty ladies as enemies."

"Not even when they think like wolves?"

For a moment he looked at her curiously; then he laughed. "Do you think like a wolf?"

"Only when I'm mad." She grinned, beginning to enjoy this banter. "Want to see me growl?"

"I don't think so," he replied. "But tell me, Maralisa, what do they call you at home? Wait, don't say it. It's 'Lisa,' right?"

"Wrong. It's 'Mara'."

He reached down beside the bench, plucked a small yellow daisy and handed it to her. "For you, Mara. Take it."

She did so reluctantly, feeling a bit puzzled.

"Forgive me," he said. "I forgot for the moment you're from so far away. In Kuba we have a tradition:

When a man first meets a woman he admires, he gives her a flower."

She twirled the flower between her fingers, feeling awkward and foolish. "Thank you. What does the woman do with the flower when she receives it?"

"If she likes the fellow, she keeps it forever."

Naïvely she said, "But it will wilt."

His face reddened. "She keeps it in her heart and in her mind."

"Oh, I see. An interesting tradition, but I like it. And I will keep your flower forever."

"Then we can be friends?"

The words were said softly, but with them came the sudden flush of reality so briefly forgotten. She looked away; her face tightened.

"Mara, what is it? Have I said something?"

"It would be better if you left me alone now."

He looked hurt. "If that's what you want."

She brushed back her hair with both hands and said, "I'm a prisoner here, not a guest. Your Rani is my jailor and Dimitri is my personal keeper. I've been threatened, condemned—Dimitri swears he'll—"

The young noble frowned and hesitantly reached out for her hand. "No harm will come to you, Mara. Can you believe me?"

She laughed bitterly. "What do you know of it? I was dragged here. Dragged! They bound my hands and drugged me so I couldn't tell day from night. Then they threw me in the hold of one of your ships and—"

"Not one of *our* ships, Mara; those were mercenaries."

Her eyes flashed. "What matter? They were under your Rani's orders, weren't they?"

"It was wrong. It should never have happened. Perhaps if I had been here, I could have stopped it."

"You? How? How well do you know Sigried? She's crazed with her lust for power. She—"

"I know her well enough, Mara. This scheme couldn't

have been her idea. I only wish I had been here when it was planned."

"What could you have done?"

Shaking his head, he replied, "I don't know. The Rani's not a fool, though. She can be made to see reason."

Mara looked up. "Ah, *you're* a fool. Sigried will kill anyone who gets in her way—even you."

He looked shocked. "I've made my share of enemies, Mara, but the Rani's not one of them. And I intend to speak to her on your behalf."

Mara folded her arms tightly around herself and shuddered. "No, don't," she said suddenly.

"Why not?"

She was frightened. This young man was sincerely trying to be her friend, she saw, and she did not want him to be dragged down with her. "I told you before: Just speaking with me is dangerous. I don't want any more trouble."

"For me or for you?"

"For either of us. If Dimitri catches us talking—"

"Dimitri can't harm me."

"But he has Sigried's ear—and her bed, I understand."

The young noble winced; that much was true. "Don't worry about Dimitri. I've seen his kind come and go. He means nothing to the Rani."

"And what if he reports you for being with me? What will be the price you'll have to pay?"

He sighed. "I'll cross that bridge when I come to it. But don't fear for me, Mara: I can take care of myself."

Glancing at his athletic body, his strong arms and broad shoulders, she was certain he could. "You seem pretty secure of your position around here."

His eyes smiled; he returned to his easy manner. "I don't worry about such things."

"You must be someone very important."

Laughing, he answered, "Not as important as a Rhonnda princess. May I tell you something, Mara? I'd give much of what I have to be able to see Rhonnda and meet with the Empire Princess."

"With your galleys?"

"Hardly. I doubt that your aunt would look kindly on that sort of gesture. But we hear so many tales of your empire *and* your aunt. I'd like to meet her just once."

Now it was Mara's turn to laugh. "What do you think you'd find?"

"A woman like you, I suppose."

Mara's eyes widened. He had called her a woman. A woman! She wondered if it were really true.

"Oh, Stacy's a lot prettier than I am," she said.

He rested his chin in his hand. "What's she like, Mara?"

The girl closed her eyes. "Dark hair, dark eyes, tall and proud. She's—" The trace of a tear ran down her cheek.

He reached over and wiped it away. "I'm sorry, Mara. The memory of home must be painful for you. I didn't mean to make you cry."

She shrugged. "It's all right. But what else can I tell you? To others she's, well, she's the *Princess;* to me she's Stacy." Then Mara smiled. "Except for her peculiarities, she's like anyone else, although sometimes she gets these strange urges."

His brows rose. "Oh?"

"You know what I mean. Sometimes at supper she howls like a wolf and looks at us strangely. Then she gets down on all fours and races across the room. And she'll eat her meat only raw."

He laughed. "You're making fun of me, aren't you?"

Mara nodded, her eyes sparkling. "A bit," she said shyly.

"Then perhaps next time you'll tell me."
"Next time?"
"Sure. We'll talk again—that is, if you like."
"Yes, I think I would, but I don't know—"
"Still afraid of my being seen?"

She locked her eyes with his and nodded.

"Don't be: It's all right." Then, to her total surprise —and delight—he took her hand in his and kissed it. As Mara gazed at him, he stood and bowed. "Are you permitted to sit in the garden at night?"

Excitedly she nodded. "For a while after they feed me—just until moonrise."

"Then I'll meet you tonight at eight."

She thought for a moment. "Are you sure?"

He winked. "I'm sure."

"All right, then, at eight."

With a smile, he turned to go.

Mara tugged lightly at his sleeve. "Who . . . I mean, I don't even know your name . . ."

He looked down at her and grinned. "Call me Quentin."

Under a hazy crescent moon the horses clomped slowly over the old rickety bridge. For long, arduous days the band had trudged silently across the Arid Lands, that desert of parched waste between the mountains of Kreel and the frontier of Kuba. The sun had been merciless, recalling for Stacy vivid memories of her experiences in the deserts of Sytherna. But now it was done: The Arid Lands were crossed. The bridge marked the border; the other side would mark Kuban soil.

Lips dry, dust swirling and clinging to their clothes, they at last paused and gazed at the distant hills, green and fertile, and the shimmering steeples of Kuba.

A few minutes' ride ahead they came to a well. Exhausted, they dismounted and lowered a bucket with eager anticipation. The splash brought grins to their faces—fresh water at last.

After drinking their fill and watering the horses, they all rested uneasily on the hard flat.

Melinda rubbed at her aching muscles and cursed softly. "*Az'i!* I think I'm ruined for life."

Alryc wiped the dust from his face and eyes and chuckled.

"What we need is a bed," said Stacy. For the past day and a half they had traveled with hardly a stop. Now they were paying the price.

"Ah"—Assad sighed—"a bed. I've almost forgotten what one feels like. Now, if there were only some tavern wench to warm me . . ."

Melinda threw a handful of dust at him. The mercenary ducked.

"That's not a bad idea," said Stacy.

Assad looked up. "What? A tavern wench?"

"Fara's kingdom! A bed, silly."

"You're familiar with these parts," Melinda said to Assad. "If we continue along this road, won't we come to some shelter?"

The mercenary scratched at his chin. It had been more than ten years since he had seen this road last; still, some memories are never forgotten. He smiled at the recollection of an amorous incident not so very far from where they were. "I think there's an old tavern with lodgings about an hour's ride away," he said. "But it's not the sort of place that, er, ladies like yourselves would frequent."

Melinda cast a wary eye at him. "More the type for mercenaries?"

"And weary travelers, yes. If I recall, pilgrims use it on the way to the Temple."

Stacy looked pleased. "Then it's a place often visited by foreigners. Wonderful, Assad. No one would question us."

Alryc sighed. "Anyway, it's a bed we're after. I vote to take it."

Melinda's eyes widened at the thought. "*Az'i!* What are we waiting for?"

Cicero growled, ears twitching. It made small difference to him; he would sleep outside, anyway.

Stacy got up with a groan, her hands rubbing at her hips. "Let's go. I don't think I can take another night on the flat."

Now the landscape changed dramatically. They rode along the banks of a small river and the hills on either side turned green and grassy. There was a tangy smell of pine in the air, and even Kuban soil was welcome after the journey they had been through.

At length Assad took a turn off the path and led them along a gravelly, badly worn road. A dim light appeared in the distance.

The mercenary grinned. "It's still there."

"Looks like an old barn," said Melinda, leaning forward in her saddle and staring at the weather-beaten wooden building.

"I told you not to expect much."

They hitched their horses to the posts, left Cicero to sniff around for danger and boldly knocked on the door. For a while there was no answer, even though they could hear laughter from within.

"Try again," said the Princess.

This time Assad banged on the door so hard it shook on its hinges. "Open up, man! It's chilly out here!"

"Hold on, hold on, I'm coming!"

The door creaked open and they were ushered in by a small, bent man whose only visible feature in the dim candlelight was a beak of a nose jutting beyond sunken eyes and jowls.

"We need lodgings for the night, landlord," said Assad.

The man looked up at him through haggard, watery

eyes. Then he glanced at the women and the tall frame of Alryc. "We don't allow women rooms of their own," he said matter-of-factly. "Be they your wives?"

Alryc was flustered. "Now, see here, landlord—"

Assad stepped forward, jingling two silver coins in his palm. "Will this meet your rules?" he asked the man.

The landlord palmed the coins and grinned. Gesturing sweepingly, he said, "Come this way, my friends. I'll see what I can do."

Just then a high, shrill voice came from the top of a darkened stairway: "More guests for the night?"

The landlord sighed. "Damnable woman," he mumbled. "Thinks she runs the place."

The voice came again: "Hope they're not drunk, and I hope they can pay their bill!"

Embarrassed, the landlord smiled wanly at Assad. "My wife," he said.

The mercenary hid a smirk. "Oh, I see."

"Well, I'm not about to reheat the food!" called the wife. "And they've got to be up before dawn. Tell them to—"

"Will you shut up? Gates of Kuba, woman, go back to sleep! I'll take care of them myself!" The landlord shook his head sadly. "Twenty-three years! Can you believe it? Oh, the Fates can be cruel to a man. They give us lovely young women to wed and then they turn them into wives."

Assad put his arm around the landlord's shoulder. "I know what you mean," he whispered. Then, with a wink: "See the fiery one behind me? She's *my* wife. Let me tell you what she does at night." He leaned very close to the landlord's ear and whispered so low that the others could not hear.

The fellow looked up, shocked. "She doesn't!"

Assad rolled his eyes toward the ceiling. "She does, every night. That's why tonight I want my own room."

Feeling sorry for the poor guest, the landlord said, "She must have learned it from her mother."

Assad nodded gravely. "I've been in this pickle for eleven years, but never mind: We all have our troubles. Tell you what: Bring us some strong wine and food and we'll sit in your parlor while our rooms are prepared."

The landlord clenched his fist around the silver coins and nodded. "Step this way," he said to them all. "I'll not be a minute."

Assad led Melinda by the arm, and Stacy went in with Alryc. The forest girl was burning with curiosity to know what Assad had been whispering but had not the courage to ask.

They plopped themselves down at a large table, sat back and waited for the food to come. The parlor was badly lit. A single candle burned on their table, the only other light coming from dull embers in the stone fireplace. The other guests were also weary-looking travelers, but a tableful of pilgrims was drinking and talking loudly, filling the air with raucous laughter and boisterous oaths.

"Rude fellows," mumbled Alryc. "Think they'd lower their voices at this time of night."

Stacy put her head in her hands. "They're giving me a headache. I think I'll just have a sip of wine and retire. I'm not feeling very hungry."

"Me either," said Melinda. "*Az'i!* They're sure creating a racket."

The landlord came in whistling, with a tray and a large pitcher of dark brew. Stacy and Melinda, after a single glass, wearily climbed the stairs to find their bedrooms. Moments after they had gone, the landlord came with the food, a hot tray filled with spicy meat and buttery potatoes. Alryc and Assad ate in silence, grateful for kitchen food after so many days of eating on the run. They cleaned their plates, sat back and sipped at the wine. The noise from the other guests had subsided some and they were able to hear themselves think.

"If we leave here at dawn," said Alryc, "how long will it take us to reach the city?"

"We'll ride through the gates before noon," Assad said.

They discussed their entry into Kuba and how best to approach the carefully guarded palace. As they spoke, Assad noticed that his companion's eyes frequently drifted off to the corner of the room where the noisy guests were sitting.

"Look at their garb," said Alryc. "Pilgrims. They must be on their way to the palace, too."

"But for a very different purpose," replied Assad. "They go to watch the High Priestess in the Temple."

"If we had pilgrims' garb," said Alryc, "it would make our entry much easier: No one would suspect us."

Assad smiled. "A brilliant idea, my tall friend. But how do you propose to find such robes?"

Alryc's eyes drifted toward the guests again. "We can use theirs."

"Steal them, you mean?"

The stargazer shrugged. "Leave it to me." Then, swinging around so as to face the others, he said in a loud voice, "Ho, good pilgrims, will you share some of our wine?"

Four swarthy men looked up.

"Come," said Alryc. "Good pilgrims like yourselves must still be thirsty and the night is young."

"Why, thank you," said one, casting his eye on the pitcher of wine. He came over with his flagon and grinned as Alryc poured. He drained it with long, throaty swallows and wiped his mouth with the back of his hand. "You treat us kindly, sir," he said.

"Bring over your friends," said Assad. "Let's make a night of it. Landlord, another pitcher!"

The pilgrims approached with wide grins. The landlord came running with a pitcher twice the size of the last one.

"Drink up, drink up," said Alryc.

"A toast, then," said the first pilgrim. He held his flagon high. "To the Rani!"

Alryc gulped as he put his cup to his mouth. "And to all pilgrims," he added, making the toast more palatable.

"Aye, aye!" cried another. "To us all!"

And so they drank, heads swiftly swimming from the heady stuff. At length a third pilgrim said, "And who are you, good travelers, so that we may drink to you, too?"

"A long tale, my friends," said Assad. "We are weary travelers from Spice Island, shipwrecked upon Kreel's shores and now on our way to Kuba."

"Then a toast to both you and our wondrous city!" called a fourth pilgrim.

The flagons were soon emptied and the landlord was called upon to bring yet another pitcher.

Alryc threw off his outer robe. " 'Tis far too hot in here for these garments," he said.

"Absolutely," agreed Assad, taking his own cloak and flinging it across the table behind him. The ploy seemed to work: The pilgrims began to take off their crimson robes.

"More wine!" called Alryc.

"Hear! Hear!" agreed the pilgrims, now becoming loud and boisterous again. They began to sing and dance.

"But what good is dancing," said one, "when there is no music?"

"Landlord," called another, "bring us your flute girl!"

"She is asleep," replied the innkeeper, himself tired and wishing all his guests would pass out and have done with it.

"Then wake her!"

The landlord shook his head and looked helplessly at Assad. "Good sir, I can't. These fellows kept her busy all evening. The poor lass is tired."

Alryc fumbled inside his pocket and drew out another piece of silver. "Nonsense, landlord! Here—and keep the change."

Moments later a sleepy-eyed young woman dressed in a soft, sheer tunic shuffled into the room, yawning and carrying a flute. She took a stance before their table and began to play a lively jig.

"That's more like it!" shouted the most boisterous pilgrim of them all. He pulled off his shirt, exposing a dirty, sweaty body, and began to dance. As the others joined in, Assad and Alryc clapped their hands in time to the music.

"I think I'm going to pass out," said Assad on the sly. "How much wine can these fellows hold?"

Alryc frowned. "At the price they pay for it, no wonder they're still on their feet. Let's see if I can hurry things up a bit." And while they danced, Alryc filled up their flagons. "Play a faster tune, girl!" he said to the exhausted musician. "Pick up the tempo!"

The girl nodded and complied.

The pilgrims twitched and cavorted, stumbling drunkenly about the floor. One grabbed Alryc by the arm. "Join us!" he implored.

"Yes, do!" cried the others, and soon poor Alryc was right in the middle of them all, his head bobbing and weaving in time with the music.

Assad groaned. This could go on all night!

After the song was done, one of the pilgrims borrowed the flute and began to play a song of his own. The flute girl was cajoled into doing a dance, and much to Assad's surprise, she danced very well. Small, but well rounded, with firm breasts and taunting thighs and hips, the flute girl swayed teasingly across the floor. The pilgrims, who had not yet taken vows to swear off women, eyed her with lust. The girl, noting this, smiled and began swaying provocatively toward them.

"*Az'i!*" mumbled Assad. "This girl begs to be raped."

The pilgrims laughed and clapped, continuing to down as much wine as the landlord provided. At length Alryc managed to break away and sit down. Panting, his old eyes red and haggard, he said, "These fellows are stouter than I thought. I can see it will take us a long time to get them drunk enough to sleep."

"Yes, but when they do, they'll sleep for a week," Assad replied.

"Let's count on it, friend. I was hoping to lift their robes before morning."

Tauntingly the flute girl began to dance virtually on top of the two gaping travelers. She shook her shoulders; her breasts, clinging wetly to her flimsy dress, jiggled inches from their faces. Then, with a laugh, she turned to face the others. The onlookers roared with delight.

"This wench is going to get us all into trouble," said Alryc, feeling yearnings he had not felt for years.

Assad sighed. "I'm tempted to come back to this tavern when our tasks are done."

The mystic nodded. "More wine, landlord, and keep it flowing!"

Sometime later the first of the pilgrims staggered into a corner, lay down and began to snore. His companions laughed and kicked at him. "Get up, you bag of bones!" they called. "The night is still young!" But so drunk was the poor man that not even the Rani herself could have aroused him from his slumber.

Assad winked at Alryc. "One down, three to go."

"From the looks of you, though, I doubt you'll be around to see it."

The mercenary frowned. "Do I—*hic!*—look that bad?"

"You look awful, good friend, but never mind. You go up to your room and get some sleep. I'll keep these fellows busy, even until dawn if I have to."

Assad looked at him groggily, the music swimming in his head. "Can you manage by yourself? I mean, it's going to take a lot more wine—"

"I'll manage," replied Alryc. "Off to bed with you!" Then, to the landlord: "What kind of a place is this? Landlord! I demand more wine, women and song!"

Assad stumbled up the stairs and down the hall, trying to figure out which room was his. The first door he opened exposed a snoring fat man lying with his belly up and his hands dangling at the sides of the bed. Opening the next door half-woke the landlord's wife, who gave a low scream at the sight of him. He shut it fast, shivering at the thought of having to hear her vile tongue again. The next door he opened just a crack; it seemed empty and he stepped inside.

Melinda poked her head from between the covers.

"Excuse me, mistress," he mumbled. "I thought this room might be mine."

The forest girl smiled wryly. "It is," she whispered, holding her finger to her mouth.

"Then what are you—"

Melinda's eyes flashed. "I've been waiting for you."

"And the Princess?"

"Shhh. Asleep in the next room." She sat up, her shoulders a silver reflection of the moonlight. "Are you just going to stand there gaping or are you coming to bed?"

Assad grinned. "Wish I'd known about this sooner."

He kissed her softly as she fumbled with the clasps of his tunic. Once in bed, he caressed her, brought her to him. And then they made love, sweetly, like young lovers embracing for the first time.

After they had finished, Melinda propped herself up against the feathery pillows. Assad rested his head against her breast, sighing as she stroked his hair.

"Melinda?"

"Umm?"

"Are you asleep?"

"Uh-uh."

"Want to talk?"

"Ummm. What about?"

He sat up on one elbow, smiling and content. "Us."

She touched his face with her finger and kissed his eyes. "What about us?"

His eyes looked sad. "Has it struck you yet that by tomorrow night we might be dead? Once we reach the palace—"

"Hush, dearest. Don't ever say that. Don't even think it." She brushed back long strands of hair from her eyes.

"But it's true, Melinda. This might be our last night."

"At least we'll share it together."

"Yes; I'm grateful for that. I'm only sorry, though, that it took us so long to find each other. Melinda, if we live, promise you'll marry me." He frowned. "I know I've little to give you. I know that you deserve—"

She kissed his mouth wetly. "I promise, dearest—the first day we reach home."

He drew a long breath and let it out slowly. *Home,* he mused. It was true: For the first time in his life he had a home. He belonged to somewhere and to someone. And secretly, in an ironic way, he thanked Sigried, for if the Rani had not committed her treacherous deeds, he would never have met the fiery forest girl and none of tonight would have been possible.

At the crack of dawn the door to the room crept open. Assad opened his eyes and stared.

Alryc, looking as though he hadn't slept a wink,

tiptoed into the room. He gaped at the sight of the sleeping Melinda in the mercenary's arms, then smiled. "The pilgrims are all asleep," he whispered. "I've taken their robes. Tricky business, Assad. The last pilgrim saw me. He wasn't quite out, you see."

Breathlessly Assad asked, "What did you do?"

"Cracked him on the head with his own flagon," replied the astronomer darkly. "Fortunes of war, poor fellow. He'll have one big headache when he gets up. But look, there's no time to talk. Get dressed quickly. I'll wake our lady. Er . . . I see you'll be able to take care of Melinda."

Assad nodded, his face growing serious. "Give us three minutes. Saddle the horses and find Cicero. We'd best be gone before the sun comes up and the landlord's wife begins to moan."

The first rays of sunlight were fanning out across the horizon as the band gathered outside.

Stacy, well rested and chipper, looked aghast as Alryc led the horses around. Outside, in the light, she got a good look at him for the first time that morning.

"Sweet Fara! What happened to you?"

The stargazer looked sick as a dog. "Too much wine, my lady; but we'll talk later. Here, take this pilgrim's robe and veil your face. We'll pass through the city gates before noon."

Stacy put it on without a word and mounted her mare.

Melinda took her robe and stared at it. *"Az'i!* So that's how we're going to do it!"

"Right," replied Assad. "We're going to make Sigried welcome us with open arms."

Mara hastily downed the bitter coffee and turned away from the small sugared pastry lying untouched on the tray. Eager for the time to pass swiftly, she took up her brush again and ran it slowly through her shining hair, counting the strokes as she did so.

For the dozenth time she smoothed her tunic, then sat cross-legged before her vanity mirror, pursing her lips and rubbing a soft touch of oil into her cheeks. Still there was time on her hands! How painfully slowly it passed. She glanced out the window at the setting sun. The sky was awash in crimson and purple hues and the spires of the city glimmered, giving Kuba a soft, mellow glow that made it much less threatening than it had been before.

Suddenly the palace bells rang. Eight times they chimed; Mara's rendezvous was at hand. Eagerly she ran to her door, flung it open and called to the stern-faced soldiers standing rigidly outside. "I'm going to sit in the garden," she announced.

"Better that you stay in your room," said one glumly.

Mara's face masked tensely. "But why? I'm allowed! Dimitri has given permission for me to exercise in the evening. You have no right!"

The soldier's face soured. "Go back before we tan your rump. You're not in Rhonnda now!"

Mara snorted defiantly; her eyes smoldered with rebellion. "I demand to see the Rani! I won't stand for this treatment! I won't!"

"Let her go."

She whirled and caught sight of Dimitri standing malevolently in the shadows. The guards bowed stiffly at sight of him. Her skirt flaring, she walked past both the guards and the grim-faced Dimitri, who rested his back against the wall.

"A word of advice, Mara," he grunted. "I know you were speaking with Quentin and I know he's waiting for you now. Watch yourself: The Rani is most displeased."

Mara seethed. "You're the last man I'd take advice from," she snapped, "you cockroach!"

"Still not good enough for you, am I? That'll change, Mara. You'll see."

"Will it?" She spun on her heels and made her way down the steps. Outside, the young Kuban captain stood waiting, his back to her.

"Quentin?"

He turned and, stepping forward, held out his hand. Hesitantly Mara took it. They both smiled.

"I feared you weren't coming," said Quentin, leading her to a bench and sitting down beside her.

"Dimitri's guards gave me trouble."

Quentin knit his brow. "Did they try to hurt you?"

"No, no; it's all right." She shrugged. "I guess I should be lucky they let me out at all." Her eye caught sight of a hound prowling along the parapet of the low wall and she shuddered. "But then again, where can I run? Your Rani keeps me well in check."

His eyes narrowed. "Mara, have you been thinking of—"

"Escape?" She laughed. "How? Look at those walls —and those dogs."

Unconvinced, he said, "Please, Mara, don't try. Don't think about it. You'll make matters worse."

The Empire girl sighed. "What can be worse? When your Rani finishes with me, I'll be turned over to Dimitri"—her shoulders sagged—"and I think I'd rather be dead."

He touched her cheek ever so lightly with his fingertips. "You mustn't say such things," he whispered. "Let's speak of other things."

Mara pressed her hand against his. "You're kind and gentle, Quentin. I like you. I shouldn't— Hel's fire! I've enough problems already."

He grinned sheepishly. "I like you too, Mara. I—"

Her smile vanished. "It's wrong for us even to be speaking. You know that, don't you?"

"But why?"

She pushed his hand away and cast her eyes to the darkening sky. Crickets sang softly from the grass. "Because of who I am."

"Ah, still enemies, is that it?"

His bitter words brought a tear to her eye and her voice cracked as she spoke: "I'm confused, Quentin. Kuba is an enemy, yes, but not you. Meeting you . . ." She wiped the tear away.

He turned her face to meet his and kissed her briefly, softly. "Do you believe in the Fates, Mara?"

She nodded, eyes gazing wetly into his.

"Then you must also believe that our meeting was more than chance. Perhaps through us our worlds can be drawn together."

Her face tensed. "You don't understand, Quentin. My aunt is to be taken prisoner here. And from my window I can see your galleys preparing to sail."

He frowned.

"Your Rani thinks she can conquer the world with my aunt out of the way. She's wrong, Quentin. There'll be war between us—terrible war. The Empire Fleet will find its way home and sweep like a hawk across the sea. Your city will burn."

Quentin winced. "Why are you saying such things?"

"Because your Rani is poisoned! Her hate is blind. Does she know what she's doing?"

He leaned back and closed his eyes. "Ah, Mara, I'm not naïve. I know what might happen."

She stared at him. "You know? You know about Stacy being forced to come here?"

Glumly he nodded. "I was angered when I heard. But believe me, Mara, Sigried will not harm your aunt. True, men like Dimitri have filled her head with dangerous schemes, but she's not a fool. She can be dealt with."

Mara laughed bitterly. "By whom? Who can sway her?"

"Maybe I can."

She looked at him incredulously, her heart skipping a beat. "You? How?"

"Sigried," he said slowly, "is my cousin; but more than that, I'm the commander of our fleet."

Mara drew back, astounded. It was *his* ships that would ravish Empire land and tear asunder all that Rhonnda had so painstakingly built! She could not control her tears. Her trust, her confidence, even her love had been given to a man who was the Empire's main threat.

"Don't cry, Mara," he whispered.

She turned away. "Leave me, Quentin. Go sail your ships! Go burn my world!"

"It's not like that, Mara, I promise you. There still need be no war. Doesn't my very being here now tell you that? Listen to me—"

"You listen to me!" she shot back angrily, eyes flashing. "Empire armies will gather all across the world. Wolves will go wild when they learn of the Princess's capture. They'll tear you apart, you and Kuba together! Kuba will be reduced to rubble."

Quentin glared. "Your heart is as poisoned as Sigried's; I can see that now. I came here to help, but very well, I'll not intrude upon your privacy any longer. Good-bye, Mara."

He stood to go, but she tugged lightly at his sleeve. "Quentin, please . . ." There was urgent pleading in her eyes.

Sweeping her to her feet, he held her close against his breast and let her hot tears run against his shirt. Running his hand softly against her hair, he whispered, "I still want to help, Mara. Let me."

She sniffed. "I must get out of the palace. I must find a way to warn Stacy."

"Sweet, sweet Mara, I can't help you do that. It would inflame Sigried. She'd make it worse."

"Then we're doomed, Quentin—all of us."

"No. I'll speak to Siggy again. I'll demand that our fleet be kept in Kuban waters."

Mara shuddered. "She won't listen. She's dreamed of this for too long. And you'll be accused of treason."

"I won't. Siggy needs me. She'll have to listen. But promise me, Mara, that until I've settled this matter, you won't try to run away."

The girl closed her eyes. With all her heart she wanted to do as he asked, but she knew it was impossible. Quentin meant well, she was sure, but there was nothing he would be able to do. Sigried had planned for this all too carefully.

"Promise me, Mara." His tone was insistent.

"I promise," she lied; "but leave me now, Quentin. The moon's rising. I have to go back. They're watching us."

He sighed and let go of her. "I may not see you for a day or two, but trust me. Can you do that?"

She smiled. "I can—I will—but take care. Be careful—please."

He leaned forward and kissed her again, not caring if even Dimitri himself were watching from the tower. Then he fled from her sight.

She watched wistfully as he disappeared into the shadows, and resolved to go forward with her plan. "Good-bye, Quentin," she whispered, her face ashen and drawn. "I pray we'll meet again. Tonight, one way or another, I'm going to escape."

Unseen from the low wall, Sigried stood staring down at the small garden below. Arms folded, hair blowing in the wind, she thought, *Dimitri was right:*

My foolish cousin has fallen in love. Ah, Quentin, you'll have to pay the price. I can't trust you any longer.

The hour was late, dangerously close to midnight. Mara stood tensely at her closed door, listening to the slow, heavy footsteps of her two guards marching back and forth in the hallway. They began to speak in murmured voices. Mara strained to hear.

"Give me about an hour," one said to the other.

"Take your time," replied the second with a chuckle.

Mara bit her lip. The time was close. She waited until the departing soldier's footsteps could no longer be heard; then she wet her lips with her tongue, pressed her tunic with her hands and threw back her hair.

Cautiously she opened the door a crack.

The soldier's eyes darted in her direction.

"Ulik," she whispered.

He looked at her quizzically.

"Ulik, come here, will you?"

"What are you doing up?" he asked curtly. "Go to sleep; otherwise I'll have to report you."

The door opened wider. Mara smiled tremulously, her eyes filled with what seemed to be unmistakable offers. "I'm frightened, Ulik. Please, won't you stay with me for a while?"

"Are you insane, girl? I'm not allowed to talk to you. You know what can happen to me."

Her breasts heaved as she sighed. "But you're alone, Ulik. Your friend has gone for an hour. I heard him say so."

His eyes darted up and down the hallway. "So you've been spying."

Seductively she put her hands on her hips and shifted her weight so that her body arched tauntingly at the young soldier. "Not spying; I just wanted to speak with you alone."

Hesitantly he stepped closer to her. "Speak with me? What for? Yesterday you—"

Mara batted her lashes. "Are you angry with me, Ulik, just because I called you a few names? What did I say?"

He frowned. "You called me a cretin—and a horse's ass."

She touched his mouth. "Hush. I never meant that, Ulik. You know I like you."

"You do?"

"Of course. I like you best of all. Will you come into my room?"

He looked about nervously. The lure of the girl was more than tempting. No one would ever believe her offer, he knew, but what did he care? The young princess Maralisa was a girl any of Sigried's Panthers would give an arm to have. Soldiers rarely had such luck, and he still couldn't believe his.

She stepped backward into the room, beckoning him to follow; he did so reluctantly. "Close the door, Ulik. Don't be shy."

He smirked and did as she asked. "If they catch me in here..."

Lithely she sat down on the edge of her bed, fumbling with the buttons of her tunic. "They won't catch you, but even if they did"—she held her arms above her head and let him gawk at her firm breasts, half exposed beneath the tunic—"aren't I worth the risk? I haven't had a man since I left Rhonnda. I'm restless."

"You... you're not a virgin?"

"Uh-uh," she lied. "Let me show you." Reaching out, she drew him close. His foul breath nauseated her as he tried to kiss her. Their lips met, and as they kissed, she caressed him with one hand and reached for her iron candlestick with the other.

Ulik groaned and slumped to the floor. Blood oozed from the gash on the back of his skull.

Mara jumped up and tossed the bloody weapon on the bed. "You should have known better than to trust a wolf, Ulik," she commented dryly. Then she ran from the room and made her way down the hallway and narrow stairs. Taking refuge in the shadows, she paused before the landing, making certain no one was about. Moments later the palace bells struck midnight. Mara wiped her clammy hands on her tunic.

She bolted across the hall and stopped short beyond the door. There were two walks, one to the garden, the other to the courtyard. High above, the Rani's rooms glowed with light. Mara sidestepped fountains and statues, slinking her way toward the courtyard path. If only she could get past the gate ...

Footsteps startled her. She bounded for the hedges and the shadows. Long minutes of lying in wait followed while a column of weary guards crossed the path where she had been standing only seconds before. Her heart leaped to her throat. Biting her lips, she waited breathlessly.

They had not seen her. The column disappeared in the direction of the distant tower. Mara dodged from her place and dashed back along the walk. More noise; she took cover behind a row of thornbushes.

A grim-faced sentry marched slowly past her eyes. Time was growing short, she knew. Ulik would be discovered any moment. With what seemed like deliberate slowness the sentry paused, looked about and rested for a moment before moving on. Mara crouched, half-considering springing on him from the bushes.

Az'i! What's the use? His friends will spring like traps!

Then, in her moment of despair, the guard suddenly straightened and, humming a bawdy tune, continued on his rounds. Mara breathed a sigh of relief. On she moved, catlike, her eyes mere slits darting about in the hazy Kuban night.

More sentries were approaching. Crouching low, Mara ran along a low winding stone wall. Her hand touched clinging ivy as the sounds came close.

Fara's kingdom! They'll see me now for sure!

Quickly she backed off a few paces, took a short run and jumped as high as she could. Her fingertips caught nicked stone. She pulled up with all her strength and swung her body across the top of the wall. Whether she was seen or not, she didn't care. She dropped down the other side and fell onto a bank of thick grass. On hands and knees she peered up. Ahead was another wall, this one higher—and impossible to scale.

Az'i! What next?

Going back was out of the question; so was going forward. Taking her chances, she ran alongside the low wall until it ended. Lights from high windows flickered. She could hear laughter and noise from above.

Servants' quarters! It must be! If only I could steal some of their clothes!

By instinct alone she whirled, poised to strike. A large slinking hound glared at her, razor-sharp fangs bared. Mara growled wolf fashion; the dog halted in its tracks and eyed her warily.

"Stay!" she snarled.

The dog yapped.

"Stay!"

A growl came from behind her. She whirled just as another hound leaped from the wall. His weight sent her sprawling, arms out, across wet grass. She rolled over, her fingernails clawlike, ready to fend him off. The dog pounced, and she tore at his throat. The second dog now joined the fray, howling and snarling.

"Freeze!"

The order was given to both the dogs and the frightened girl. The hounds stepped back, their eyes still fixed on their prey. Mara didn't move a muscle.

Her eyes focused on the man approaching from the shadows.

"Well, well, what have we here?" He laughed loudly.

Mara gasped. It was Dimitri!

The dragoon stood over her, a thin, cruel smile on his lips. "Poor litle princess," he rasped, "wants to run away, doesn't like it here."

As he spoke, a host of running soldiers surrounded her, swords fixed at her throat. "Put your weapons away," he told them. "She won't be any more bother at all. Isn't that right, Mara?"

She sneered.

"I could let the dogs have you, you know. They'd fix up your face so that Quentin would never want to look at you again." He kneeled down beside her and grabbed her throat with his hand. "Would you like that?"

She spit in his face.

He slapped her hard and brought tears. Wiping the spit away, he clenched his fist and she flinched. "Oh, I'll not hurt you now, girl—not yet; later, when this business is done. But we can't let you go running about like this, can we? Sigried will be most displeased." He stood and faced his men. "Take her to the dungeons!"

"Lord? The Rani hasn't said to—"

"I'll take care of the Rani. This girl almost killed one of our soldiers. She needs to be taught a lesson."

Two guards dragged her kicking and screaming to her feet.

"I'll kill you, you bag of offal—" she began. Stars flashed before her eyes as Dimitri's fist smacked against her jaw. She groaned and slumped.

"Take her away! Chain her to a wall! And if she screams, gag her! She's caused enough trouble. When I'm done, she won't be able to cause any more."

* * *

Above the fertile plains, below the contoured mountains that climbed majestically against the sea-blue sky, rose the walls of Kuba. The towers and steeples of the Opal City shimmered in midmorning heat. A cool sea breeze set a multiple array of black and gold imperial banners to fluttering. The walls appeared softened in faint haze, like polished marble.

In the east, Stacy could see the harbor, with its many ships, and the massive interconnecting seawalls towering above it. From each wall rose lofty towers, with squads of keen troops to watch every vessel that sailed into port.

Slowly she dismounted and stroked her horse's mane. "So that's Kuba," she whispered, both awed and shaken by the sight.

Assad dismounted at her side and nodded glumly. "And look, my lady: There must be two dozen galleys on the bay."

The Princess shaded her eyes, frowning. From here they looked like small toys bobbing in a tub; but she knew all too well what such toys as these were capable of.

"Best we keep moving," said Alryc, his face shaded by his pilgrim's hood. "We don't want any passing patrol to see us standing and gaping."

Stacy looked down from the grassy knoll to the wide road that curved along the bottom of the hill. Merchants' and traders' wagons were rolling past in a steady stream of two-way traffic.

"We can pass through the gates in an hour," reminded the mercenary.

The dark-eyed Princess shivered. *The gates of Kuba! How the very words frighten me*. Aloud she said, "Then we'll do as planned."

Alryc grimaced. "Are you certain?" he asked. "Won't you reconsider this hasty plan of yours?"

Stacy shook her head. "It's the best way. We can't afford to attract any attenion. Anyway, Assad knows the city."

"But you'll have need of us, my lady! What if you're stopped by soldiers?"

"Three pilgrims—especially if two of them are women—won't cause a single eye to turn, but having you and Cicero beside us just might. We can't chance it. Both of you will wait outside the walls."

"I fear for you, my lady."

Melinda fingered the concealed knife, which she had managed to keep hidden since the night of the "insect feast." "Stacy's right. We can slip through the city much faster on our own. We mustn't arouse suspicions."

Alryc lowered his head. His eyes looked pained. "Where . . . where will you leave us?"

Stacy reached out and took his hand. "Here, Alryc: Better we part company now." She handed him her mare's reins. "Take care of her, my friend. She's a fine animal and we'll have need of her tomorrow."

The astronomer winced, hoping there would be a tomorrow to share.

The Princess kneeled and ran her fingers along Cicero's thick red fur. "Watch over him, Cicero. Keep your eyes keen. With luck, tomorrow night we'll be back."

Cicero turned his face away so that she could not see the tears come to his fierce hunter's eyes.

"It's time," said Melinda, hair tossing in the wind.

Stacy nodded and stood. She pulled her veil up to her eyes and let the hood fall. Assad clasped Alryc's hand and petted Cicero. Melinda kissed the astronomer and the wolf; then, flanking the Princess, she began to walk down to the road.

Alryc watched forlornly as his three companions began to move in the direction of the towering black gates. His physical presence was very much at the top of the hill, but his heart had gone with the Princess.

Through the maze of streets and bazaars they roamed. The scent of cheap perfumes filled the air; milling crowds lingered beside vast arrays of stalls and shops; merchants hawked their goods above the din, calling and cajoling passersby. Assad led them along a labyrinth of back alleys east of the central plaza, barely in sight of the palace.

"Where are we?" asked the Princess.

"The Japouri, my lady," he replied, "the Street of Beggars. Here we can mingle freely and wait for the palace gates to open."

Stacy looked about nervously. The gutter was lined with beggars and prostitutes; the low two-storied stone houses on each side seemed decrepit. From dark doorways swarthy men kept watch on the crowds in the streets.

"Pickpockets," mumbled Assad. "The Japouri teems with them."

Stacy looked at him incredulously. "And Sigried allows this to go on right under the shadow of her palace?"

"This is Kuba, my lady. Pickpockets are the least of it. Within these streets are some of the basest men and women you'll ever see: brigands, cutthroats, murderers..."

A tall red-headed prostitute ambled by, swung her hips and winked at Assad. Melinda grew livid and reached toward her knife.

"Don't start any trouble," warned the mercenary.

The prostitute laughed at the glowering pilgrim and slowly crossed the street to where a drunken soldier had beckoned.

Just then they heard screams behind them. Stacy

spun around: Two beggars had begun to fight, each wielding a curved dagger. The men grappled and fell to the gutter. No one tried to stop them. A small crowd of onlookers began to egg them on—a grisly bunch, who laughed as the combatants drew blood.

"They'll kill each other!" cried the Princess.

Assad took firm hold of her sleeve. "Don't try to interfere. They'll kill you for it. This isn't Rhonnda, my lady. Life is much cheaper here."

Stacy shivered. "Take us away from this place, Assad. Where do pilgrims gather?"

"In front of the palace at dusk, when the gates open for evening prayer at the Temple. We can't enter the palace until then."

A low gurgle emitted from one of the beggars. Throat slashed, he slumped in the gutter, lying in his own blood. The victor laughed, spat on the man, then he picked his pocket and fled down the street.

"The man's still alive," gasped Melinda. "Won't anyone try to help him?"

Assad sighed. "Not in the Japouri; no one cares. But come, let me take you away from here."

Crossing a stinking tangle of back alleys, Assad led them down a winding street and onto a spacious boulevard. Here there were small parks filled with fountains and statues. They rested beside a flowing fountain. Suddenly Stacy grew tense. Heading their way strode a tall helmeted soldier. He wore a crimson military cape, his hand on the hilt of his glittering scimitar.

"What are you doing here?" he asked curtly.

Assad replied, "We wait to enter the Temple, my lord. We are weary pilgrims come from the Kreelian border this very day."

The soldier eyed them suspiciously. "Pilgrims, eh? Don't you know that this street is forbidden to you?"

"Forgive us, sir, but we're still strangers."

The man scowled. "Pilgrims must wait at the gates,"

he said. "If you need somewhere to stay, stay there. Now, don't let me catch you around here again."

Assad crossed his hands over his chest and bowed, and hastily they headed back in the direction of the Street of Thieves.

Once the soldier was out of sight, Stacy stopped. "That man was a mercenary, wasn't he?" she asked.

Assad nodded. "A Panther. Sigried surrounds herself with such foreigners."

The Princess sighed. "How will we ever free Mara? The palace will be crawling with men like him."

Assad smiled. "That place is a rabbit warren of secret tunnels. After prayer, Sigried will hold audience for pilgrims. When she does, we'll sneak away and find the passage we need."

"But Mara might be in any of a hundred different places," protested Melinda. "How will we know where to look?"

Stacy tightened her grip on her concealed dagger. "Sigried will tell us. Assad, can you lead us to her private quarters?"

He nodded gravely. "It will be risky. As you said, mercenaries will be all over."

Her dark eyes flashed with anger. "No power on earth will stop me from dealing with Siggy this very night."

The Temple priestess held her arms out for the last time, swaying as she chanted, and kneeled on the floor at the foot of the stone icon. The multitude of pilgrims got up from their knees and bowed. Crimson sunlight slanted down from the high narrow windows. The first evening stars had begun to twinkle.

Lost in the crowd, Stacy, Assad and Melinda followed the procession to the audience hall.

"Let's go in with them," whispered Melinda, her

hood covering her eyes. "We can kill her right here, right now. Just one throw of my knife . . ."

Stacy tightened her veil. "To what purpose? We'd never find Mara. No, Melinda: My plan is best. Assad, what now?"

The mercenary looked around in the fading light. They crossed the wide walk with the others, then paused at the vestibule entrance. "There's a side door," he whispered.

"And a guard in front of it," reminded the Princess, noting the soldier standing stiffly under a torch.

Suddenly Assad clutched at his stomach, doubled over as if in terrible pain.

Stacy understood the ruse right away. She put her arm around his shoulders and half-carried him over to the soldier. "Please," she rasped, "this brother is ill."

Assad moaned.

The soldier helped take hold of him.

"He needs a physician," said Melinda. "Where can we find one? Where does that door lead?"

The soldier looked doubtfully about, searching for some comrade to help straighten the matter out. "No one can enter this way," he said. "You'll have to go back to the Temple."

"Ohhh . . ." Assad acted as though he would pass out.

"Please," pleaded Stacy, "just let him rest somewhere while I fetch help."

Before the soldier could reply, Assad's fist knocked the wind out of him. Melinda covered his mouth with her hand and stifled his cry, and Stacy pushed the door open and led them all through, dragging the soldier after them.

It was a dark hallway they found themselves in. No one was about. Off to the left, there was a small stairway leading down into what appeared to be a black abyss.

Melinda threw back her hood. "Where does that stairway lead?" She hissed at the soldier.

He glared back defiantly.

Stacy whipped out her dagger and pushed it toward his neck. "Tell us, and be quick! There's nothing I'd like more than to slit your throat!"

"It . . . it leads to the cellars."

"Will it take us to the imperial quarters?"

He stared incredulously.

The knife pressed and drew a trickle of blood. "Will it?"

The soldier nodded slightly, his eyes straining to keep a fix on the shiny blade.

Assad shoved him harshly into dark shadows. "Show us the way."

"We'll need a torch; it's dark."

"Uh-uh," said Stacy, "no torch. Feel your way—and no tricks. Now move!"

Slowly the trembling man felt his way to the steps and led them down. Dust stirred at their feet; wood creaked. At last they came to a landing deep under the Temple grounds. "This way," the soldier said, gesturing for them to follow along a dimly lit passage.

Assad glanced at Stacy.

The Princess nodded. "Strip," she said.

The soldier turned. "What?"

"Strip! Take off everything!"

He did so slowly, first his belt and weapon, then his bright tunic.

"Underwear, too," whispered the Princess.

Reluctantly he did as she asked. Naked, he stood before the pilgrims, shivering.

Stacy threw off her hood and pushed aside her veil. "Lie down on the floor."

Assad's sword teased at the man's ribs. "Do as she says, my friend."

The soldier gulped and lay down on his stomach.

Stacy gagged his mouth with his sash while Assad took cord and bound both his hands and feet. Then, making certain he could not wriggle out of his bonds, Assad hit him hard with the hilt of his sword. The soldier groaned and sprawled limply on the floor.

Dashing from shadow to shadow, they followed the passage for what seemed like hours. The air became hot and dank; their lungs wheezed with dust.

They came to a junction where two separate tunnels lay ahead.

"Which one?" asked Stacy.

The mercenary shrugged. "Both wind upward. Either should take us out of here."

Stacy nodded. "All right. This one will do." She chose the one on the left and they began the ascent. Soon the air freshened. Above their heads, iron grilles let in cool night air. They could even catch a glimpse of the stars.

Noises grew louder, muffled sounds of men speaking. The three pilgrims froze. Stacy leaned forward and strained her ears. Above one of the grilles, several soldiers were talking and laughing. "Serves her right," one said. "The bitch," said another. Then their footsteps moved on.

"There's a door," said Assad, pointing to where the passage ended. Stacy moved lithely toward it and pushed ever so slightly. She peered beyond the crack into what seemed to be a huge, opulent dining hall. The room was brightly lit by both globe and candle, the walls laden with long, intricately woven tapestries. Bidding her friends to wait, she tiptoed into the room and stood perfectly still. Feeling safe, at least for the moment, she opened the door.

Assad's eyes widened in recognition. "I know this place," he whispered. "A stroke of luck, Stacy: Sigried's chambers should be just above us, on the next landing. These rooms are for the Rani's banquets. Sigried likes to entertain in fashion."

"So I understand," drawled Stacy as she peered at the lavish decor. The bark of a dog cracked whiplike through the air. Stacy whirled, drew aside the drapes and peeked out the window. "What was that?"

"Siggy's hounds prowling the walls."

The Princess cursed softly under her breath and glanced at the empty courtyard below. Suddenly, across the path, she saw several shadowy figures emerge from what seemed to be the back wall of the Temple. She narrowed her eyes and stared. Faces were impossible to discern, but the flowing yellow hair could not be mistaken. Stacy held her breath. "It's Sigried!"

Stealthily Assad moved to her side, careful not to let himself be seen through the glass. The woman walked with a brisk gait, her head up, her hair tossing in the breeze. Assad felt a shiver run up his spine. It was the Rani, all right, and she was every bit as beautiful as he remembered her.

"Her audience must be over. She's returning to the palace."

"Will she go directly to her rooms?"

"If I'm right," Assad said, "she'll first go to her throne room."

"Now? At night?"

"She's a strange woman, my lady. Many was the time I saw her sitting alone upon her ebony throne, staring. She enjoys solitude."

Stacy smiled. "Old habits die hard. How can we reach her throne?"

The mercenary rubbed tensely at the side of his face. "It's on this level. We might reach it from the balcony—it circles virtually this entire wing—but it's dangerous. Her troops can spot us at almost any point."

The Princess looked to the sky. "There's no moon, Assad. We'll be less than shadows."

"Don't waste time," hissed Melinda to the mercenary. "How do we reach the balcony?"

Assad sighed, then moved stealthily across the room and parted another set of curtains, which concealed huge glass doors. Beyond them was the balcony, a wide stone platform with a low wall, extending as far as they could see around the palace. "This is the way," he said, gesturing.

Stacy grinned. "You know your way around here pretty well, don't you?"

He flushed as he said, "Once upon a time I made it my business to know such things, but never mind that. Let's hope these doors aren't locked. Shattered glass is going to make an awful lot of noise."

Stacy reached for the brass handle, closing her eyes as she did so. The hour was at hand, she knew, and nothing must go wrong. Hesitantly she grasped the handle and turned. The door opened and she was greeted with a welcome rush of cold night air. She sighed with relief: Fortune was still on her side.

Assad crouched low and stepped out first. Nestled low against the wall, he signaled for the others to follow. Stacy moved deftly, darting across the balcony to the wall and taking hold of a twirling ivy vine that twisted over it. Melinda was at her side instantly.

The mercenary put his finger to his lips and peered over the wall. A towering guard post stood too close for comfort. "Do as I do," he rasped, and without waiting for a reply, he began to move along the wall, hugging it closely, and made his way around the first turn.

Stacy followed close behind. At every turn, there seemed to be another tower. Suddenly she froze. Walking slowly atop the closest parapet was a great vicious hound. Though it was moving away from them, Stacy slid her hand up her sleeve, clutching at her dagger. "How much farther?" she whispered to Assad.

"Not far. Beyond the next turn. Let me go first."

The Princess nodded and grasped his hand. "Be careful, Assad."

He smiled; then, hunching his shoulders, he crept ahead.

Minutes seemed like hours. Stacy nervously tapped her foot, her eyes still on the hound. Assad crept round the turn and was gone from sight. The hound barked. Stacy felt a tinge of panic. *Dear Fara, please!*

A soldier in the tower whistled and the dog ran toward the sound. Stacy relaxed. For the moment the danger was over. But where was Assad? Why didn't he signal?

A chirp of a bird came softly from around the corner, a pretty nightingale's melody.

"That's him," said Melinda, grinning.

"Praise Fara for that! Come on."

The two women cautiously moved on. Around the turn they were finally able to stand, as the wall was higher here. The balcony had widened spaciously into a semigarden with benches and shrubs. Assad was waiting just around the corner.

"Now what?" said Melinda, uneasily looking about.

"It's just past the garden," said Assad. "But we'd better go slowly. Someone might enter the chamber at any moment."

Siggy paced the room, her arms folded and her face darkened by a scowl. The stones of her diadem sent colorful gleams around the hall as they caught the dim globelight. Her sandals echoed hollowly against the polished floor. She walked briskly, ignoring the dark figure at her side. He was speaking constantly to her. Finally she stopped, looked up at him and said, "I don't want to discuss it! Is that clear?"

The man smirked. "You saw with your own eyes, didn't you? Well, didn't you?"

Icy eyes flashed angrily. "You're a pig, Dimitri, lower than a gutter. I should send you back to the Japouri, where I found you. Your whores are all you deserve."

Boldly he took her by the arm.

The Rani winced. "Don't touch me. Get out of my sight!"

"You need me, Mistress," he gloated, "now more than ever—and you know it."

Siggy fumed. She looked at him contemptuously.

Callously he returned the sneer. "Why not confront him about it? If you don't believe your own eyes, why don't you ask?"

"I don't have to ask," she answered coldly.

"Then you admit it? Ha! A fine mess this is! The commander of the Kuban fleet swooning before a bitch from the Rhonnda palace!" His eyes darkened as he spoke. "You must relieve him of duty at once!"

"Are you now giving orders to me, dragoon?"

"Rot in Hel, Sigried! We're in this together, are we not? Do you expect your ships still to sail when their commander aids and comforts the enemy? *Your* enemy, Sigried, not mine. Your grudge and yours alone."

Burning with rage, she put her hands to her ears. "Enough! What do you want of me?"

Dimitri smiled wickedly. "Kill him. Kill them both."

Her eyes widened. "Are you insane?"

"No, I'm realistic. Quentin is no longer any use to us; you know that. A man who can't be trusted is a threat. Be done with him—now. And be done with the girl, too."

The Rani smiled sardonically. "You hate the child, don't you? Why?"

"For the same reasons you hate her aunt. Get rid of them."

Siggy laughed. "Ah, I see. And who will command my fleet? Don't answer—you, of course."

His face twisted; cold eyes glared back at her. "And why not? I've served you well, haven't I? Taken risks no other man would have taken for you? Yes, I want the fleet. Quentin's lost the right—"

" 'The right'? What do you know of it, dragoon? Without him, Kuban waters would be rife with . . . with bastards like you."

"A bastard like me hasn't turned against you, at least."

The Rani bristled. "Quentin's not turned against me!"

"No?" he said with raised eyebrows. "Then confront him. Make him swear allegiance to you."

"I don't have to. I know he will."

"Then make him swear he has no love for the girl."

Here Sigried tensed. Her cold eyes betrayed her worry and her fears. Although it pained her to admit it, she had indeed seen her cousin take the young princess into his arms: Maralisa—Anastasia's niece, the blood of her hated rival.

"Bring him to me," she whispered.

Dimitri smiled smugly. "As you will, my Rani. I'll have my Panthers—"

Siggy retorted with a smug smile of her own. "No, Dimitri, not with your guards. Fetch him yourself. Let's see if you're man enough to call him out."

"You'd like that, wouldn't you? You'd like to see him spill my blood. But I promise you'll be disappointed. I'll break his spine!"

"Do so and I'll have your head, I swear by the Fates, Dimitri! I told you to bring him and nothing more."

The dragoon crossed his hands over his chest and bowed. "Yes, Rani. Shall I bring him to your quarters?"

"No. Bring him to the throne room. I'll speak with him there."

Stacy peered through the glass doors of the throne room. The chamber was dark; none of the globes or candles had been lit. The ebony throne stood tall in the center of the room, rising majestically like a black snake coiled to strike. *Like Kuba itself,* thought Stacy bitterly. *Like Sigried.*

The entrance door opened. Stacy held her breath. She signaled for Assad and Melinda to back away from the glass doors. With glowering canine eyes, Stacy watched the Rani enter alone and shut the door behind her, dismissing attendants as she did so.

I come like a thief in the night, Sigried, as you came for Mara.

The Rani paced for a few moments, then swung back her crimson cloak and slumped onto her throne. Elbow on the armrest, chin resting on clenched knuckles, she seemed deep in thought. Stacy wondered just what might be racing through her mind—what new scheme, what new lust for the glory of her city, her empire.

Restlessly Sigried looked about. She bit pensively at her lips, drummed her fingers, crossed and uncrossed her legs. Suddenly she caught sight of a fleeting shadow on the balcony, beyond the glass doors. She leaned forward on the throne, clutching at the arms. She felt a deep chill overwhelm her. "Who is it? Who's there?"

The form of a pilgrim showed itself behind the glass, face completely masked by hood and veil. Only the eyes could be seen—cold eyes, locking Sigried's gaze.

Siggy stared for a long moment. It would have been easy for her to cry out and have this intruder arrested and killed on the spot, but something about this pilgrim intrigued the Rani; something fueled her curiosity. She motioned for the pilgrim to slide open the door.

Stacy did so and took a single pace inside.

"How did you get here?" hissed Sigried. "Speak!"

"I found my way from below. I hid from your guards." There was no hesitancy in the reply.

Siggy smirked. At least the woman was honest. "You know I could have you punished for this."

"I know."

The Rani threw back her head and glared at the intruder. "And still you came? Why?"

"To speak with you, my Rani."

"The audience is over. Come to the Temple tomorrow. Perhaps I'll have time for you then." With a wave of the hand, feeling benevolent for not punishing the reckless pilgrim, Siggy dismissed her; but the pilgrim made no move to go. Sigried looked astonished. "Did you hear me? Go! Go now!"

Stacy shook her head.

"You refuse, pilgrim?"

"I have urgent matters, Rani, matters that must be settled tonight."

The chill returned. Siggy leaned forward again, eyes straining to catch a glimpse of the hidden face. "Step closer, pilgrim. Let me see you."

Stacy took a cautious step forward, then stopped in dark shadows.

The Rani shifted her weight uneasily and slid her hand slowly toward her sheathed dagger. "What is this business that is so important?" she asked.

Stacy crossed her arms and bowed Kuban fashion. "I need your wisdom, my Rani. My problem must be resolved. Only you can solve it."

Siggy frowned. "I cannot be bothered with personal matters. You waste your time, pilgrim. Find your answers at the Temple."

Once more Stacy shook her head. "I need *you*, Rani. Will you listen?"

"Very well," she said with a sigh, "speak. What is so urgent that brings you here like a thief?"

"A matter of another thief, my Rani. There is one who has stolen the possession I cherish the most—

willfully taken it from me, with malice. I seek a way to retrieve it."

Sigried smiled. It was such a trifling matter; but this pilgrim was too ignorant to realize that. "The answer is easy," she said irritably. "Seek out your thief and demand your possession back."

"And if the thief refuses?"

"Then you must take it by force."

"And kill the thief if necessary?"

The Rani laughed loudly. These countryside pilgrims were such children. "Of course. The crime must be punished."

Stacy smiled. "Thank you, Siggy."

The Rani grew livid at the use of her familiar name. "How dare you! I'll have your head shaven for that!"

"No, Siggy, I don't think you will." Stacy boldly threw back her hood, pushed aside her veil and stepped from the shadows, exposing herself fully.

The Rani's eyes grew large with shock and amazement. "Stacy!"

The Princess smiled. "Yes, Siggy, it's me. I've come to punish the thief."

Seething, Siggy half-rose out of her seat. Stacy drew back a step, poised to fight, but much to her surprise the Rani made no threatening move; instead she sank back easily onto her throne. A thin smile crossed her lips as she stared at the Empire Princess. "Ah, Stacy," she whispered, "I should have known it was you. I should have known you'd find your own way of reaching here. But here you are, and I'm glad."

"You won't be so glad before the hour is done, Sigried. Acting upon your advice, I'm going to kill the thief who stole my niece."

Siggy sat back. "Of course: Mara is your only concern. I knew she would be, Stacy. But come, step closer to me. Let me see you better. How long has it been?"

Without fear or hesitation, Stacy stepped before the throne. "More than seven years have passed since we've seen each other, Siggy. I see the years have treated you well."

Siggy dismissed the compliment with a haughty wave of her hand. "So you intend to kill me, eh?"

Stacy nodded. Her eyes looked uneasily toward the doors. They were tightly shut.

"My attendants are gone," confided the Rani, "and I'll not scream for my guards, if that's what you think. In fact, I rather like the idea of the two of us facing each other again, Stacy. I've waited a long time. I've even dreamed of it. Remember, I still bear my scar."

The Princess glared. "I'll not toy with you, Siggy. I have little time for your games. Where's Mara?"

Sigried stared at her incredulously. "Do you really think I'd tell you? Ah, Stacy, who else but you could be so rash? Who else but you would dare to dream you could slip into my palace and escape with your niece at your side?" She smiled caustically. "You have courage, though, I must admit—more than the spineless mercenaries who fly my banner and steal my gold."

"Gold stolen from Rhonnda ships, you mean," Stacy replied. She glanced toward the balcony. Her two companions slipped inside between the shadows.

Siggy gaped.

"I'm not alone," said Stacy with a thin smile, "as you can see. But time's running out, Siggy. Where's Mara?"

Ignoring the demand, Siggy examined the other "pilgrims." Her lips parted in a sinister smile. "Is that you, Melinda?" she asked.

The forest girl threw off her hood. "It's me, Sigried."

The Rani clapped her hands delightedly. "Joyous day! I've been doubly blessed! But who's the other? Surely not Elias?"

Stacy shook her head. "A friend. Leave it at that. Now, tell me, Rani: Where's my niece?"

Slowly the Rani rose from her throne. Her hand slid to her knife.

Stacy drew her silver dagger.

Sigried eyed her and smiled. "One shout from me and a hundred guards will converge on this chamber. You realize that, don't you?"

The Princess met her gaze. "You'll be dead before they come. Now, for the last time: Tell me where Mara's being kept!"

The curved blade glittered as the Rani whipped it from its scabbard. Melinda and Assad moved forward.

Stacy waved for them to hold back. "You were right, Siggy," she whispered. "It was meant to be this way: you and I, alone."

The Rani laughed. She began to circle the Princess, moving with slow, catlike steps.

Stacy crouched, her dagger poised at arm's length. "I promise you, Siggy, before you die you'll tell me what I need to know."

Sigried grinned devilishly. "We'll see, Stacy; we'll see."

The Rani lunged. Her thrust was parried, the knives clashing loudly. Both women pulled back sharply, each watching the other's eyes. The Rani feigned a thrust, but Stacy twirled out of harm's way.

Sigried's eyes glowered. "Fast as ever, aren't you, bitch?" she hissed through clenched teeth.

Stacy smiled thinly. She hunched her shoulders, moving lithely in a slow backstep. The silver dagger glimmered dully in the shadows. A rapid flash of it caught Sigried off guard and she jumped to the side, precariously close to losing her balance. Stacy closed in and they grappled hand to hand, the knife of each threatening the throat of the other. Stacy tightened her grip, a look of cold satisfaction crossing her face as she realized the Rani's strength was waning.

With a sudden shove, Sigried freed her left arm and

brought her elbow smashing into Stacy's throat. The Princess staggered for an instant, then seized Sigried's knife arm, yanked and sent the Rani of Kuba sprawling against her ebony throne. The bejeweled knife clattered to the tile floor.

Siggy countered with a swift kick, a low blow that caused the Princess to gasp in pain, and then hit Stacy with the back of her hand, causing blood to flow from the side of her mouth. Stacy slashed and Sigried ducked. This time it was the Princess's knife hand that was twisted. The Rani made a desperate attempt to wrench the knife from her fingers. Stacy held on and the two of them twisted together, grimly dancing across the floor.

Sigried pulled at Stacy's flowing hair. Head yanked back, Stacy pushed an open palm against Sigried's chin and forced her to release her grip. Then Siggy tripped Stacy and both of them lost balance and fell to the floor against each other.

Rolling, writhing, Sigried managed to knock the silver dagger from Stacy's hand. The Princess struggled and arched her back up, her sharp nails scratching at Siggy's face. Panting, sweating, gasping for air, they leaped to their feet. The silver dagger lay between them. The Rani bent to reach for it.

"Don't even try!" growled the Princess. "The second you take your eyes from me I'll kill you with my bare hands!"

Siggy looked at her with hard eyes. "Maybe you're right, slut. Maybe I won't need your dagger." She straightened up, tossing back her golden hair. "I'm going to strangle you, Stacy, watch you turn purple and your eyes bulge, hear your lungs burst, hear you squeal—"

Suddenly the room was awash in soft light from the antechamber. Both women twirled, startled. Two men stood gaping in the doorway.

The Rani screamed with rage, *"Get out!* Both of you, get out!"

Quentin and Dimitri exchanged incredulous glances.

"But, my Rani," Dimitri said, "this woman means to kill you!"

The Rani smirked. "How observant you are, Dimitri. But your bravery won't be needed." Her tone was sarcastic. "And neither will yours, dear cousin."

Stacy suppressed a gasp as she recognized one of the men. *Fara's kingdom! It's Quentin!*

"Turn on the light, Quentin," Siggy said. "I see you need to be introduced.

Awkwardly he did as she asked. Soft globelight illuminated the room. "Lady Kesa!" he cried with amazement. "What are you—"

The Rani turned her head to him. "What did you call her?"

"Lady Kesa, of Glowing Mist in Satra. This is the woman I told you about, the one I saved from the pirates."

Her laugh was drowned out only by that of Dimitri. She glanced at Stacy. "It seems my cousin has saved your life twice, now. The least you can do is explain things to him."

Sourly Stacy nodded. "I've lied to you, Captain," she admitted.

"You're not Lady Kesa?"

Stacy shook her head.

"Then who are you?"

She threw back her head and stood defiantly. "I'm Anastasia."

He stared at her, dumbfounded.

Sigried grinned. "Yes, Quentin, the Empire Princess —the woman you so nobly saved! And the other one: Do you know her, too?"

He nodded. "They were companions—"

"Companions indeed!" flared the Rani. She grinned

with genuine amusement. "Allow me to introduce you to Mistress Melinda, the captain of the Rhonnda Guard." She peered at the hooded man. "And who, pray tell, are you? Not Alryc, that's certain."

Assad pushed back his hood and met the Rani's eyes with a glaring gaze. "My name is—"

"Assad!" gasped Dimitri.

The Rani whirled. "You know him?"

He smiled acidly. "I do, my Rani, and so should you. He is a traitor. He once flew your flag; now he sells himself to Rhonnda."

Siggy pursed her lips. "I see."

"Kill them all now," said the dragoon. "Have done with it."

Quentin's mouth gaped. "Siggy, you can't!" he cried. "You must not!"

Ice-blue eyes flashed. "Why?"

"Because . . . because the Princess came here in peace."

"In *peace?*" she huffed. "Ah, Quentin, Mara has you blinded!"

At the mention of Mara, Stacy grew tense. "Do you know Mara?" she asked the youthful lord, a pleading look in her eyes.

"I do. And she's well, I promise you."

"Know her?" The Rani laughed. "My foolish cousin has gone and fallen in love with her!" In a fit of anger, she spun on her heels and shouted down the hall. A squad of burly Panthers came running, weapons drawn. "Take these three prisoner!" she commanded.

"Kill them now!" cried Dimitri. "Have you lost your senses? We need no martyrs in our dungeons! As long as the Princess lives, she's still a threat!"

"No!" shouted Quentin. "Listen to me, Siggy. Dimitri's poisoned you. No good can come of this. Free the Princess, avert this war—"

Hands on hips, the fiery Rani replied, "Now? After

so many years of planning for it? Quentin, you're a bigger fool than I thought." Then she threw back her long yellow hair and looked to her guards. "Take them away! Chain them if you like, but get them out of my sight!" And stone-faced, she watched as Stacy, Melinda and Assad were marched out, swords at their backs.

Soon the clamor of footsteps disappeared and the stillness of the night returned.

"You've made a terrible blunder," Quentin said frankly. "You underestimate the Rhonnda Empire. Her forces will rally, even without Elias and the Fleet. Anastasia's wolf army will—"

She faced him with a smirk. "Matters of war are no longer your domain, Quentin," she rasped.

He looked at her oddly. "What are you saying?"

"You're no longer our fleet Commander. You've been relieved of all duties and confined to the palace. I brought you here to give you a chance to justify your rash actions with Mara, but what you've already said has been plain enough."

"Ah, at last it's come," he said scornfully, looking first at the Rani and then at the grinning dragoon. "I need not ask who takes command in my place."

"Consider yourself lucky, Quentin," Sigried said. "If Dimitri had his way, you'd be sharing the same cell with the Princess."

"I'm sure," he said. "But this time you've gone too far. You and your mercenaries have bitten off more than you can chew."

"Get out, Quentin," she hissed. "Don't make matters worse for yourself."

He bowed stiffly, ignoring the dragoon, spun on his heels and strode from the room. For a long while the echo of his boots could be heard from the hall; then they were gone.

Dimitri came close to the Rani's side and reached for her hand. She drew away and folded her arms tightly about her. The wind was blowing more chilly now and she felt a shudder. Eyes gazing wetly at the sky, she felt a lump of sadness rise in her throat.

"I told you Quentin was against you," said the dragoon after a while.

Siggy shook her head slowly. "He's young. Perhaps tomorrow I can speak with him. He's no fool. He'll understand."

"You delude yourself, Sigried. He's made his choice, and it's a fatal one."

She looked into his eyes. "What do you mean?"

Dimitri drew a deep breath. "Our fleet must sail. Time is of the essence. Who knows how long Elias will labor to find his fabled island? We must strike immediately. And we cannot afford to let Quentin be an albatross around your neck." He touched her throat lightly and ran his hand up the side of her face. "Quentin," he whispered, "will have to pay the price for his foolishness."

Siggy bit her lip. "I know."

"There isn't much time, Mistress. I can take care of it for you." His words trailed off slowly.

The Rani winced. The thought of Quentin's blood being spilled made her quiver. *Butchered by a foreigner! Fates above! I can't let it be!* "No, Dimitri. Leave him to me. I'll do it my way."

"And the Princess? You'll kill her, too?"

She nodded, pain drawn across her pale face.

He looked at her mistrustfully. "Are you sure? It will be easier for you if I do it."

"Don't crowd me, Dimitri! These woman's feelings will pass."

As she spoke, she put her hands to her face and desperately tried not to weep. Her closest blood relative must die—her lifelong friend, the one man she had still trusted, the voice of her conscience. Even now Quentin's voice gnawed at her and sent goose bumps rising across her flesh. But no, Quentin *had* betrayed her. There was no doubt; he had virtually admitted as much. Now there was no one, no one at all, except for the scavengers—except for Dimitri.

The die was cast. On one point Dimitri had been right: There could be no turning back. The ships must sail. The vacuum of power must be filled even while the Princess languished in her cell.

Drying her eyes, she looked up at the impulsive dragoon. *You and I are from the same gutter, Dimitri. When this venture is done, I know you'll try to wrest my throne away, but you won't—even if I have to slit your throat myself. I'll not let Quentin die only to replace him with someone like you.* "Set to sail," she said impatiently. "Satra must be taken quickly. Then you'll converge on Rhonnda."

His eyes grew bright. "You won't regret this, Rani," he said, "I promise you. I'll smash the Empire. Elias himself will grovel at your feet."

She smiled bitterly. *Will he? Will all this be so easy, my gutter companion?* "Best you leave me now, Dimitri." There was fatalism in her voice. "I need to be alone with my thoughts. Go and make your preparations."

He bent down to kiss her, but she turned her head. Ignoring the slight, he bowed. "And when do we sail?"

"As soon as you can—the moment the fog lifts."

The young Princess Maralisa sat huddled atop a pile of straw in the corner of her cell, her knees up, her arms wrapped tightly around them. Her face was drawn and pale, her eyes sunken and red from long hours of crying. Desperately she tried not to allow her surging terror to rise to the surface. Her cries would only be mocked by the swarthy guards outside.

It was cold in the dungeon, bitingly cold. She had no cloak, no blanket, only her soiled tunic, the one she had been wearing when she was caught. The cell was damp and dark, fueling her misery. The only light was a dim glow that seeped under the door, coming from the brackish tunnel outside.

Spiders crawled at the corners of the ceiling and roaches moved swiftly between matted layers of straw. The stench of the cell was nauseating, from what she realized could only be the vomit and urine of the previous occupant. She knew that the best she could hope for now was a quick death. But she also knew that Sigried would deny her even that.

With trembling hands she lifted the small bucket of fresh water placed at her side by the kind-looking turnkey and forced down a few pitiful swallows. The stale bread still lay at her feet, where she had left it, and already the roaches were scrambling to nibble at the crumbs.

Again she began to weep softly. At the age of seventeen, she wished never to live to see another day.

Miserable and aching, she rubbed at her shackled wrist, trying to ease the dull pain of her bruises. Being chained like a wild animal was the cruelest cut of all. Even Sigried would not order that. Her heart pumped faster as malice and hate grew within her. *Dimitri!* Only the thought of somehow being able to repay him was keeping her from losing her sanity.

She drew back in fear as the lock of her door began to turn. A thin beam of light slanted across her face and she closed her eyes against its brightness. *They've come for me! Fara above! Please don't let Dimitri have me!*

"Mara?"

She hid her face and trembled.

"Mara? Are you—"

She peered through the curtain of her hair and gasped, "Quentin!"

He stood over her, a look of shock written across

his handsome features. "Dear God, girl! What have they done to you?"

She turned from his stare. "Don't look at me, Quentin, please."

He took her hand and forcefully pushed her face toward his. There were welts on her shoulders and a large blue-black bruise on her chin. "Mara, who did this?"

She sobbed. "It was Dimitri! He came last night, drunk. He ... he ..."

The young noble closed his eyes.

"It's not what you think, Quentin. He wasn't interested in touching me, but he had a whip—"

"Now I've two scores to settle," he vowed.

Her eyes opened wide. "What?"

"Never mind. Can you walk?"

"I think so," she said excitedly. "But how—"

She tensed at the sight of the old turnkey standing in the doorway.

Quentin smiled. "Don't worry. He's a friend. I still have a few in Kuba, you know. These mercenaries aren't running the whole show yet. But look, there isn't much time. The turnkey is going to unlock your shackles. I'm taking you out of here."

Her eyes burst with love. Then suddenly she became frightened. "No, Quentin, you mustn't. They'll make you pay with your life. Leave me here to die."

Tears welled in his eyes. "Oh, sweet Mara! Do you think I could ever live with myself knowing you were suffering like this? I'd rather die myself!"

"They'll rack you, Quentin! Please—"

A soft kiss ceased her protests. "I love you, Mara."

Sobbing, she threw her arms about him. "I'm frightened, Quentin. Where will we go? How can we escape? The hounds—"

"Shhh. Leave that to me." He glanced over his shoulder. The turnkey came running with his key chain.

Kneeling down, he hastily began to free the girl. "I should have listened to you before," Quentin said ruefully. "I *was* a fool. Sigried *does* mean to kill the Princess—and you and me."

She gasped. *"Az'i!* We've got to warn her!"

"Too late. Oh, sweet Mara, how can I tell you?"

Her eyes narrowed. "Tell me what?"

"The Empire Princess has been caught, just hours ago. She's been taken—"

Mara, now free of her chains, put her hands to her face and wailed.

"But she's all right," he added hastily. "At least so far. Right now I think the Panthers are looking for *me*."

She shook off her tears and looked at him with anguish. "You? But why you?" Her shoulders slumped. "It's because of me, isn't it? Oh, Quentin . . ."

He smothered her in his arms and kissed her again and again.

The turnkey nervously darted his eyes to the passageway. "We've got to go, my lord," he said.

Quentin nodded and took Mara by the hand. "All's not lost quite yet," he said, forcing a grim smile. "I've been able to free one of your aunt's companions—a man called Assad. With luck, we'll free your aunt, too."

Mara squeezed his hand. "I believe you, Quentin. Fara above! I must already be insane, but I believe you! Tell me what has to be done and I'll follow you to the ends of the earth."

He put his arm around her, sheltering her with his cloak. They moved swiftly down the passage, the turnkey in the lead. Quentin's jaw was set in grim determination. At all costs he would kill the dragoon, he knew. He must! And if Sigried stood in his way, he would have to kill her, too.

Seconds later they turned a corner. Torchlight dazzled above their heads. Mara caught sight of a man approaching and tugged at Quentin's arm.

"It's Assad," Quentin told her as the man reached them.

The girl stared. "He looks like a mercenary!"

Assad chuckled good-naturedly. "I am, young princess, but one on your side. It makes me shudder to think of the dangers I've encountered to gaze upon your pretty face."

The girl flushed and smiled, liking him instantly.

"We'll get to know one another better a bit later," said Quentin. "Right now we've got to find the Princess and Melinda."

The old turnkey's eyes sparkled. "I know the way," he said, "but first . . ." He led them inside a dark room, where he tossed a sword to Assad and a small knife to Mara.

Quentin grinned. "Can you use it, my lady?"

"As well as Stacy," cooed the girl as she fingered the blade and felt its weight.

Assad whistled. "Then I'd hate to meet you on a dark night, young princess. I've seen what your aunt can do."

Mara tossed aside her hair. "Just give me the chance," she hissed.

The turnkey frowned. "You'll have plenty o' that," he said darkly. "Princess Anastasia is being held on the upper level. There'll be Panthers enough for all."

Quentin bit pensively at his lip. "Perhaps it would be better if you led Princess Mara to safety," he told the turnkey. "I don't want any risk of her being hurt."

"Not a chance!" snapped Mara with flashing eyes. "You said you had your scores to settle; well, so do I! Lead on, turnkey!"

Off into darkness they slinked, carefully following the footsteps of the old, wizened turnkey. At a turn in the corridor, they stopped while Quentin peered around the corner. A group of mercenary guards stood beneath dim torchlight in the distance. Quentin quietly drew his blade from its sheath. "Let me go ahead. Follow as soon as the fun begins."

Assad wiped his mouth with the back of his hand and nodded. It was about time!

Quentin turned the corner and strode toward the guards.

"Halt! Who goes?"

"Quentin—Fleet Commander!" he replied.

They eyed him suspiciously. "What are you doing down here, my lord?" queried one, keeping careful watch on the sword he carried. As mere dungeon guards, they had evidently not yet heard of Quentin's dismissal or of his pursuit by the Rani's Panthers.

"Stand aside!" he called. "I'm releasing a prisoner."

The soldiers gaped. "Lord? We were given no such instruction—"

The young noble's blade spoke for him. The first guard gurgled as the blade cut through his belly. He staggered back, fell against the wall and slowly slid to the floor.

The fight was brief but furious. Assad and Mara came running, weapons in hand, and plunged into the melee. Assad wrenched a guard against the wall and plunged his sword through the man's lungs. Quentin parried one blow, dodged and met head on the thrust of the next. A knife came whistling by his head. He crouched, watching as the man before him clutched at his heart and tried to pull out the blade. From over his shoulder Quentin could see Mara standing proud and defiant, pleased to see that her throwing arm, despite her bruises, was on the mark. The guards had been eliminated in less than five minutes.

Mara pulled loose her knife and wiped the blood on the slain man's tunic. She stared down at his twisted face. This was the first time she had taken a life, and the thought of it nauseated her.

Quentin pulled her away. "It's better not to look,

Mara," he said softly. "No matter how much blood you spill, you'll never get used to it."

Assad grunted; he looked at the turnkey. "Which way now?"

The old man put a finger to his lips. "Follow me," he whispered. Then he led them away and back into shadows.

After anxious moments in the dark, they came to an aging set of steps under bright-glowing globes. "Up to the next landing," rasped the turnkey. "There's only one cell and it will be heavily guarded."

"For sure," agreed Quentin. "Dimitri will have stationed his best troops to guard Anastasia. And there'll be dozens crawling about at the entrance to the passage."

"Four against Sigried's Panthers," said Assad, sighing.

"There's no other way," assured the turnkey. "Keep your blades in hand. Once we reach the top . . ." The thought needed no finish. Everyone understood his meaning all too well.

The turnkey smiled grimly and, hefting his own sword, began the ascent. Assad was next. As Quentin made ready to go, he took Mara by the hand and looked into her eyes. "Mara, I just want you to know—"

"Shhh. I do know." She kissed him gently and felt her own passions rise. He tightened his fingers around hers and led her by the hand.

They heard the shuffle of feet from above. For barely an instant they froze before flooding the steps like the fury of Hel, weapons flashing.

Three guards came racing from the arched cell door, swords in hand. The hilt of the turnkey's sword slammed forcefully into the belly of one, knocking the wind out of him and sending him sprawling across the floor. Assad followed through, sending his blade into the man's back. Quentin quickly dispatched the second.

The third guard made to run. Again Mara threw her knife. Her victim stopped short, straining and twisting to reach the blade stuck cleanly between his shoulders. Then he fell with a thud against the stone.

Quentin glanced quickly about. There were no more guards to be seen, but that was deceiving, he knew. At any moment a dozen more Panthers would come stumbling down the hall.

"Quick, where are the keys?"

The turnkey peered about; then he smiled. Dangling from the waist of the man Mara had felled hung a small chain. Swooping down like a vulture, he grabbed it and went to work laboriously on the locks.

Quentin wiped beads of sweat from his face as the turnkey worked feverishly. "Can't you go any faster?"

The turnkey shook his head. "Patience, m' lord."

Assad gulped as he peered down the long hall. "I hear footsteps!"

Quentin groaned. He snapped his fingers impatiently. "Faster, man, faster!"

Anxious and frightened, Mara kneeled beside the door. "Let me help," she said.

"Not much you can do, my lady," replied the turnkey. "These locks are old. One bad twist and they'll jam. Then we'll really be in a fix."

Just then the first lock clicked. The second was quick to follow. The turnkey's usually nimble fingers trembled as the third and last key was placed into position. It too turned with a click. He grinned at Mara; then, with all his strength, he pushed with his shoulder and the thick wooden door creaked open.

A nervous guard leaped from the cell, sword flashing. The blade caught the turnkey across the throat and the old man staggered and dropped heavily against the floor. Quentin ducked, then thrust. The guard's sword clanged hollowly to the floor. Bleeding profusely, the Panther did a slow dance before he fell.

"Fara's kingdom!" cried Stacy as Quentin entered the cell. She leaped to her feet.

Quentin drew a long breath and sighed. He held up the keys. "My ladies, I've come to free you."

Melinda shared an incredulous glance with the Princess. "*Az'i!* He means it!"

Stacy beamed. "I think he does."

The Kuban noble dropped to one knee and began to work.

"How can I ever repay you for this?" said Stacy with tears in her eyes. "How can I—" The sight of Mara standing in the doorway cut short her words. The chains dropped to the floor and she ran and embraced her niece.

"No time for that now, my ladies," said Quentin, now freeing Melinda of her chain. "The fight's far from over."

"*Az'i!*" squealed Melinda. "Get me done so that I can help!"

"Take your choice of weapons, Mistress," chuckled Quentin. "You'll have a selection waiting for you all over the hall." He stood up, put his hand inside his tunic and drew out a small dagger.

Stacy's eyes widened; she threw back her head and laughed. "My silver blade! Where did you get it?"

Quentin smirked. "Like any good Kuban sailor, I lifted it." He winked as he tossed it to the outstretched hands of the Princess.

Assad popped his head inside the door. "Let's get out of here, fast!"

Quentin took firm hold of Mara's hand. "I know my way from here," he told the Princess. "We can make it down from the palace. But where we'll go after that . . ." He shrugged in dismay.

"I have . . . er . . . friends waiting outside the city. You should remember them: Alryc and the wolf Cicero."

The lord grinned. "It's almost dawn. We'd better hurry."

Stacy shook her head. "You go, all of you. I have unfinished work—"

Melinda looked at her wildly. "Stacy, no! Please!"

The Princess was firm. "I made a vow, my friends. Sigried must be punished and so must Dimitri."

"I'll settle the score with Dimitri," said Assad. "He is my account."

"You're both wrong," said Quentin. "Both the Rani and the dragoon must first be accountable to me. Remember, Kuba is my land, not yours. The deeds wrongly done are my shame and mine alone. I have the right to payment."

Stacy knew he was right. She nodded quickly. "Very well."

Quentin let a faint smile cross his lips. "Assad, take the women to safety. I'll show you the way."

"No!" cried Mara, reaching out toward him. "Don't let him do this alone! They'll kill him! They're looking for him now!"

The Kuban noble shook his head sadly. "Mara is a wonderful girl, Princess Anastasia, and it's been the brightest moment of my life to know her, but she's young—a child. She doesn't understand."

Gravely Stacy nodded.

"No!" screamed Mara. "No!"

Quentin bowed stiffly. "Good-bye, Mara," he whispered. "May the Fates one day bring us together again."

Assad whirled, sword in hand. "The stairs!"

Racing up the old stairway at a frenzied clip came a band of fierce and frantic Panthers. Quentin and Assad dashed to the top of the landing.

The two men wove a wheel of flying steel about them, each blow bringing forth screams and gurgles as the Panthers were stopped from reaching the landing.

Their bodies tumbled back down the narrow stairs, blocking the advance of those below.

Wildly, savagely, the Panthers pressed on, a wall of breast armor inching ever upward. Assad recklessly positioned himself on the first step and met the charge. Thrusting madly, he sent three square-jawed mercenaries reeling backward. Pools of blood made the steps slippery; those yet unhurt began to stumble and slide.

Quentin yanked the enraged Assad by the sleeve. Grinning at him, he said, "If you wish to live to fight another day, my friend, you had best leave your position now, while you can, and come with me to safety."

Assad smiled. He kicked high, caught a single rushing soldier in the face and sent him toppling back down. "Lead the way, my lord!"

Down the corridor they ran, hearts pumping wildly, Assad and Quentin leading the rest. Then it was up yet another stairway and along a brightly lit corridor. Twice they paused to deal with startled guards; twice they were forced to leave crumpled corpses in their wake. They passed through a large oval door and ran madly through the palace kitchens as servants and cooks gasped, dropping pots and pans.

Once out and away, Quentin paused to catch his breath. He turned to the Princess. "Here I will leave you, my lady. Godspeed to you. I go myself to the Rani's throne room."

This time it was Stacy who spoke without care of personal safety. "We'll not let you bear this burden alone, Quentin. We all knew the risks when we undertook this venture."

"My lady!"

She held up her hand. "No, Quentin. We'll go together or not at all. Now, which way from here?"

Dawn was breaking dully across the Kuban sky. The grim haze that had set in the previous evening was at last beginning to break. Siggy stood at the balcony wall, staring down at the formation of ships beginning to stir from their moorings and edge their way toward the seawall.

The Rani drew a deep, exhilarating breath. At dawn her head was always clearest. Her thoughts were no longer tangled and filled with self-doubt.

My ships sail! My dream is fulfilled! Kuba will rule forever!

Hollow footsteps clicked on stone. Siggy turned to see a frightened mercenary bow low before her. She glared at him. "What is it?"

The soldier lowered his eyes. "The prisoners, Rani—they've escaped."

Sigried's eyes flashed. "Find them! Dispatch every man you have!"

He crossed his arms. "Yes, Rani. And I'll have guards sent for your protection."

She smiled a fatalistic smile. "You need not worry for me, soldier. Look! See our ships? They sail to claim the world! Nothing can stop Kuba now. No force can halt her glory. Now leave, and scour the palace until they're found!"

He departed at a dead run, and again the Rani of Kuba was left alone. Then she heard more steps from behind her and frowned, expecting to see the mercenary come back. It was with total shock that she saw Stacy standing tall and poised in the doorway, a bitter smile on her lips, her silver dagger in her hand.

Sigried stared at her with utter disbelief. She threw back her head and glared. "You *are* a fool, Anastasia! You could have escaped. Instead you've thrown your life away to find me."

"My debt must be paid, Siggy. I told you I'd kill you."

The Rani laughed hauntingly. "It would do you no

good, Princess. Here, come to the wall and see for yourself." Stepping aside, she gestured grandly.

Stacy warily stepped out onto the balcony and gazed down at the fog-shrouded harbor. Two dozen galleys were on the move, slinking like cats to the seawall entrance.

Siggy chuckled. "So you see, Anastasia, taking my life will no longer matter. It's too late. My navy will reach Satra in days, and despite what may happen to me, they're going to crush your empire like an insect."

Stacy held her breath. The sight of the warships made her cringe. With the Empire Fleet still on its fool's errand, there was no force in the world capable of dealing with the Rani's powerful navy.

Siggy laughed. Her eyes sparkled with madness. She turned to Quentin and Assad and Mara, who had entered behind Stacy. "Come, come," she told them all, gesturing for everyone to take a look at the malevolent sight.

"Is there any way they can be recalled?" Stacy asked Quentin frantically.

Sadly he shook his head. "They sail on imperial directive, Princess. Even Sigried could not call them back."

"You see?" flared Siggy. "It makes no matter if I die. The glory of Kuba cannot be stopped."

"*Az'il!*" spit out Melinda. "You're insane! You don't know what you've unleashed! When Lord Blood hears of this—"

"It will be too late, Mistress," retorted Sigried. "By the time word reaches Azura, Blood's army will be hard-pressed to defend itself, let alone recapture Rhonnda."

Stacy gasped. "You plan to attack *Rhonnda?*"

The Rani's eyes flashed. "And burn it to the ground. When this crusade is done, there will be nothing left of your empire."

"A 'crusade,' she calls it!" cried Mara. "It's massacre!"

Quentin took the girl and cradled her in his arms.

"You gave up the chance to rule half the world, cousin," sizzled Siggy. "And for what? For *her?*" Sigried's eyes focused contemptuously on the frightened girl.

"I pity you, Sigried," he replied acidly. "You've never known real love, have you? Only men like Dimitri warm your bed."

Sigried's eyes filled with tears; her lips trembled. It was true, too true. Love—the one thing she had never had and never would. Her breasts heaved as she spoke: "Why don't you kill me, Anastasia—now, while you can? You've wanted to for years." She spat the words.

Stacy looked at her with amazement. "I begin to understand you now, Siggy, and in my heart I feel sorry for you. Your selfish lust for power has turned away even those who did love you. You'll die as you've lived—a lonely woman."

"Save your pity, Rhonnda bitch! Look again at my ships and weep for your lost empire."

The haze was breaking fully now; the sun began to peek down from the morning sky, the sight of the ships became harrowing indeed. From the west, beyond the seawall, came yet more ships, dozens more, swiftly bearing down to join the fleet. An armada that was invincible.

Quentin gaped at the sight. "Where in blazes did they come from?" he muttered.

Siggy leaned over the wall and caught sight of them, too.

"Fates above!" cried Quentin. "They're not ours!"

Stacy's mouth dropped. "What?"

"The sails!" shouted Mara through wet eyes. "Look at the sails and the banners!"

"My God!" It was Melinda who gasped. "They're flying maroon and blue!"

The Rani visibly paled, she swept aside her cloak; her knuckles turned white as she clutched at the wall.

Assad raised his brows. "Those are Empire ships!"

Quickly they came into full view: sails of gold and ocher, each emblazoned with the crest of Rhonnda—frigates, galleys, warships all. And in the lead, bearing down hard against the choppy waters, came a long, triple-masted vessel, sails rising high against the blue sky. A hundred maroon and blue banners flew proudly from prow to stern. Twin sleek battering rams gleamed at her sides.

Mara stared transfixed. "It's the flagship!"

Stacy marveled at the sight. "Elias! Elias and the Fleet!"

"Look to your pitiful ships now, Rani," blustered Assad. "They're in for more of a fight than they bargained for. Gods below! I wish I could be there now!"

Shoulders straight, jaw set in determination, Elias stood at the prow, hands on hips. The seawall loomed high on the port side, and Kuban galleys were streaming toward him from starboard. But it was on the Kuban palace itself that his eyes focused.

"They're bearing down fast, Captain," came a call from his aide.

Elias nodded. "Give the call for battle stations." His eyes danced grimly as shrill blasts gave the signal on each and every ship. Hundreds of sailors, weapons in hand, took positions along the rail. Predator birds—fighting hawks and falcons trained for combat—perched restlessly atop the yards, wings fluttering, beady eyes glowering, awaiting the call to action.

Elias smiled in satisfaction. All grew quiet as tense men prepared for combat. The only sounds were the groans of well-aged wood as the ships drew closer. At Elias's right foamed the swells from his rovers, sturdy vessels whose decks carried naught but catapults, ships especially designed for the brutal task of storming cities and seawalls.

These past weeks had been a nightmare for Elias. First, mere days out of harbor, the Fleet had encountered such hazardous gales that it made its search for the elusive island of riches virtually impossible. Wracked by the storms, tattered by the gusty winds, they had to abandon the task—but to his fortune, he mused grudgingly, for it was upon his premature return to Rhonnda that he heard of the events that had transpired in his absence. The kidnaping of Mara had sent him into a furious rage, and his anger had only deepened when he learned that the Princess had taken matters into her own hands. "We sail for Kuba at once!" he had barked.

And sail they had, half the Fleet, the rest in harbor awaiting repairs. The very thought of his being duped away from home so that the Rani of Kuba could hatch her plot made his blood boil. And now with the walls of Kuba in his sight, he itched for the moment he would reach her accursed palace. "Opal City indeed!" he rasped. "If either Stacy or Mara has been harmed, I'll turn it to rubble."

An aide approached and saluted smartly. "The Kuban galleys are coming about, sir."

Elias watched as the enormous warships cut an agile swash through the blue water. Across the enemy bows, Elias could see crimson-cloaked Kuban captains shouting commands up and down the lines. Ranks of enemy archers stood three deep from forecastle to stern, and behind them, grim squads of dragoons with gleaming scimitars in their hands.

"Signal the rovers," said Elias coolly. "I want that

seawall out of action before noon. And have three escort ships swing wide to starboard. Those galleys may be bigger than us, but they can't maneuver half as fast, I'll wager."

Moments later the three Empire escorts, *Snapdragon, Bittersweet* and *Jasimine,* trimmed their sails and began to move abreast at a new tack. The cat-and-mouse game had begun.

To port, off Elias's bow, four grim roundbottoms—hulking support ships that comprised the workhorses of the Kuban fleet—began to turn counterclockwise to meet the bold Rhonnda tactics. Black banners aflutter, they fanned out menacingly across the bay.

The Rhonnda flagship, *Southwind,* and her sister ship, *Royal Lady,* slowly began to bare their yards in anticipation of greeting the two galleys running straight off their stern.

As the fighting ships poised for battle, the six devastating rovers cut a sharp angle and made full speed toward the looming seawall. All across the wall amazed soldiers scrambled frantically to take battle positions. Warning trumpets blasted throughout the city, telling all that Kuba was under bold attack.

War machines quickly rolled into position along the wall, a line of catapults with throwing arms cocked back. But it was with desperate gloom that the shirtless operators watched. Even should the seawall hold, they knew, there was little chance of their lives being spared once the rovers had swung into action.

From far to the west, distant thunderclouds rumbled. A squall would soon be upon them, adding fury to the battle.

"Hard alee!" called Elias to his officers on the *Southwind* bridge. "And signal the *Lady* to follow."

Message flags fluttered and the *Royal Lady* was fast to comply. Sleek sails pulsed with flowing winds.

Elias felt the rush of salt water on his face as the swells pounded across his rails.

"Poor weather for fighting, sir," grumbled his aide, eyeing the fast-approaching squall.

"For Kuba, too," he replied darkly. "It gives neither side advantage. But let's see if we can strike the first blow."

The young aide grinned.

From the bridge of the Kuban flagship, Dimitri looked on with disbelief. He gripped the rail and stared at the maneuvering Rhonnda ships. "What's Elias doing?" he said, half to himself. His captains looked on with long faces. "The fool's spreading his forces too thin!" said the dragoon, chuckling. "We'll smash right through his lines." He turned and smiled at his companions, crimson cloak flapping high in the breeze. "Bear hard, my friends. Soak your arrows well. I'm going to set the *Southwind* ablaze and watch her sister ship run."

The sky began to darken and the air grew eerily calm. And then it began.

Whoosh!

The first rover catapult let loose. The iron-spiked ball sailed toward the first tower and hit with incredible impact. Stone and wood alike gave way; screaming men, faces mangled and twisted, hurtled to the sea below.

Furiously the Kuban catapults returned in kind. Half-ton balls of iron went crashing down into the sea in near misses, but one struck its mark. A rover's mast smashed at the block, the iron ball crunching through the sturdy deck as though it were made of glass, and men were thrown into the air like paper dolls.

A thousand arrows whistled down. Another Rhonnda catapult sounded, then a second and a third. The parapet was squarely hit and flying debris rained down like mighty hailstones. Heads and limbs flew through the air like soaring birds. Decapitated bodies splattered as they fell from the towers onto the crenellated walls.

Kuban catapults unleashed in revenge. A second rover was hit, taking three terrible blows within a single second's time. Timber was crushed amid the wails of maimed and drowning sailors. The ship seemed to gasp, her very life draining from her, her fractured body sinking swiftly down into the cold, deep Kuban waters.

The rain began; the wind started to howl. Waves lashed furiously against the seawall and the rovers bobbed and came reeling about. Lighted Kuban arrows tore across the bleak sky, trailing flames and thick black smoke. A third rover's sails began to blaze. And again the Kuban catapults roared. The fight had hardly begun and three of the dreaded rovers were already out of action.

A fighting ship appeared at the face of the wall: *Jasimine!* The discouraged rover sailors shouted gleefully. The escort could not have come at a better time. Having successfully rammed and sunk three Kuban roundbottoms and one archer-infested knorr, she had seen the peril of the rovers and had fought her way to their side.

Jasimine archers let their bows sing in unison with rover catapults. All across the wall there was bedlam. The walls ran red with mercenary blood. An iron ball slammed hard into a Kuban war machine splintering it like kindling. Towers, men, flaming canisters of oil—all tumbled through the air. Two more balls of iron smashed into a squad of dragoons, caught unaware. Bodies cartwheeling, they fell down into the frothing waves.

From *Jasimine's* yards flew the birds. Hawks and falcons soared high into the sky, then, screeching, fell upon the Kuban defenders. Like spitfires from Hel, their talons ripped at the faces of the disconcerted Kubans. And as the men tried to fend them off, more *Jasimine* arrows sang into the line of Kuban troops.

Roaring fires rose higher and higher in the remaining towers. The rovers pressed in and sent their fiery balls now completely over the wall, spreading death among those cowered behind it.

Down on the bay, the sailors of the *Southwind* prepared to throw grappling hooks across the rails of a burning galley. Elias, sword in hand, stood ready to lead the assault. The rain slanted down harshly, partially dousing the fires that had spread across both decks. From the corner of his eye, Elias could see the *Royal Lady* come charging down upon the Kuban flagship. He had wanted to take that one himself, but a twist of Fate had given it to the *Lady. Very well, then,* he thought. *This fine Kuban galley will be prize enough.*

Wood ground bitingly as the sides of the two ships grated together. Rhonnda sailors leaped from one deck to the other, while two hundred mercenaries, eyes wild, came running to meet the new threat. A line of *Southwind* archers brought down the first rank.

Thunder clapped. The galley reeled under the onslaught of massive waves tearing over the rails. Elias tripped and fell as a Kuban mercenary charged him; from his knee, he slashed the man across the belly, nearly cutting him in half. Soaked with blood and sea water, Elias staggered to his feet. The slain mercenary slid clumsily along the deck and over the side. All around, bedlam reigned. His sailors swept past him, whooping and shouting, tearing into the disarrayed Kuban ranks.

Across the bow another galley was desperately trying to fight her way through the squall to reach her beleaguered ally; but before she could, the escort *Bittersweet,* steel rams glistening in the wet, cut across from starboard and smacked bow first into the galley's hull. The ram's teeth ground solid wood into pulp. The galley heaved and slowly began to flounder. The *Bittersweet* drew back and, like a hovering cat, watched as the galley began to sink from the deep, enormous gashes in her side.

All over the bay, fires were raging. Many Empire ships had been damaged: The *Snapdragon* was barely afloat, and the *Royal Lady*'s masts had been split in two.

Lightning flashed. In that grim moment of light, Elias could for the first time see the magnitude of carnage. Swimming sailors from the fired and sinking roundbottoms were being picked off by marksmen at the bulwarks of other escort ships. The rovers, now only two, had all but turned the mighty seawall into rubble. Catapults were still flying and this time far past the wall, far past the harbor—into the city itself.

Dodging blades and arrows, Elias made his way back to the deck of the flagship. Aides rushed to assist him and attend to his small wounds. Elias brushed them off angrily. He stared at the flaming towers of the Opal City. Had Sigried had her way, he knew, those flaming towers would have been Rhonnda's.

The winds continued to howl. Pitiful survivors along the seawall lost their footing and fell, screaming; their necks and backs were broken on the piles of jagged rock and rubble below. The wall itself was a blackened, gaping maw crumbling before his eyes. Little spirit for fight remained among the remaining defenders. Faces tormented, bodies raw and bleeding, they stood almost passively as the two rovers, *Jamimine* still at their side, made their way past the last of the seawall and sailed slowly into Kuba's harbor.

"It's done," hissed Elias through clenched teeth. "Maybe now the carnage can stop." But he knew better.

Waiting at the quays would be Sigried's crack Panthers —men sworn to die rather than let the hated enemy be given free access to the fabled city.

Suddenly Elias felt his aide tugging at his sleeve. "The Kuban flagship," cried the youth, "she's beaten off the *Royal Lady* and is headed toward the harbor!"

The Empire captain shot like a bolt to the bridge and directed his steersmen to pursue; but the squall was still at its peak, and there was no way his ship could negotiate the choppy waters in time to intercept the Kuban ship.

He wiped rainwater from his eyes and peered darkly out at the fires. "Move all our ships down to the harbor," he growled to his aide. "We've got to get to the palace."

Already they could both see that the fight on the quays between the Panthers and Rhonnda's sailors had begun.

"We'll have to fight our way in," replied the aide. "The palace will be the last stronghold. At any rate, if we turn now, we'll leave too many Kuban ships still afloat."

With a grimace Elias peered over the bow at the remains of the powerful Kuban fleet. The bay was aglow with smoldering fires. Those few ships that were not aflame bore deep ram gashes along their hulls, and those very few unscathed were doing all they could to battle the squall and stay clear of the prowling escorts.

"Sigried's fleet is no longer any threat," he told the officer calmly, "but the Rani still is. She cannot be allowed to escape. At all costs we must reach the palace."

The aide nodded and saluted. "Aye, aye, sir." Spinning on his heels, he gave the order. Message flags were raised, and the other ships began to converge as fast as they could in the direction of the harbor.

* * *

Siggy drew away from the wall and returned to the throne chamber. Flinging back her cloak, she slumped upon her throne, a bitter smile upon her lips.

Stacy leaned against the back of the divan and gazed into the Rani's eyes. "It's over, Siggy. You've failed. Without your navy, Kuba is powerless."

Sigried looked up at the Princess. Slowly her hand slipped to her waist. She stood from her throne. "But *our* fight isn't done yet, wolf bitch."

Stacy lowered her eyes. "No, Siggy. There's no need for me to kill you anymore."

The Rani laughed bitterly and drew her knife. "I want it this way, Anastasia." Stepping closer, she waved her blade menacingly before Stacy's eyes.

Mara turned from the wall and gasped. Quentin moved to intercede, but Assad blocked his way.

"Leave them," drawled the mercenary. "The seeds of this enmity were sown too long ago. They must settle it in their own way."

Quentin was aghast. "But you don't know the Rani! She's deadly with a dagger. She'll kill your princess!"

Melinda shook her head. "That is for the Fates to decide, young lord."

Stacy drew her silver dagger and moved back toward the center of the room. Siggy thrust. The Princess caught the lunging blade with the tip of her own and pushed Siggy back. "I don't want to do this, Rani. You're forcing me."

"Ha! Have you lost your nerve, Anastasia?"

There was a strange glow of elation in Sigried's eyes, Stacy noted. It made her shudder. She knew full well that the Rani would kill her if she could; yet she felt somehow that Sigried was secretly wishing for her own death. A noble ending to a tragic life.

Siggy whirled and slashed high. Stacy parried.

"Where are your wolf tricks, Anastasia?" rasped the beautiful Rani.

"I won't need them," replied the dark-eyed Rhonnda Princess.

The two circled and stalked, Stacy like a wolf, Sigried like a cat. Siggy probed and faked a quick lunge. Stacy drew back, sidestepping it with ease. Sigried shifted the knife to her left hand, then back to the right. Closing the space between them, she feinted a low blow, then swung the blade upward. Stacy grabbed her wrist and the two women grappled hand to hand. Siggy suddenly pushed and Stacy tumbled backward to the floor.

Mara screamed as Sigried's blade plunged down. Stacy rolled and caught the Rani's arm just as the blade rushed by her face. Then she brought her knee up and hit the startled Rani squarely on her jaw. Siggy fell back. Stacy was all over her, elbows smashing her in the ribs. Siggy, with her free hand, pushed hard against Stacy's throat and sent her toppling back onto the floor. Both women leaped tiger like to their feet.

Their stalk intensified. Siggy swung, the point of her knife missing Stacy's chest by the slightest fraction.

"My Rani, all is lost!"

Whirling, they both turned and stared. Dimitri had come breathlessly into the chamber, drenched in perspiration, his cloak and tunic smeared with blood.

At the sight of him Assad jumped forward, sword in hand.

Dimitri's eyes glowered. "By the Fates," he said. "This is the second time I've interrupted—and I'll make it the last!" His own sword whipped from its scabbard and he lunged for the Rhonnda mercenary.

Assad drew in for the kill, his eyes burning.

"Dimitri is mine!" It was Quentin who spoke. Pushing both Melinda and Mara aside, he leaped to the center of the room. "Give me your sword, Assad," he hissed.

Assad shook his head, held his ground.

"Give it to me! The dragoon is mine!"

Dimitri scowled. "I'll kill you both!"

Quentin met his gaze squarely. "You'll have your chance, dragoon. Assad, I'm waiting. . . ."

Reluctantly the mercenary complied. No sooner had Quentin clutched the hilt than Dimitri lunged. The clash of steel was shattering. Sparks flew.

"I've longed for this moment, *Commander Quentin,*" snarled the dragoon contemptuously.

He pressed in close and the two men grappled. Quentin shoved him away and, sword thrusting wickedly, forced him backward. The dragoon attacked; Quentin crouched and brought his sword high to parry. Steel blades quivered in the abrupt shock of meeting. The young noble swept forward and, with a series of devastating blows, managed to push Dimitri back until he was almost against the far wall.

Everyone held his breath as Quentin now seemed to have the upper hand.

Dimitri swung around, and as Quentin lunged, the dragoon yanked the curtains from the wall and threw them at him. The young noble tried to sidestep, but for an instant his vision was blocked. That instant was all the time the dragoon needed. With a savage whoop and a wild lunge he brought his blade across in a broad arc through Quentin's belly. Quentin stood motionless, eyes staring at the gloating dragoon. Dimitri drew back his blade and spit. Quentin dropped his sword to the floor. He staggered forward, hands outstretched, as if trying to clasp them around Dimitri's throat. The dragoon laughed as Quentin's body crumpled to the floor.

Mara ran to him, weeping and screaming.

Assad knelt down and swept up Quentin's fallen

sword. Veins bulged from his neck. "It's our turn to fight now, you swine!"

The dragoon wiped his mouth with the back of his bloodied hand. "I'll make you wish you were never born!"

Steel clanged against steel. Grim and equally determined, the two mercenaries began their fight to the death. Mara still slumped over the still body of Quentin, sobbing, oblivious to the deadly combat in the room.

Dimitri fought with renewed zeal. Left, right, left, right, his blade sang wickedly and soon his powerful blows had put Assad badly on the defensive. Assad tried to parry, but Dimitri laughed lustily, eyes aglow. Assad made a desperate lunge. The dragoon quick-stepped to the side and brought his own blade around hard, knocking Assad's from his hand. The weapon clanged hollowly across the stone.

Stacy gasped. Assad took a few cautious steps backward. Dimitri's face twisted into an ugly scowl, his eyes narrowed as the kill drew close at last.

"First you, Assad," he hissed vengefully, "then the women—all of them." The wild, frenzied look on his face assured Assad he meant to keep his word. Recklessly, putting hopes of saving himself aside, he threw himself at his adversary. Dimitri's fist shot out, knocking him to the floor. Then, holding the sword above his head with both hands, a vicious grin upon his lips, he stood over Assad's crumpled body.

Suddenly Dimitri's eyes grew wide; he stood stock-still, a look of disbelief rising across his dark features. Behind him, Mara drew her blade from the small of his back and plunged it in again, upward and deeper. The sword slowly left Dimitri's grasp and fell harmlessly to the floor. Assad rolled to the side, scooped it up and bounded to his feet. The dragoon did a pirouette, his hands awkwardly reaching behind his back, trying to pull out the embedded dagger. Mara stood breathlessly before him, trembling at the realization of what she had just done.

The dragoon feebly moved toward her. His arms stretched out; veins bulged from his sinewy neck. A thin stream of dark blood trickled from the side of his mouth. He was trying to form words, Mara could tell.

Mara lifted her chin and glared at him. "I told you I'd kill you," she said coldly.

Dimitri swayed and fell to the floor with a dull thud.

Hands on hips, Mara spit on the corpse, then, face as white as a sheet, turned away, buried her face in her hands and began to sob.

Melinda and Stacy rushed to Quentin's side. He was breathing, they saw, but little more. Sigried was kneeling at his side, weeping openly.

"He's dying," whispered Stacy, casting the Rani a long, hateful side-glance. "And his blood is on your hands. Are you satisfied?"

Sigried looked up through pitiful eyes. Then she buried her face upon Quentin's bloodied chest and continued to cry.

Cinders blew high above the Opal City, scattered by the chilly night winds. In the small hours before dawn the last of the fires was still smoldering, leaving a dull orange glow across the horizon.

Quentin lay quietly upon the bed, satin sheets pulled up to his chest. On one side kneeled Mara, clutching his cold hand with both of hers. Stacy and Elias stood across from her, near the recessed windows. Their faces were sad, their eyes downcast and forlorn.

As Mara wept, a sparkle of recognition slowly came into Quentin's glassy eyes. A small smile came to his lips and he reached out and dried her tears. Mara pressed his hand firmly against her cheek.

"Why are you crying?" he whispered painfully.

She sniffed and closed her eyes. "I'm remembering a flower someone once gave to me—a flower to cherish forever."

There was a faint sparkle in his eyes as he remembered their first meeting in the garden. "Ah, sweet princess . . . a fine Kuban tradition. You should adopt it in your own land."

Mara squeezed his hand harder as he strained to stroke her long flowing hair. It was then that his eyes caught sight of the shadows cast by the two visitors beside the window.

"Dear Anastasia . . . you look well."

Stacy came forward, smiling warmly at him. She glanced at the tall, handsome man at her side. "Quentin, I'd like you to meet Elias."

Elias lowered his head in a respectful bow. "It's good to meet you, Captain Quentin. Stacy's told me all you've done. I don't know how to thank you."

Quentin waved his hand weakly. "The honor is mine. Captain Elias. I've always hoped to meet the commander of the Empire Fleet. Alas, I wish the circumstances had been different." He began to cough. Then: "I trust all is well, then? Dimitri—"

"Dimitri is dead," Stacy said. "All mercenaries have been taken prisoner. You can rest easy, Quentin. Everything is being taken care of. The fires are out and your city will be back on its feet in no time."

He closed his eyes and sighed. "Good . . . good." He smiled thankfully. "And my cousin?"

"Sigried is well. Alryc is watching her. No harm will come to her, I promise you. Do you want to see her?"

Quentin gazed into Mara's wet eyes and shook his head. "Not now—perhaps later."

It was all Mara could do to keep from breaking down. She mustered all her strength and courage and fought back her sobs.

"We'll leave you two alone," said Stacy, motioning to Elias. "But you need rest. Don't let Mara keep you too long."

"Ah, Princess, would that she could keep me forever."

Stacy smiled at the brave youth and, taking Elias by the hand, slipped quietly from the room.

Quentin turned his head and stared out at the sky. "Mara," he whispered, tears rising in his own eyes, "you know I'm going to die. . . ."

The girl swallowed hard. "Don't say such things, Quentin. You mustn't. Kuba needs you—a new, strong leader. And I need you, too." She couldn't contain the burst of tears.

Quentin began to stroke her hair again, toying with the long locks. He sighed wistfully. "I would have wished nothing more, my love; but Dimitri's blade cut a bit too deep, I fear."

Mara put her head on his chest and wept openly.

"Shhh, my princess—and you *are* my princess. . . . In Kuba there is another belief. When a man dies, his soul is whisked to the heavens to rest with the Fates, but his flesh remains behind. And from his flesh there one day will spring a garden filled with flowers"—Mara cried as he spoke—"flowers to be picked by carefree lovers—"

"And cherished forever," said the girl, finishing the thought.

He smiled. "I see you know the rest. Oh, Mara . . ."

She looked up in despair. "Quentin? Oh, Quentin! No! Fara, please! *No!*"

Her sobs echoed throughout the long hall.

* * *

In the antechamber, Elias raised his head and looked searchingly into his beloved Stacy's eyes. The Princess looked away, grief-stricken, then she shook her head. "Leave her, Elias. Let her be."

"But she needs us. She needs someone to turn to."

Stacy smiled softly, "Later she'll need us, but not now. Now she needs to be alone, to deal with her pain."

Elias touched Stacy's chin with his finger and swung her head around to face him. "I see you're crying, too."

The Princess leaned forward and kissed him gently. "Mara was brought here a child; she leaves a woman."

Elias frowned. "A woman perhaps, but she's so young, so vulnerable."

Stacy kissed his hand. "Her pain will mend, I promise you, just as my pain always mends after you've gone away."

They were suddenly interrupted by a soft knock on the door. Alryc cautiously stepped inside and bowed. "Sigried has been sent for. She'll be here any moment."

Stacy sighed. There was just one loose end to tie before the nightmare could end—one small matter yet to be settled.

The Rani walked tall and poised into the antechamber. She was as beautiful as ever. Only the dull pall of her ice-blue eyes betrayed her true feelings and the pain she had brought upon herself.

Stacy nodded curtly to her, then sat easily upon a low couch. Siggy met her eyes, and for a long minute the two of them stared at each other: the victor and the vanquished.

"You may sit," said the Princess, gesturing toward the cushioned seats set randomly throughout the room.

"I'd rather stand."

Even in her hour of grief she still stands proud, mused Stacy. Few others could have their entire world shattered and still be defiant. Stacy knew all too well that she herself couldn't.

It was the Rani who spoke first. "I would ask you a favor, Anastasia," she said in a clear voice.

Elias stirred angrily. Stacy held up her hand, once again slipping back into her role of Empire Princess. "What is it you want?"

Siggy sighed. "To be allowed to pray in the Temple before you kill me."

Stacy's eyes widened. "To pray for your soul?"

The Rani winced, then evenly met Stacy's gaze. "Yes," she said, "to pray for my soul and for those others who believed in my cause, Kuba's cause, and died for it."

Stacy leaned forward in her seat, still meeting Sigried's eyes with her own. These past days in the Kuban palace had not been lost on her, she now realized. She had learned much from this bitter experience. And, strangely, she saw that her hatred for her rival was now suddenly and unexpectedly gone, despite the knowledge of how much grief and suffering the Rani had caused both her and the ones she loved. Stacy had come here with a solemn oath to put Sigried's life to an end. Now, though, she wondered if such a punishment would best fit the crimes. Sigried was no longer a threat to Rhonnda and could never be one again. Her death would serve no purpose. Surely enough blood on both sides had been shed already.

Abruptly she said, "My counselors advise me to spare your life."

Elias looked at his beloved with amazement. If anything, those closest to the Princess had advised the opposite in no uncertain terms.

If Elias was surprised, Sigried was stunned. Her body noticeably stiffened. She looked at the Princess with total disbelief. "After what I've done?" she asked. "After condemning Mara to death in my dungeons?"

Stacy smiled thinly. "There will be conditions for your life, Rani," she said imperiously. "I know that as

Rani your title can never be taken from you. But know and understand this: You will never sit upon your throne again. Another will be given the charge, one who bears none of your malice toward either me or Rhonnda. Had Lord Quentin lived, it would have been he. Now, though, my ministers will have to select another."

"And what is to become of me? Am I to languish in your own dungeons as revenge?"

Stacy shook her head. Condemning Sigried to a cell would have been the easiest course for her to take. Stacy had not sought an easy way; instead she had wisely chosen another.

"No, Rani. No dungeons. No prison cell." She met Sigried's ice-blue eyes and smiled. "Your own words have spoken your punishment." Her smile turned to one of satisfaction as the Rani showed her bewilderment.

"The Temple, Sigried. Do you understand me now?" Stacy leaned forward, her hands formed into a pyramid. "Among your many titles is that of priestess, is it not?"

The Rani nodded slowly, cautiously.

"Then the Temple is to be your domain, where you will live out your days as a priestess of Kuba. You will dance before your gods, but never again set foot outside into the world. The Temple gates shall be your bars, your unrealized dreams and ambitions your tormentor. You'll have a whole life in which to reflect on the grief and pain you've caused others."

Sigried threw back her head and glared coldly. "What do you know of grief?" she whispered. "The suffering I may have caused is far less than that I've lived with every day of my life."

"I know," said Stacy sadly. "It took me until now to understand, but I'm glad I finally do. The biggest tragedy of all, though, is that you've always spurned those who truly did love you and wanted to help."

The inference was clear. The memory of Quentin brought a brief wet look to Sigried's eyes. She closed them momentarily; then once again she looked at her hated rival with shrewd, calculating eyes. "You know you're making a mistake in sparing me, don't you?" she said. "You know that some way, somehow, I'll rid myself of the bonds and restrictions you impose and regain my rightful place—"

Stacy waved a hand, cutting her off. "I know you'll plot and scheme as you've always done before—that much I suppose can never be changed—but I'll take the risk, Sigried. The Temple will be well watched and not by men. I'm too well aware of your beauty and seductive charms. Melinda's forest girls will be your jailors. Your wiles will mean nothing to them."

We'll see, thought the Rani. *We'll see.*

Stacy sighed, putting down her own doubts with the conviction that she had done the right thing. "There's no more to be said, Rani. Gather your most needed possessions and be prepared for my guards to escort you to the Temple tonight. You may leave."

The Rani bowed curtly. Skirt swirling, she strode from the room.

It was a fair and bright morning when the *Southwind* unfurled her gold sails and moved slowly out of Kuba's bay. Hundreds of gulls flew above the masts, crying shrilly as they dived down into the water. Merchant ships were once again plying the sea lanes, carrying their goods to the Opal City. Save for the crumbled seawall, there was little evidence of the terrible battle that had taken place only seven days before.

Gone were the crimson-cloaked mercenaries who had patrolled Kuba's streets; gone were the squad's of

Panthers who had sworn to give their lives to the Rani's cause.

Kuba was serene and peaceful, a quiet city again, graced with bountiful resources and lush landscapes. Even Sigried would be able to admire it from the Temple steeples. And Mara knew that somewhere from above, Quentin would also be watching, peering down at his beloved homeland and smiling. He would be pleased.

Stacy and Elias stood hand in hand upon the bridge. They smiled at the sight of Assad and Melinda standing close together at the rail and gazing out at the diminishing city the same way they were. The two were deeply in love; at least one good chapter had come from this adventure.

Alryc, as usual, was busy peering up at the angle of the sun and plotting his courses, while Cicero lay at his feet, happy to be going home again.

Only the sight of Mara made them sad. The girl was alone at the aftcastle, head low, hair blowing freely in the wind. She had been withdrawn and brooding this past week but at last had finally begun to come out of some of her sorrow. The wounds would always be there, Stacy knew. Sigried's never healed; Stacy knew Mara's would. When you were seventeen, the world was a wondrous place and your life had yet to begin.

For Mara there would be other love, love without pain, one day soon—another sweeping adventure to lift the girl off her feet. Stacy corrected herself: not the girl; the *woman*.

"You look depressed."

The Princess smiled at Elias. "No, love"—she sighed—"not at all. Happy. Happy is what I am."

He kissed her lightly and put his arm around her shoulders. "Are you sure?" he asked.

She laughed and pushed him away teasingly.

He drew her close and kissed her hard, much to the consternation of some of the officers.

Stacy's eyes danced merrily. She looked at him with mock astonishment. "Why, Captain! You are bold!"

His face may have reddened, but his eyes couldn't help lingering on her supple body. *Fates above!* he thought. *We've been so preoccupied with matters of state that we've not even slept together!* He pulled her close and whispered in her ear.

Now it was Stacy's turn to grow red. She felt so embarrassed that she wanted to crawl away from the grins and stares of the officers. "You wouldn't dare!" she squealed girlishly.

Elias laughed. "Oh, wouldn't I? Princess or no, you left home without telling me and now it's your turn to be punished! Forgive me, my lady, if I seem rash, but your royal behind is going to get a bloody good tanning!"

"No it won't!"

"Damn sure it will! A rump is a rump, royal or no!"

"Well, if that's your attitude . . ." She leaned close and whispered a few choice remarks to him.

"You'd do that to me?" he asked.

"Damn right!"

"In our cabin? Now? Alone?"

She grinned. "Damn right!"

He grabbed her by the hand and nearly whisked her off her feet. "What in Hel are we waiting for?"

And as they ran off to the captain's quarters, he called to his wide-eyed officers, "The Princess and I don't want to be disturbed—not today, not tonight, not even tomorrow. In fact, don't bother to knock until we can see the towers of home!"

Stacy leaned against the gangway, her face aglow. Home! What a word, what a magical word: "home"! *More than anything in the world, I want to go home.*

Elias kissed her right then and there and she felt her heart leap. All the pains, all the frustrations somehow were swept away and she could think of nothing else but him.

A nightmare was over. A sweet dream had yet to begin.